Artificial Gravity

B. L. Gillette

First Edition 2026

To Gabby Gillette, who lent me an ear so many times, and Morgan Gillette, who gave me the dream of writing.

Acknowledgement

To the editor who fixed so many errors, my friends and coworkers who inspired my characters, and my Nana who believed in me.

Table of Contents

Chapter 1 Nothing Lasts Forever....................1
Chapter 2 Asteroid Dust.................... 19
Chapter 3 At Least Two Weeks.................... 31
Chapter 4 The Round-Up 47
Chapter 5 Six Business Cycles 56
Chapter 6 The Gravity of the Situation.................... 75
Chapter 7 Sector Six.................... 87
Chapter 8 Until Further Notice.................... 106
Chapter 9 The Coffee Maker.................... 123
Chapter 10 Secret Squirrel.................... 142
Chapter 11 Business as Usual.................... 150
Chapter 12 Processing….................... 166
Chapter 13 Five White Boxes.................... 183
Chapter 14 A Thread of Blood.................... 195
Chapter 15 Next Cycle.................... 208
Chapter 16 Big John.................... 227
Chapter 17 One Hour.................... 241
Chapter 18 Counting to Four.................... 260
Chapter 19 What the Stars Don't Owe.................... 271

CHAPTER 1
Nothing Lasts Forever

Beyond the porthole, the stars stretched forever—cold, bright, and utterly indifferent. Ethan barely noticed them anymore. He sank into his chair, rubbing his eyes, finally released from the mind-numbing slog of inventory tracking. Another work cycle done. Another twelve hours before it all started again.

Three on, two off. That was the grind. Not exactly the nine-to-five Dolly sang about, but he was with her in spirit. It didn't matter if you liked a song at first on Foxtrot. Eventually, you learned to love them all because they played *Earth's Greatest Hits* on an endless loop. But Ethan only needed seconds to love Dolly Parton.

The cycle had been endless, made longer by a mountain of computer work. Transactions. Move this here, log that there, zap everything with the guns—except the guns were useless. The barcodes they scanned were just as bad. Maybe, if the stars aligned, they'd actually work as intended, but even then, he'd still have to find a free computer to finalize everything. Unfinished transactions? Big no-no.

Bin-to-bin movements were the only thing the guns did right. But zone transactions? No chance. Worse, sometimes the gun failed while the computer worked fine, for absolutely no reason.

Ethan muttered to his reflection in the porthole. "There has to be a way to make them work better."

If there was, he hadn't found it yet. He carried the gun for appearances, but his computer was the beating heart of the warehouse. It was far easier to move boxes first, take notes, and then do the computer stuff on the back end. That's how he got stuck playing catch-up, madly beating on a keyboard at breakneck speed. But that was all behind him now.

For twelve glorious hours, he was free. Ethan could sit in his chair and look at the stars, sipping his slushie, feet propped up, completely relaxed. Let his mind turn off. Maybe look at his cat book again. Think about anything but work, or how this place was falling apart.

Anything.

Sadly, he couldn't get it out of his mind. As beautiful as the many stars in the porthole were, they were nothing he hadn't seen before. The endless vista had been a constant companion for years. That, and the bleak, metallic grey walls that defined every ship in the fleet, they'd been with him longer than not now.

Good old Foxtrot. It was his home, his chariot through the stars, and his prison—all in one. Ethan wasn't sure if that was depressing or not.

"I could always transfer to Delta," he mused. "Drive an air trawler all cycle." He snorted. "Yeah, right."

Not that it wouldn't be good work. The Delta crew wasn't so bad; it was just that Foxtrot was all he had known for years now, and he was getting old. Ethan had invested a lot of his life here in this ship. What was the point of leaving? Change for change's sake?

Just because working the front half of the ship was infuriating and the back half wasn't much better? Delta was dumb in her own ways, too. By all accounts, every ship in the fleet was. There was nowhere to escape to.

Ethan tried not to think about that, either.

He received shipments from Delta every cycle. At least, he was supposed to. Most cycles were pretty consistent: three, maybe four shipments arriving every few hours. The process was simple. One-man freight haulers docked, hunting a hot cup of coffee as much as the signatures they needed, while the lifters hovered around on their air trawlers, loading and unloading their cargo holds with boxes. Brown boxes. White boxes. Big boxes. Little boxes.

So many plastic-wrapped boxes.

Then, they flew away again.

The lifters stacked the off-loaded pallets in various places, hopefully with all the paperwork or stickers attached somewhere to the cocoon. Ethan had to triple-check all the pallets to make sure he didn't miss one.

A sudden hiss of air jerked Ethan out of his brooding. He stood up, setting his drink down on his cat book like it was a coaster on the chair, and then hurried toward the door. Normally, he heard her coming down the hall. Rose was home.

"Babe, I'm back," she called out, stepping through the auto-door and collapsing into Ethan's waiting arms. "How was your work cycle?"

Rose melted into his embrace, warm and smelling faintly of plastic and lavender. She kissed him, quick but lingering, before breaking away and making a beeline for her true love—the couch. It sat next to Ethan's chair, dividing their room in a way that reminded Ethan of a tipped-over lowercase "i." Lounging upon her beat-up, baby blue sweetheart, Rose proceeded to unclasp her bra. She unbuttoned her pants and then kicked off her shoes. She turned toward him with a knowing smile. "Let me guess. It was a boo-boo."

Ethan nodded, returning to his chair with a little smile of his own. "Every cycle, babe. Every cycle. How was yours?"

"I've been dying to tell you for hours!" Rose exclaimed, fingers curling into happy little fists that punched the couch repeatedly. "Guess what!"

Ethan picked up his drink and took another sip. Then he asked the obligatory question. "What?"

Rose's honey-brown doe eyes gleamed. "You're never going to believe it!"

She had a triumphant look on her face as she batted her eyelashes at him. The way her auburn hair spilled around her shoulders never got old to Ethan. Her smile just kept getting bigger, and she punched the pillow again, still running hot off of whatever happened.

"It was so great!"

"Well, spit it out already." Ethan reached out and squeezed her hand, his gaze beginning to drift toward the porthole again. "What happened?"

"They finally moved him! They moved Eggplant!"

Ethan blinked, suddenly giving her his full attention. "When?" he asked, cracking a grin. "Think they'll move Myrtle too?"

"After lunch," Rose beamed. Pointing to his drink, she added, "Make me one. And you wish! She hates you."

Ethan hurried to fetch her a glass. "No kidding—you take one roll of tape!" He jabbed a finger in the air for emphasis. "Anyway, tell me what happened with Eggplant!"

"Jim came out of his office—no ice for me, thanks."

Ethan winced. "I always forget, sorry." He poured her two fingers of vodka, then filled the rest of the rocks glass with orange juice.

Rose made a face. "You're just weird. No one else puts ice in a Screwdriver."

Ethan shrugged. "Slushies are the best. Anyway," he added, handing her the drink and returning to his seat. "What did Jim do? And I thought you liked Eggplant—why are you so excited he got moved?"

Rose was practically giddy about the whole thing. "Jim told him he was supposed to start on the dock last week! And I do like him," she added, "but now, the pink keyboard is mine!" That revelation made her squeal. "I won't have to race him for it anymore!"

Ethan just laughed. "Wow. Aren't you glad you got up and went to work after all?" he teased.

Rose cut her eyes at him. "No. My one true love is sleep."

Ethan laughed at that too. "And here I thought it was the couch."

Rose shook her head solemnly. "No, no, that's just my side piece."

Ethan's eyes drifted toward the window again, his mind wandering back to his racks, where a host of problems always seemed to be waiting—problems his own boss couldn't save him from. "Where does that leave me?"

"Baby," she said tenderly, placing her hand on his. Rose smiled sweetly, gazing into her husband's milk chocolate eyes. "You carry my stuff."

Ethan hung his head. "Right," he chuckled. "That's all I'm good for, huh? Good to know."

She winked at him and cleared her throat. "Well," she said slowly, "there is one other thing you're really good at, too."

Ethan tore his eyes from the stars, his interest fully piqued. "Oh? And what might that be?" His voice was hopeful. Playful, even.

Rose stood slowly, stretching just enough to draw his eye before leaning down and kissing his cheek softly, her lips lingering. Then, as her body brushed against his, she whispered in his ear, her breath warm against his neck. "Why don't I show you after my shower?"

Ethan reveled in the afterglow, flushed and sweat-slicked, his limbs pleasantly heavy. Rose lay beside him, still breathing hard.

The bed they shared dominated the space. Rose had maxed out her credits for it, getting the biggest one available. In addition to the standard sheets, her side featured a heating blanket, which she lay on top of, and a faux fur blanket, which she lay beneath. Two giant pillows propped up her head. She slept on her back, just like that, an arm's length away, in a cocoon she wove every rest cycle.

Bedding was one of Rose's love languages, which explained why Ethan slept under a fake fur blanket of his own and a duvet. The thread count of everything on the bed combined was some obscene number like a hundred million.

All of that lay in a heap on the floor now.

Ethan didn't care about the wet spot, either—if anything, he was a little proud of it. What he really cared about was Rose's head on his chest and the peace he felt inside. Deep, resonant warmth vibrated through his body. It felt good to be in love.

Rose rolled over then. "If I get pregnant, what do you want to name the baby?" she asked, facing him, her eyes boring into his.

Ethan tried to kick-start his brain again, but it protested. All that came out was a monosyllabic, half-formed grunt. "Ugh…"

Rose snickered. "I know I got that fire, but don't get all caveman-ish on me now."

Ethan chuckled back. "Sorry. Give me a second," he laughed again. Not nervously. More like he couldn't believe this was happening. Lying beside your wife, thinking of baby names? That was always something he had imagined, more of a concept than reality. Now that he was living in the moment, it almost didn't feel real.

She tried rephrasing the question. "Do you know any baby names you like? In general," she added. "If we have a girl, I like Elizabeth."

Ethan ran his hand down the curve of her back, savoring the moment. It felt like his heart might beat out of his chest. "Oh, not that!" he chuckled, adding dryly, "Please. Have mercy on me, my queen."

Rose sounded shocked. "Really? You love that game. I thought for sure you'd be all over that one!"

"That's just it…I don't want to name her after Queen Elizabeth or someone from the *Time Traveler game.*"

Rose whined playfully. "Whyyy? We could call her Lizzy!"

Ethan shrugged, trying to articulate his thoughts. "Because." He scratched his head, letting his brain buffer. "I don't want to be like that. If it's a boy: Do you like Sage?"

Rose made a face. "Sage. Like the seasoning?"

Ethan smirked. "It's a name too, you know."

"Yeah, but…I don't want our kid to sound like a spice rack, either."

That drew a genuine chuckle from Ethan. "Fair enough. What about—" He paused, thinking. "Aspen?"

Rose considered it, rolling onto her back and stretching out as she stared up at the ceiling. "Aspen…" she repeated, trying it out. Her fingers idly traced a heart on Ethan's belly. "It's got a nice ring to it. "

Ethan nodded. His heart absorbed the tenderness of the moment like a dry sponge in water. "Right? It's strong but not, like, old-man strong."

"You like the idea of naming them after things, don't you?"

Ethan nodded again. "Things I like, yeah."

Rose asked, "What's an aspen?"

He let his fingers play with her hair; the strands reminded him of the last smears of sunset on Mars. He searched for an explanation. "There were these trees on Earth. They're in my cat book."

Ethan sat up and switched on the overhead light. For another long, glorious moment, Rose lay spread out before him on her back, and he was mesmerized by her raw, natural beauty. She was pale. Petite. In a word, perfect.

Then he slipped on his breeches and retrieved the picture book. Flipping to the page by heart, Ethan pointed to the trees behind the big white fluff ball of a kitty in the foreground. "See."

Rose smiled as he returned to bed. "I do. They do look pretty. If he comes out blond like you, it will be perfect. The dark spots even kind of look like your eyes…" she trailed off for a moment, her fingers tapping on his chest as she thought. "But what if it's a girl?"

"Not Elizabeth," Ethan repeated. "Not Kitty, either," he added, closing the book and pushing it aside.

Rose giggled. "Alright, alright. What about…Celeste?"

Ethan cocked an eyebrow at her. "Like the stars?"

Rose gestured lazily toward the porthole. "I mean, it fits, doesn't it?"

Ethan let the name roll around in his head. Celeste. He imagined a little girl running through the ship's halls, hair like a flame, eyes bright with curiosity. A child raised among the stars. It felt fitting.

He smiled at her. "I like it."

Rose grinned. "Good. Then it's settled."

Ethan's grin consumed his whole face. "I still can't believe we're actually doing this."

Rose leaned in close, her voice dropping to a whisper. "Let's go again. Maybe if we go twice a cycle, we'll have twins."

Ethan's eyebrow nearly hit his hairline. "We'd get transferred to Delta for sure then. They don't have enough rations here for a couple with two kids."

She shrugged, tracing little hearts on his chest this time. "You're not too old to go again, are you?"

Ethan swallowed hard, feeling his heart accelerate again. "I'll never be that old."

"Good," Rose cooed, straddling him, her hips settling over him with practiced ease. "Well, how about I sit right here then, and we'll talk about the first thing that pops up."

Twenty minutes later, Rose opened her bedroom door, slick with sweat, her hair twisted into a careless knot on top of her head with a blue scrunchie. Then she collapsed onto the couch with a satisfied sigh. "We haven't gone at it like that in a while, babe." She stretched out, still trembling, and pointed out the obvious. "I'm shaking."

Ethan kissed the top of her head. "Let me turn the heat up then."

Just then, the soft blue glow of the wall screen flickered. A new alert throbbed in the corner:

System notice - maintenance alert.

Zone heating at 67% efficiency.

Maintenance notified. No action required.

Status: Green.

Ethan snorted as if he'd just heard a terrible joke.

Rose didn't acknowledge the warning. She barely even noticed them anymore. System alerts proliferated now—low power warnings, sensor recalibrations, and comms interference. They were always labeled 'no action required.' It was easier just to ignore them since she didn't have to do anything.

She just adjusted her robe and settled on the couch. "It has nothing to do with the heat." She winked meaningfully. "I told you you were good at that. Now I need another drink just to steady my legs."

Ethan chuckled, but his eyes lingered on the alert. He couldn't remember the last time everything had been running at full capacity. "That sounds good."

He crossed the room in four steps, rinsed out their cups, and pulled out the alcohol and orange juice again. He dropped soft ice into one cup, poured two fingers of vodka into both, and then tossed the empty juice container down the trash chute with a disappointed shake of his head.

Clearing his throat, he grabbed their drinks and returned to her. "I know Eggplant got on your nerves, but three times in one cycle?" He handed her a glass. "I didn't know you hated him so much."

Rose rolled her eyes but grinned. "It's not just that. They moved Autumn, too."

Ethan let out a low whistle as he sat back down in his chair. "That makes, what, four people this month?"

Rose nodded. "One a week, so far."

Ethan shook his head, caught somewhere between excitement and fear. "Who's next? Do you know where she's going?"

"Who cares? She called me a bitch, remember?"

He nodded. "Yeah, I remember." Ethan sipped his slushie, his gaze drifting to the stars streaking past the porthole. "I thought she was finally getting her act together."

"She was, but then Jim caught her sleeping at her desk. Again. I watched him ream her out for a good five minutes before personally escorting her out of tech support. Last thing I heard, HR's gonna review it."

"Ouch," He agreed. "Yeah, she's gone."

Rose shrugged. "She's young. They'll probably ship her back to Delta."

"They've been sending a lot of people to that ship lately," Ethan noted, stretching out in his boxers, the only thing between him and the cool air. The ship's vents were humming, making the room smell faintly of dust. He propped his feet up on the wall, trying to get comfortable. "Are they ever going to bring Gigi back?"

Rose shrugged, her face twisting into a grimace.

"I still message her at work. She says no one knows. A lot of them don't even want to come back. It's smaller rooms, but more food."

Ethan frowned, swirling the ice in his drink. He repeated, "Smaller rooms, but more food? I don't know if that's a good trade or not."

Rose took a sip, her expression thoughtful. "Yeah. Gigi says it's 'different.'"

Ethan glanced at her. "How?"

She shrugged. "They use different BCT programs to do the same things, and apparently, there's a union. Gigi said something about 'stricter rules,' but it's also 'more laid back,' somehow."

Ethan's stomach tightened. "You know, John was supposed to go over there and drive a lift for a few weeks, but he still hasn't come back."

"I know." She sighed, running a hand through her hair. "We used to go months without a single reassignment. Now it's every few weeks."

Ethan set his drink down, the slushie momentarily forgotten. "It's been like this ever since those guys from the Mike ship flew here with their big plan. Everything has changed so much—and not just the warehouse."

A silence stretched between them. The ship's vents hummed, filling their 400-square-foot home with soft, mechanical breath. Ethan shifted in his seat, suddenly restless. "What if they're not coming back because there might not be a place for them to come back to?"

Feeling a touch paranoid, he licked his lips. Something about the recycled air made them crack in here. Ethan added, "The cabal from Mike had a plan, and it didn't work. They said they were going to double our output with automation." He shook his head sadly. "That promise was too good to be true. Remember that tour they gave the Fleet Admiral last week? The one that went nowhere near the back?"

Rose gave him a pointed look. "What? Do you think our ship's going to fail as Golf did? Is that it? So, they're finding reasons to send people away? And they don't want to tell us yet because they're scared people will panic? Is that what you think?"

"Something like that. Sounds like you've thought about it, too."

"I don't know what to think," Rose answered, "but the Admiral's trip makes me nervous. All I know is they are taking away more computers, and they want more people to use the scanners. I'm always fixing errors they make in the system. Phantom bins, mostly," she explained, waving her hand. "They like to invent places to send things. All it takes is for the WiFi to go out for a second…and it does all the time."

Ethan rubbed his shoulder, feeling stress start to knot his muscles into steel cables. Rubbing did little to help, but he did it anyway. He added, "Seems like we're getting to the point where we're going to have to use them. I don't know how much longer I'm going to get away with letting people use my computer."

Rose fretted, her brow furrowing. "Do you really think the ship is failing? Why would the captains try to hide that from the Admiral?"

"I don't know, babe. Wish I did. My best guess is there's a fear that the Admiral will shut us down. Scrap the ship as they did with Golf. Foxtrot's over a hundred years old now. It was built to last forever—but you know how that goes. Nothing lasts forever."

Rose took his hand in her own. "They're probably just trying to figure out how to fix things. No one wants to lose another ship from the fleet. No one." Ethan wasn't sure who she was trying to convince. She added, "Besides, if the ship really was failing, they wouldn't have given us permission to have a baby. We're probably worrying about nothing."

Rose reached up and brushed a lock of hair from his forehead. Her touch was light, but it grounded him, pulling his thoughts away from spiraling uncertainty. She flashed him a reassuring smile.

Ethan wanted to believe that. He just wasn't sure if he could. "I hope so." Then he kissed her forehead. "I love you, babe. You're probably right. Everything is going to be OK."

A long stretch of silence followed.

Rose broke it. Still feeling chatty, she said, "You're awfully quiet all of a sudden. Don't tell me I've finally worn you out."

Ethan took a deep breath, trying to push aside his lingering concerns. He smiled at her, but it didn't quite reach his eyes. "I'm good. Just…you know, thinking."

"You always overthink everything. You know that, right?" Rose smiled warmly and leaned in closer, shifting her weight so she could be nearer to him. "Let's put on a show—get your mind off it." She squeezed his fingers. "What do you want to watch?"

Ethan asked hopefully, "How about the *Time Traveler* Pro Tour?"

She shot him down gently. "Pick something else."

Ethan snapped his fingers with mock disappointment.

"Worth a try. I already know who won, anyway. Kraven played Queen Elizabeth into a spy and got 15 fame all in one turn."

Rose smiled. "Cool." Then she batted her eyelashes, changing the subject. "Let's put on *90 Cycles*," she suggested.

Now Ethan let out an exasperated chuckle. "Is there a new episode out?"

Rose grabbed the remote and switched on the tube. The far wall flickered, shifting from transparent to opaque as the screen warmed up. A static burst crackled before the screen sharpened into focus.

"Yes, there is," she beamed as a bright, bubbly title screen flicked into place. Technicolor letters flashed.

"90 CYCLES - NEW EPISODE LOADING…"

A peppy announcer's voice kicked in. *"Welcome back, Cycle-heads! This time, Mickey takes on the lower decks—and things don't go exactly as planned!"* A musical number played with gusto alongside the show's opening montage.

Ethan breathed out slowly. He tried to turn his brain off, to step out of the weight of reality and into the manufactured absurdity of the show. "Well, I guess you did just rock my world." He half-smiled. Letting the glowing screen wash over him, he hoped these people's problems would distract him from his own, if only for a little while.

"That's right." Rose agreed happily, grinning ear to ear. "Buckle up, big boy. Lavender and Mickey are the new couple this week."

On the tube, a low-angle shot showed Mickey, a balding, heavyset man, crouched beside an open panel, bathed in flickering warning lights. His red vest was already smeared with black grease, and his drone hovered closely at his heel. The machine's two stubby mechanical arms twitched from its boxy core, trying to hold out tools to him as needed. Trying and failing.

Mickey exclaimed, *"Come on, not you too!"*

The drone gave a stuttering beep, its stabilizers whining. Mickey shot the camera a look—half amused, half exhausted. "*People think maintenance is all about fixing things. It's not. Routine maintenance is essential to preventing issues before they start.*"

Ethan looked away from the tube, back out at the stars, wishing they had more orange juice for another screwdriver. They were all out of red and purple juice, too. "What ships are they from?" He was only half-interested at best.

Rose didn't miss a beat. "Mike and Whiskey."

Ethan chuckled. "Kind of an opposites attract sort of thing?"

She nodded. "Sort of. She models for Mike. He's…well…"

Rose cut her eyes at him and just giggled.

Ethan sighed. "Gotta love Reality Toobies. Let me guess, he pays for everything?"

Rose just grinned. "You called it."

"How much younger than him is she?"

"Worse than us. He wants to have a baby, but something tells me she's not feeling it as much as he is."

"Dang!" Ethan chuckled and shook his head. "That's rough. What makes you say that?"

Rose thought about it. "Well, they met on a sugar baby site. She probably has another one over there on Mike right now."

He just shook his head. "Why do you watch this stuff?" Ethan asked for the thousandth time. He knew the answer; he just couldn't wrap his mind around it yet.

Rose let out a slow, content breath, wiggling into her favorite corner of the couch with delight. "You can't look away," she explained.

The tube cut to a camera feed showing narrow metal halls, halogen lights, and exposed pipes dripping condensation. A robotic intercom droned in the background, making announcements in a foreign language, distorted by static.

The producer asked, *"Lavender, tell us about your life here on Mike."*

The woman appeared to be in her mid-thirties, sitting on a twin-sized cot, adjusting a flickering light, trying to get it to stabilize. The walls behind her were paper-thin, and somewhere nearby, you could hear a baby crying through the air vents. "*Mickey says it's hot and humid here, but, you know, I love it. I love being a model and getting paid to wear bikinis.*"

The producer asked, "*So…is that how you met Mickey? Bikini modeling, I mean?*"

Lavender giggled. "*Oh my, well, not exactly. Okay, so…we met online. Mickey messaged me, and he was sooo sweet. He even helped me fix my scanner! I didn't know how to clear the cache." She admitted that sheepishly, with a smile. "It worked so much better! Not that I need to use one anymore.*"

Ethan, who had been only half-listening, suddenly perked up. He glanced at Rose, then back at the screen. "The multi-user cache? Is that what she meant? You can clear that?" Any given scanner had a dozen different accounts logged in to them at any one time. If you could clear the cache, all those accounts would go away; more importantly, all the things they were remembering would too, and then the scanner could focus solely on doing what you wanted it to do.

"Shhh!" Rose hissed, swatting at him. "Quiet! This is the price you pay for loving me!"

Ethan sighed, but his mind wasn't on the show anymore. "Clear the multi-user cache," he muttered more quietly. "I'm going to have to figure out how to do that."

CHAPTER 2
Asteroid Dust

Ethan's work cycle began at 05:00 sharp. That meant his alarm jolted him awake at 03:00. He was part of A-shift, and he gave himself an hour to make coffee, shower, shave, and ponder life's mysteries over a morning constitutional before heading out to join the crew. That cycle, clearing the multi-user cache on the scanners was high on his list of things to do, but more than anything, he hoped his pay was right. That was part of the grind, too.

His uniform was uncomplicated: a yellow vest. The color held meaning. Everyone wore fluorescent yellow vests for visibility, so the forklift operators could see you. The vests also denoted rank. Yellow was the standard-issue color. Ethan's supervisor, Buck, wore orange. Their department head, Jim, wore blue. A simple, effective system.

For most men, freedom of expression came in the form of hats. Ethan had a dirty orange bill, a black crown, and the symbol of his childhood hero, a bullseye, on the forehead. For Ethan, though, real freedom came from his socks. His left sock was red with white polka dots. His right sock? Blue with white stripes.

He buckled his belt, clipped his badge, grabbed his gloves, and slid his safety glasses over his hat. By now, he was usually working on his second cup of coffee while Rose combed her hair. They'd have fifteen minutes to play with.

Usually.

Not this cycle.

This cycle, Rose stood frozen in front of the dryer, staring at a pile of soaking-wet clothes.

Her morning routine was efficient. She woke up, brushed her teeth, used the bathroom, and laid out her uniform after Ethan finished showering. Then she stole thirty more precious minutes of sleep before rising again to wash her face with witch hazel, moisturize, and do her hair and makeup. Putting on clothes was the last step.

The dryer had betrayed her. The clothes weren't damp or slightly cool. They were wetter than a dog-eared romance novel in the tub.

Ethan stood there, his gaze momentarily caught by her form, bent over in her underwear, fruitlessly rummaging through the dryer. She yanked her uniform shirt out of the dryer and wrung it viciously between her hands, watching the water drip, before hurling it back inside the machine.

Rose looked up, rubbing a spot on her neck. Irritation gleamed in her eyes as she demanded, "Help me!"

Ethan hesitated for a moment, still half-distracted by his half-naked wife. He stepped forward, offering cold comfort in an attempt at reassurance. "I put it on the highest setting when I got up."

Rose shook her head, her voice sharp with rising frustration. "You didn't even notice, Ethan." Her eyes flickered toward him, then back to the pile of damp clothes. "You should have checked!"

The words stung more than he'd expected, but he didn't want to argue. Besides, she wasn't wrong. He could have checked. He could have gotten a jump on the problem, but the real enemy here was time. Their attendance wasn't exactly sketchy, but it was far from exemplary. Too many tardies added up to disciplinary action. Punishment: that was what she was really afraid of.

On Foxtrot, being sent out an airlock was the equivalent of a death sentence. No one volunteered for those details, because half the people who drew them never came back. Asteroid mining, for instance. The station needs metal, and someone has to go out into the black and get it. Every so often, security would round up the people with the worst attendance, load them on a haulage freighter, and send them out to do just that.

The average miner lasted approximately fifteen minutes. Ethan knew all about that. A couple of years ago, he had been sent out himself; all the way to Beta, which specialized in that sort of work. It was more of a prison than a ship. Ethan had watched good men die out there in the void, one by one, sometimes several at once, and had nearly been one of them.

"I should have checked," he agreed, a little too late. "I just assumed it worked." Ethan crouched beside the dryer, examining the dials again, trying to piece together the puzzle. He twisted the knob and hit the button, but the dryer didn't respond. Ethan checked the time again. Ten minutes. Not much, but enough—if they moved fast.

The dryer had shut down mid-cycle, its tiny status screen flashing a stubborn error code. Rose kicked it with a frustrated grunt. "Stupid outdated technology!"

Ethan pressed a few buttons, then smacked the side. The machine gave a pathetic beep and went still. He said carefully, treading lightly on every word, "We need another plan."

Rose crossed her arms, tapping her foot impatiently. "Yeah? Got one? Because unless you've figured out how to magically dry these, I'm screwed! I can't walk in there wearing a wet t-shirt! I've got meetings today, Ethan!" She rubbed her temples and glanced up at the clock. She wasn't angry at him, not exactly. It was just…everything piling up.

Rose added anxiously, "I don't want to be asteroid dust!"

Ethan flinched. Just a little, but enough that Rose noticed. If they missed too many shifts, there wouldn't be more warnings. Just reassignment.

Outside.

Ethan still had nightmares about that experience. As he tried to sleep, he could still hear the voices crackling over the comms before fading to silence for good. The nightmares came and went, lancing through his subconscious suddenly like a comet streaking by.

Rose's frustration dimmed slightly. "Hey," she said, softer now. "I didn't mean to stir up bad memories."

Ethan rubbed his neck, feeling the weight of her disapproval settle like a heavy yoke around his shoulders. "It's OK." He shook off the thought and tried shaking the dryer. When that didn't work either, he tried unplugging and plugging it in again.

The dryer wasn't the best. It had been on its last leg for a long time, but the maintenance request queue was higher than a giraffe's eye. Whatever those were. He had never actually seen a picture of giraffes, but judging by the saying, they must have been some kind of bird.

Try as he might, Ethan could never keep the dryer running long, and no one ever showed up to fix it. "This isn't cutting it. Let's hang the clothes near the vents so they don't get musty. The airflow will help them dry while we're gone. You'll just have to wear some of my clothes."

Rose hesitated for a beat, then nodded. She didn't say anything, but the sudden, relieved exhale told him enough. They worked quickly, draping the damp clothes along the warm air duct, the fabric fluttering slightly in the artificial breeze. The minutes ticked down. Seven. Then four.

"This sucks…" Rose muttered, pressing a palm over a shirt. It was still damp, but better than before. Not perfect, but they were out of time.

Ethan patted her on the butt. "I'd fistfight that dryer for you if I could. Just know that."

Rose gave him a small smile for his effort; then, pressing her fingers to her temples, she turned to the small closet that was wedged between the wall and the dresser, yanked the door open, and scanned the hanging clothes for a potential candidate.

"These are all against the dress code," she muttered, her voice heavy with defeat.

Ethan leaned in beside her, flipping through the shirts. "What about this one?" he suggested. "It's clean."

Rose hesitated. "It's the wrong color." The shirt was a white v-neck, one of the spares Ethan kept stowed away. "I guess that will have to do," she sighed. "Hand me my vest."

Ethan grabbed the bright yellow vest off the hook near the door and tossed it to her. She slid it on over the t-shirt, smoothing it down while eyeing herself in the vanity mirror wedged in the other corner of the bedroom.

"If anyone says anything," Ethan advised, "tell them it's a casual cycle."

Rose snorted. "What if they call me on it?"

His solution was simple and immediate. "Then act surprised. Play stupid."

That earned him a smirk, the last traces of her frustrations momentarily fading away. She grabbed her work gloves and clipped on her badge, giving herself one last glance. "Alright. Let's go before the shuttle leaves without us."

Right on cue, a final announcement blared over the intercom outside, loud enough that they could hear it in the living room. "Final boarding for Shuttle 3 in two minutes. All personnel must report immediately."

Ethan grabbed a plasma cutter from the shelf and passed one to Rose. She took it without a word, slipping it into a side pocket of her vest. For a moment, they just stood there smiling at each other, while the steady hum of the ship filled the quiet between them.

"Yeah," Ethan echoed. "Let's get this over with." Then he added, "After you, Lady of the Lake," and opened the door with a dramatic sweep of his arm.

Rose shot him a quizzical look. "What?"

"From Arthurian legend. Her clothes were wet, too." Ethan chuckled, scratching the back of his head with a shrug.

She chuckled, too. "Come on, nerd."

It was a short walk to the tram station—short enough that sometimes, from their quarters, Rose and Ethan could hear the train rattling down the tracks. The door to their quarters slid shut behind them with a quiet hiss. Outside, the corridor stretched in both directions, a long, ribbed tunnel lined with exposed pipes and faltering overhead lights. The ship's artificial gravity thrummed beneath their feet, a faint vibration that never quite faded into the background.

Rose adjusted her vest self-consciously, tugging at the hem. "You really think I can get away with wearing this white T-shirt?"

Ethan shrugged. "I'm telling you, just play dumb."

She shook her head but let the subject drop. Ethan could tell she was still on edge. They fell in step together, their boots clanging against the metal grated floors.

The corridor was already filling with workers shuffling toward the tram station. Further down the tube, a red-vested maintenance worker knelt beside an open panel, half his body disappearing into the wall as he enthusiastically cursed the wiring. Rose and Ethan exchanged a knowing look. The guy could be Mickey's brother. Maybe he was. He was definitely new. The fleet seemed big at first, but the crew was a small town. By now, Ethan knew most of the other Foxtrotters, or at least recognized them.

Rose slowed, clearing her throat. "Hey, any chance you'll get to our work order today? Busted washing machine. In 402. We put in a request cycles ago."

The red-vest slid back just enough to glance up at her. "A dryer in section four?

"402," she repeated. "It's been on the fritz for weeks. "

He snorted, shaking his head. "Look, lady, we've got a backlog the size of the ship, half as many hands as we need, and more problems piling up every cycle. Life support. Gravity." He gestured at the open panel for emphasis. "I'm busy."

Rose shot out a foot, blocking him from climbing back inside. "I get it. Just…you know, laundry's important, too."

He scowled. "I didn't say it wasn't, but keeping us all from becoming floating corpses is a little more important. Don't you think? Come on." He pointed at her boot, exasperated. "Move it, would you?"

"I will!" Rose snapped back. "Because I'm running late! Because I have no clean clothes! Because my dryer has been broken for weeks!"

The red-vest sighed, scratching at his short, grizzled beard. "I'll see what I can do—but no promises."

She gave him a tight, thin-lipped smile. "Thanks. We'd really appreciate it."

Ethan echoed. "Yeah, thanks."

The Mickey look-alike grunted before disappearing back into the wall, muttering something about stripped screws. Ethan wasn't sure if he was talking about the machinery or them, but they didn't stick around to find out.

As they passed the cafeteria, the sterile scent of recycled air mingled with the bitter tang of instant coffee and powdered eggs. There was no time to stop for breakfast, though Ethan stole a few wistful glances at the coffee urn. He could only hope Buck would make a fresh pot. After last night, he needed caffeine. Lots of it.

At the end of the corridor, they reached the tram station. It wasn't much. Just a platform wedged between two bulkheads, the floor scuffed with faded yellow caution lines. A small overhead screen flickered with the route map, and some kid had managed to climb up and scrawl "Marty eats erasers" on the monitor with a marker.

Rose gave him another look. "You'd think you wouldn't have to beg to get an appliance fixed."

Ethan shoved his hands in his pockets. "If the gravity goes out for a little while, that would suck. If it goes out for a long time, we'll all end up on dialysis." He shuddered. "Being hooked up to those machines looks terrible."

Rose tossed him a quizzical look. "Who do you know that's on dialysis?"

Ethan grimaced, his jaw tightening at the memory. "Some guys back on Beta."

She shot him a sideways glance, unimpressed. "Well, the gravity would have to go out for years here before that happened." Her tone was arid. "In the meantime, I still need clothes. I don't know what to tell you."

As they stepped onto the platform, a chime echoed through the station. Ethan barely had time to register it before Rose stiffened beside him.

"Did you hear that?" she asked. "That's the train—the doors are about to close!"

In a split second, something took over Ethan's shoulders, something he had felt before when the stakes were 'move or die.' He grabbed Rose's wrist and yanked her forward. Boots pounding against the metal floors, they darted through the crowd for all they were worth. Ethan tugged Rose along behind him. The train was already at the platform, its doors hissing shut.

Ethan's eyes widened. "No, no, no—"

He lunged forward recklessly, jamming an arm between the closing doors at the last second. The impact sent a jolt shooting up his arm. Then the safety sensor tripped, and the doors slid back open with a frustrated hiss. They were in. For a second, they stood there breathless, taking in the half-full cabin lined with steel benches.

Ethan gave her a thumbs-up. "We did it."

Rose blew out a breath, straightening her vest again as if it were nothing. "Next time, remember the laundry."

They grabbed the overhead handrails tightly as the doors closed again. The long, narrow car smelled faintly of sweat, its worn-out polymer seats scuffed from years of use. The magnetic rails groaned, sending a faint vibration through the floor as the tram picked up speed, swaying slightly with each lurch.

Overhead, the dull white lights flickered in their sockets, as if chuckling along with them in Morse code.

"There are so many errors to fix," Rose deadpanned. "820 errors are easy. 822s, though? It's technically a three-step process, but technically, we've all kicked a pregnant woman. "

Ethan snorted. "Nailed it!"

She smiled. "Thanks. I've been sitting on a lot of morbid jokes lately."

"On a scale of one to ten, just how morbid are we talking here?"

Rose bit her lip and looked at him guiltily. "How do you fit a hundred dead babies in a bathtub?"

Ethan blinked. "Wow, Rose."

She pressed on, her expression a little guilty. "A blender." Rose offered a sheepish smile.

He shook his head in disbelief, looking somewhere between horrified and delighted. "That's about a twelve. Are you sure you want to have a baby with me?"

"Of course," Rose said, her smile fading. "It's just...well, I'm scared. That's all. It's going to hurt, and you know." She lowered her voice, conscious of the other passengers. "People die from this. I don't want to die."

"What did you say? I can barely hear you," Ethan said, leaning in. "The tram is kind of loud." He tapped his ear. "I don't hear as well as I used to—"

"Ever since you worked around those loud machines on Beta," Rose interrupted, raising her voice. "I know. You've told me." She winked at him. "I'll tell you after work. Right now, just know that I'm still glad our relationship got approved, and I still want to have your baby."

He chuckled. "OK, good." Then, more somberly: "With a little luck, my paycheck will be right this time, and we'll actually be able to afford to have one."

The rest of the ride passed in a dull roar; the rhythmic clatter of the tram, the occasional crackle of the intercom, and the passengers filtering in and out at each stop all blended together into a numbing white noise. Rose stared at the scuffed floor, lost in thought, while Ethan tapped absentmindedly against the pole, his mind drifting back to the scanners. She exhaled, rolling her shoulders when the tram arrived at her stop a few minutes later. The cabin lights dimmed slightly as the tram slowed, gradually coming to a halt as the brakes were applied unevenly with a dull hiss. Then the doors slid open with a reluctant chime.

She kissed Ethan's cheek. "I love you, babe. And I'm sure your paycheck will be right this week. Have a good cycle."

Rose stepped off with a backwards wave, and the door slid shut behind her. Ethan gave her a small wave back. Then, the tram jolted into motion again, carrying him further down the line.

Three stops later, Ethan sighed again. Heavily.

Time to go to work.

CHAPTER 3
At Least Two Weeks

The platform leading to the warehouse was cold and dark, but after roughly two dozen steps, it was over. The moment Ethan passed through the department doors, the temperature spiked nearly thirty degrees. The sudden shift made his skin crawl, and he was still shivering as he pushed through the door.

A warehouse stretched out before him—ceilings six stories high, bright white lights stinging his eyes, still dilated from the dark. The waxy tile floors reflected the glare, while row after row of shelves, stacked with parts in boxes, formed a labyrinth Ethan navigated as instinctively as any minotaur. Taking a hard right from the time clock, he vanished into the BA-racks, took another right, then a left through the W-racks, crossed the hall, and reached the back of the SM-racks, where he was assigned.

He didn't stop there, though. No, of course not. There was no coffee machine in the SM-Racks. So he kept going, weaving through the UB-racks, the 180-lines, and the BS-lines, all the way to the break room. That's where the coffee was. To Ethan, it was more than just coffee; it was the literal nectar of the gods.

By the time he returned to his desk, he had three good sips in him. He took a fourth, tapped on his keyboard, pulled up his email, and opened BCT. As the system loaded, he bounced his knee impatiently. His mind was blank. A total void. He couldn't think of a single thing.

Actually, that wasn't quite true. He could think of one thing. His paycheck was probably wrong. Ethan didn't have the stomach to verify that depressing thought yet. He just smiled wryly and took another sip. While waiting for his brain to engage, he absentmindedly tapped his foot, scanning the area for the handheld scanners. Normally, they were charging on one of two stands beside the console, their numbers always totaling eight. Now, there were none.

He frowned, then slid open his desk drawer. A black plastic brick with a pistol grip lay inside, tucked beneath a stack of safety cards. "That's not supposed to be there." Ethan grabbed it.

Adding insult to injury, the trashcan by the desk was overflowing. A few crumpled napkins were perched precariously at the rim. Usually, it was emptied before it ever reached this point. Stan was probably running behind.

He tried to focus on the problem, but his mind wouldn't cooperate. All he could think about was the *Time Traveler* tournament. The last big game had been legendary—and he'd missed it because of work. Kraven played Queen Elizabeth, Ethan's favorite card, "Earth's coolest virgin", and won. Would she have been able to figure out the scanner situation? Probably not.

He took another sip of coffee and walked over to the UB-racks, glancing at the surrounding desks, but saw nothing. Not even spares. All sixteen scanners were missing. That was weird.

"Hey, Buddy, " Ethan greeted Shaggy as he approached. The scrawny, beanpole-thin young man scratched his cleanly shaven chin, ran a hand through his long, thin copper hair, and then turned his tired blue eyes toward Ethan. Shaggy looked like he'd been awake for all of thirty minutes. His gaze lingered on Ethan's face with unnerving focus.

"Hey there, Guy," Shaggy offered, his voice quiet and even, his gaze unblinking. "Have you seen the scanners? Me and Shaye-Shaye have been looking for them."

Ethan shook his head no. "I was just looking for them, too. D-shift must have done something with them."

Shaggy nodded vigorously. "Uh-huh, uh-huh, yes, that's what I was thinking too." He pushed his glasses back up the bridge of his nose, a gesture of habitual thoughtfulness. "D-shift likes to hide things. People hoard what they think they'll need later. Or what they think someone else will need." He shrugged. "What do you want to do if we can't find them? Go back to paper logs? "

Ethan took another sip of his coffee. "What do *I want to do*?"

Shaggy looked at him a moment, long enough to acknowledge he knew Ethan didn't *want* to be the one making the call.

"I want to go home and watch the rest of the *Time Traveler* tournament. Did you see it?"

Shaggy shook his head. "Nah. My buddy told me some guy won with a Fame victory for the first time in ages, but I was up all night playing *Bot Hunter*."

Ethan nodded vigorously. "Yeah, all in one turn! Apparently it was insane—or so I'm told."

Shaggy nodded along. "You ever play *Bot Hunter*?"

"Nah. The wife and I are hooked on *90 Cycles*, but that's about it." Ethan took another sip. "Tell Shaye-Shaye to print out the replenishment list. Have everyone log everything they move on paper and do their transfers while I track down Buck. You seen him?"

Shaggy shook his head. "Nuh-uh, nuh-uh, no. I haven't seen him either. But I'll go pass that along."

As Shaggy scurried off, Ethan took another sip of his coffee. This wasn't good. Normally, Buck was already here by now. You couldn't miss him. At 0500 he was already jacked up and knee-deep in something, wheeling skids around, or up on a lift, getting after it. How Sandy kept up with him was a mystery to Ethan.

If Buck wasn't here, that meant Ethan was in charge until he got here. And if his kid was sick, he wouldn't be coming in at all. Which meant Ethan was going to have to do a ton more extra work for exactly the same pay.

That went against his religion.

He took another sip and weighed his options. Like the brown water, none of them seemed particularly good. Ethan truly believed that if he started doing that, he would never stop. After all, why pay twenty-five credits an hour if you could get the same job done for twenty?

Of course, he could always go home. Just walk out. Security would drag him back eventually, but he might be able to catch the *Time Traveler* game first. Thinking like that was a good way to end up shipped back to Beta.

He could quietly rebel. Do the bare minimum, let his emails pile up, and ignore messages from Jim and everyone else. After all, he was still technically an MH1, and filling in for a lead wasn't in his job description. They couldn't touch him for refusing to do his job, but that didn't mean Jim couldn't get angry. Bosses can always find a way to write you up if they try hard enough.

Ethan took another slow sip. Every option tasted like garbage.

Then there was the baby to consider. Barely a twinkle in Ethan's eye, but even now, the baby complicated things. He needed the extra credits now, more than ever.

This pay cycle would mark eight weeks since Ethan had received his last two-credit pay stipend for taking on the responsibilities of an MH2. For reasons unknown to him, Ethan couldn't get fully promoted to the position, but he could be put on a spreadsheet and receive a pay stipend. Sometimes. If Jim didn't forget, something didn't go wrong with the old system, or whatever excuse they had cooked up that week.

It wasn't a life-changing amount of credits, but it was significant. After all, Ethan and Rose paid eight hundred credits a month for their home, and those two credits each hour added up to a healthy chunk of that payment. Ethan had been running on empty promises for twice that long, but they were getting hard to swallow. When would enough finally be enough? Was it this cycle?

His family needed him to keep this job. Where was the line? Was he supposed to perform like a circus bear and just be thankful not to be back on Beta Mining? That felt like a big pill to swallow, and he didn't exactly have a tall glass of water handy. Ethan didn't know if he could manage it.

Then again, mining an asteroid had nearly killed him. Twice. And for what? A lot fewer credits. If he got sent back there now, his daughter might never know her father. Would Rose ever forgive him if he failed?

Once again, his thoughts were churning. At Delta, he could just drink his coffee and mindlessly count boxes all day. No stress. They would probably even pay him what they promised and everything.

He muttered to himself, "I should probably go check my paystub. Maybe it's all there this time."

Two credits an hour. It was death by a thousand tiny cuts. Thinking about it was giving him indigestion. Ethan scowled and took another sip, then impulsively hurled the half-empty cup into the trash. It had turned lukewarm.

Ethan stood in front of the bins, his scanner glowing in the dim light. The first step in counting bins was to check BS03 and look them up. If you skipped this, you wouldn't know what was actually supposed to be in there. Somehow, and don't ask Ethan how, it was never the kitters' fault. (That was sarcasm.)

It is their fault. Not all of it, but yes, a big chunk, especially on the bottom shelves. Kitters loved to take things out, but updating quantities? Putting things back where they were found? Apparently, that was asking too much. It was like they woke up five minutes before their alarms, looked in the mirror, and decided, *"I'm going to do as little as possible this cycle."*

Ethan hadn't always been so cynical. Back when the White Vests from upper management first pitched their plan, he had been one of the few people who bought into it. The new shelving. The improved AI-guided drones. The bonus pay made him feel all warm and hopeful inside. For a while, Ethan thought he was going to be part of building a better future. He had truly believed.

The plan had been simple. Build big shelves, stock the lower bins with a cycle's worth of work, and stock the upper shelving with enough parts to last all week. The dock would bring back pre-sorted cages from Delta, and then Ethan and the others would replenish the bins. Little robots would zip around and kit all of the orders for them.

At first, it seemed like it was going to work. The most frequently used parts went up front, and the ones used the least went in the back, but then everything seemed to need to be in the front. The upper shelves were supposed to line up with the lower bins, but halfway through, the lower bin team changed the configuration without notifying the upper shelves team. No one had measured the lower bins, either. No one measured a thing. So, parts didn't fit in the new bins, and the old ones had been long gone. The list of problems stretched on and on.

Ethan didn't know what hurt more: losing the bonus pay or watching the renovations he had worked so hard on make things worse. There were many excuses, of course. *"It's a temporary setback. We're still ironing out the kinks."* He couldn't repeat it with conviction anymore.

A small voice in the back of Ethan's head whispered that he was being unfair. Half the kitting bots didn't even have BCT accounts installed; how were they supposed to make bin-to-bin transfers when IT took months to process requests? That wasn't the machines' fault. They *could* use Buck's communal login, but that would require the drones to be programmed to problem-solve. But kitters couldn't do that. They followed routes, grabbed parts, and if anything went wrong, they generated an error that humans had to clear. Sometimes it was an easy fix. Often, it wasn't.

BCT is a fickle mistress. Eight-twenty-ones weren't that bad. If you got off easy, all you had to do was click one button to confirm it. But triple eights? Those were the worst. No one had ever formally taught him how to use BCT. It was the blind leading the blind.

Still, even if the kitters were off the hook, the system wasn't off the hook. AI was supposed to make things easier, so why was everyone left in the dark about it? What was the point of gatekeeping information from the people who actually work with the programs? The AI was smarter than everyone in the fleet; shouldn't it be teaching them?

Ethan sighed heavily. But the bins weren't going to count themselves. Ethan exported the file and pulled it up on his scanner, enlarging the text to a size his aging eyes could handle. If the rows looked neat, he might get away with not pulling everything out. But one quick glance told him this wasn't one of those cycles.

The parts came in all shapes and sizes, a disorganized mess. The smallest boxes, about the size of a small shoe, were stuffed with thousands of O-rings. The big, square behemoths, weighing fifty pounds or more, were full of pumps and motors. Then there were the plastic totes, a category unto themselves. Literally anything could come in those. The red ones were short, square, and supposed to be neatly packed with foam liners. The blue ones were longer, with yellow foam and solid-bottomed interiors. They were supposed to hold big parts. Instead, people used them as catch-all bins for whatever they pleased. They just tossed stuff in. It was easier to do that and walk away than to identify it, hunt down exactly where every little thing actually went, and update stock for them.

Ethan exhaled through his nose in a long sound of resignation.

Bin LB1007A1 was supposed to have 96 pieces. He counted 83. Bin A2 should've had 19 but held 347. He counted that one three times just to be sure. Bin A3 was miraculously correct. From A1 to D6, only A3 matched the stock in BCT.

He tried not to let this constant annoyance get to him, but it wasn't working. He just kept his head down, focusing on consolidating similar parts, labelling boxes, and updating counts.

He hated how mind-numbingly predictable it was. How this job, this whole fleet, made him feel so frustrated.

Ethan muttered to himself, "Sweeping cobwebs isn't a long-term solution. We need to kill the spider."

People walked by and asked him questions. He answered them, but he kept his radio turned low. Too low. He ignored the constant stream of requests and emails waiting for him at the computer desks. Being the boss often felt like putting out little fires before they became bigger ones. Ethan drank enough coffee to stay awake all cycle putting them out.

He was halfway through counting another bin when the radio crackled to life again. He barely noticed. When he finally did notice, he turned it down. They probably wanted someone else.

The *Earth's Greatest Hits* sang, *"We're two of a kind, workin' on a full house."*

Ethan couldn't carry a tune in a bucket, but he loved this song. And when you worked in the back of the warehouse, that's what mattered most. It was just him, the bins, and golden oldies from Earth. Or so he thought.

A familiar voice chimed in, "You missed your calling, you know."

Ethan turned to see Darnell floating up beside him on his air-trawler, the lift purring as it hovered just a foot off the ground. Darnell had been around the warehouse longer than most. His beard had turned more silver than black, and he always wore a bandanna on his head. Some cycles it was yellow or red. This cycle, it was orange.

Darnell leaned an elbow on the side of his rig and grinned. "You must've been one of those lounge singers, crooning to folks sipping cocktails in a past life."

Ethan snorted and played along. "Yeah? Is that why I've been eyeing a sequin jacket?" He set his box down and added, "Did you hang a hammock up in here somewhere yet?"

Darnell chuckled. "Overtime is good for you." Then he jerked a thumb over his shoulder. "You wouldn't happen to know where LB1107B is, would you? It says here it should be in this row, but I've already done two laps and haven't seen it."

Ethan glanced at his scanner. "Yeah, it should be three rows down, but someone probably stuffed it in the wrong spot." He scanned the bins quickly, then pointed. "Try behind that blue tote."

Darnell grunted as he maneuvered his air-trawler a little closer. "They really need to get this labeling mess sorted out. It feels like every week, they change something and expect us to know it automagically."

Ethan nodded. "Yeah, well…why make it easy?" He glanced at his scanner. "You know, if you don't get some rest, you're going to crash that shuttle you love so much one of these cycles. Even God took one cycle off a week."

Darnell gave a dry chuckle. "I don't get tired flying Six."

They worked in silence for a moment. Then Darnell tapped the side of his trawler. "Alright, I appreciate the help. Did you know that Jim's been calling you on the radio?"

Ethan turned up the radio. "Oh, I must have bumped it," he lied. Darnell just shook his head, laughing.

Ethan waved as he glided off, then turned back to his bins, sighing at the mismatched counts. Bin LB1007A1 was wrong too, but at this point, he was ready to give up. He consolidated a few more scattered parts, labeled what he could, and tidied his area. Then, with the kind of resignation that came from knowing exactly what awaited him, he trudged toward the computer desk to submit his counts.

Greeting him was a stale, sour smell that clung to the air near the desks, where the overflowing trash can sat untouched. People had started balancing their garbage on top, creating a precarious little tower. Where was Stan? The old trash collector was really running behind now.

The moment he stepped up to the computer terminal and signed in, the waiting messages beeped at him like a nest of hungry birds. Someone had left a sticky note on the monitor that simply said, *"Transfer 37 pieces of 1326464."* Something. What finish was it? He wasn't sure. He could barely read the note. And where was he supposed to transfer it, anyway?

He muttered, "Whose handwriting is this?"

Then he exhaled slowly and sat down. The scanners were still missing, so at least he had an excuse to use the keyboard and manually enter each adjustment. That helped a little. The whole system was supposed to streamline inventory, but right now, it felt like he was trying to hold water with a cracked bucket.

Just then, a new email popped up from Jim. The subject line read: *Answer your radio. See me before lunch.*

He stared at the email for a long moment, fingers hovering over the keyboard. Then, with a quiet exhale, he went back to submitting his counts. Whatever Jim wanted, he was sure it wasn't going to be, "You're promoted, effective immediately. Here's your back pay, too."

Before he could log out, another message popped up, this one from Rose. He clicked it and read: *Ugggh … work blows. Why couldn't we be born rich? Lots of love, Nerd!*

Ethan smiled and typed back. *We didn't draw Nepo Baby. Lots of love!*

Then he logged out and pushed himself up from the chair. He flexed his fingers, then smoothed a wrinkle on his vest. Then he forced his arms to stay still at his sides.

"Shaggy!" he yelled across the floor. "I'm going to go see what Jim wants! Be right back!"

Jim's office was just past the break room. Ethan topped off his coffee before heading in. Sometimes, that first sip set the tone for the rest of the cycle. If it was better than expected, the cycle might hold a pleasant surprise. If it was worse…well, you know the rest.

He took a sip and scowled.

With a sigh, Ethan left the breakroom, turned right, and knocked twice on a white door a dozen steps down the hall before stepping inside. The reception area was empty, save for two desks, a few cabinets, and the door to Jim's office. His door stood open.

"Come in," he called.

Jim sat behind his desk, squinting at his monitor. He was a wiry man, his frame a size too small for his vest. His dark hair was in that awkward stage midway between a fresh buzz cut and a grown-out style. His scraggly beard looked like it had surrendered for the cycle. As Ethan entered, Jim finally looked up from his screen.

Jim's eyes weren't cold, abyssal pits of villainy, nor were they a warm, heroic shade of chestnut brown. They were simply, profoundly tired. Deep bags hung beneath them. Framed pictures of his kids crowded the desk's surface. He mustered a tired, strained smile. "What's all that huffin' and puffin' for?"

Ethan raised his polymer coffee cup slightly. "Coffee in the break room is off. Too watery."

Jim cleared his throat, searching his memory. "I like my coffee like I like my deadlines. Strong and impossible to ignore."

Ethan smirked. "Nice one."

Jim gestured toward his dry-erase board. "I had to keep up with you." The joke Ethan had scrawled there last cycle, in grease-marker green, with letters three feet high, was still there. "Geology rocks, but geography is where it's at." He paused, squinting. "That's what it says, right?"

Ethan nodded, glancing at Jim's photos. "Just helping you work on your dad jokes." He nodded toward the frames. "Cute kids."

Jim snorted, erasing the board with a sweep of his arm. "Thanks. The little one's sixteen months and just figured out how to run. Can't keep him out of anything. His brother's eight, and he tries to climb everything. The wife says our apartment looks like a warzone. Not that I'm home enough to see it, now that I'm on salary."

Ethan wasn't sure what to say. He settled for, "I can only imagine. Rose and I are trying, too." He hesitated. "How'd you settle on names?"

Jim's grin faded into something weary but warm. "We named Marty after my wife's father, Martin." Jim tossed the eraser aside and turned. "Honestly, I wanted to call him Junior, but she cared more than I did, so I didn't fight it. Wasn't worth it. You'll learn that one cycle. Gotta pick your battles."

Ethan half-smiled, unsure if it was genuine advice or a subtle warning.

Jim cleared his throat and pointed at Ethan's radio. "And check your mic," he added, his voice hardening. "People have been calling you."

Ethan nodded, reaching for his belt. "Anything else?"

Jim nodded toward his screen. "Yeah. Check your IMs and emails. Then hit these bins, verify the counts, and pull as many of these parts as you can find. Haul them over to plating. We've got to get those panels coated so we can fix the gravity."

Ethan looked down at the list loading on his scanner and paused, his fingers tightening around his cup. "The glowing ones? Don't they go on the hull?"

Jim had already turned back to his screen. "Yep." He cleared his throat, a telltale sign the conversation was over. "That's all."

Ethan didn't move.

Jim glanced up, his impatience now visible. "Something else? "

Ethan shifted his weight. "Jim…it's been two months. I still haven't seen my bonus pay."

Jim frowned. "Really? I could have sworn I put you on the spreadsheet last week."

"You didn't. HR verified it." Ethan held his gaze. "Eight weeks now. First two of the year were fine, then nothing. I haven't calculated taxes or overtime, but every credit counts. "

Jim sighed, rubbing his temples. "Alright. I'll see what I can do."

Ethan's stomach tightened. He'd heard that before. "I know you're busy. I asked HR if she could help sort it, but she can't approve anything without a written statement from you. Each week." He added, his voice flat.

Jim shook his head, straightening in his chair. "I've got enough on my plate… I can't promise that. But I want to promote you and be done with the damn spreadsheet."

"I'm glad to hear it. I don't want to bug you every week, but I need those credits, Jim. We're talking about a new dryer."

Jim nodded. "I understand," he replied, his tone cooling. "You're still our top candidate. Unfortunately, the interview process is taking longer than expected. I have to interview every applicant. People from all over the fleet want to be MH2s here."

Ethan asked. "So when can we schedule mine?"

Jim leaned back in his chair. "How about right now?" he offered. "What makes you think you're qualified to be an MH2?"

Ethan blinked. "Now?"

Ethan squared his shoulders. "Well, I use multiple BCT programs every cycle. I work closely with inventory to reconcile the stock. Pull up my transactions and see for yourself."

Jim nodded slowly. "Good answer. Do you know what BCT stands for?"

Ethan blinked again. "Business...Coordination Tool."

Jim grinned, looking genuinely surprised. "That's right! No one ever gets that. How'd you know?"

Ethan shrugged. "My wife watches *90 Cycles.* That dating show. Some guy on it mentioned that little factoid."

Jim chuckled, grabbing a pen and jotting something down. "That random factoid stuck with you? That's funny. Well, Parks,

I'm glad you learn fast. You're *still* our top candidate. I'll try to wrap up the other interviews as soon as I can."

Ethan stared at him. "That's it?"

Jim held his gaze for a long moment before speaking. "Just remember to stay positive. We have plenty of problems around here. What we need are hard workers with the right mindset to come together and execute the solutions. I'll make sure you're on the spreadsheet this week."

Ethan drained his cup and dropped it in the trash. "Yeah. Thanks. Before I go, how much longer do you expect to be interviewing?"

Jim's answer was, "At least two weeks." He said it like an afterthought, eyes already drifting back to the screen. "Now, will you *please* go get those parts?"

Ethan nodded. The words, *"at least two weeks,"* rattled around in his skull like a couple of loose screws as he left.

CHAPTER 4
The Round-Up

The radio station's music had shifted to pop by the time Ethan exited Jim's office. It wasn't until he was storming through the SM-Racks, ducking beneath a hovering kitting drone in the narrow aisle, that he finally noticed. Truthfully, Ethan wasn't hearing the music. He was hearing Carolina singing it.

She was belting it out. Something about a pink pony club in Hollywood.

Ethan waved as he got closer. "Every time I hear this song, I always wonder what West Hollywood looked like back then."

Carolina munched a chip and waved back. "I don't know, but I love this song! It makes me feel so free!" Her short, pink-and-blonde beaded dreads clicked together as she finished typing. "What's up?"

She had as much energy as a Labrador that's just found a tennis ball.

Ethan shook his head and chuckled.

"What?" Carolina asked.

"I swear, if you had a tail, it'd be wagging. I was just thinking you must've been a dog in a past life. A retriever, maybe."

She laughed. "I can see that. You were probably a border collie."

Ethan snorted. "Probably. So Jim gave me a project, and I need some help." He highlighted a few parts on his scanner and sent her the file. "Can you pull these for me?"

Carolina pulled up the file in a couple of clicks. Seconds later, the printer started coughing up paper. "Sure thing." She agreed, crumpling her now-empty bag of chips. "I've been bored, so I'm glad you asked. Honestly."

"Thanks. I really appreciate it. Have you seen Shaye-Shaye? Or Shaggy?"

She shrugged and hopped out of her chair. "Barry's over there. Hey, have you seen the scanners?"

Ethan shook his head. "I was hoping you'd have by now."

"Nope! Let me grab my harness and I'll go pull these parts. You want me to stage them back here?"

Ethan nodded. "That'd be great. Leave 'em on the skid, please."

He left her to it and headed across the floor, scanning for Barry. Like most cycles, he was on an air trawler working the bent aisle. Barry was in his late twenties, with sandy, shaggy hair and a fresh shave under a backwards ball cap. He returned with a clean pallet moments later, glistening with sweat.

Barry unhooked himself from the machine and adjusted his cap. "What's up, bro?"

"Not much, buddy. Jim gave me a project."

Barry's reply was as dry as the grit in the sandblasters. "Tell me it doesn't involve me crawling in a bent rack." He stepped off the machine and was still taller than Ethan. Here, Barry was taller than everyone and bigger, too. He had a lot of old Viking genes still rattling around in him.

"I wish I could." Ethan tapped his scanner and flicked the file to Barry. "Can you pull these for me? They're all bent."

Barry took a swig of water. "Sure."

"Thanks. Carolina's pulling some from eight, and she's staging the skid by the computer desk. Put yours on the same skid with hers." Ethan nodded at the air trawler. "You look busy. Where's Shaggy?"

Barry wiped sweat from his brow. "Mercedes grabbed him for mini-orders. Momma was here a minute ago, but she's looking for the scanners now."

Ethan nodded. "Alright, thanks. I'm heading to the FS-Racks if you need me." He tapped his radio. "I got this thing turned up."

"Alright, bro. No problem. Hey, I tried cooking steaks," Barry interjected quickly. He was excited; Ethan could see it in his eyes. "We went to the park and rented a grill for a few minutes and everything!"

"Oh, sweet," Ethan replied. "What kind?"

"New York strips. Momma's came out great, but I don't know about mine. I accidentally did that blue-rare thing you're always talking about. It was like a crime scene on my plate."

"What temp did you set the grill to?"

"Four fifty. I used up most of the time on Momma's, so I cranked the heat and tried to finish mine quick. I got a good sear on both sides, but the middle was still cold. Juicy, though."

"Did you like it?"

Barry nodded vigorously, clipping himself back into the airlift. "I would've preferred medium, maybe medium rare, but it was good. Bloody, but good."

Ethan smiled knowingly. "Rose loves 'em that way. I know what you mean, though, I prefer a little less moo myself. You ever wonder what New York looks like now? There's this old-timey card, Lady Liberty, she's a huge statue. Sometimes I wonder if she's still standing."

Barry shook his head. "Nah, not really. Mostly I just think about playing *Bot Hunter*. It's about shooting evil robots." With that, he fired up the machine and was gone in a rush of air.

Ethan lingered a moment longer to send Shaye-Shaye an email. Subject line*: Look At Me.* He copied the message and sent an IM, too. The messages read: *"Any luck with the scanners? Need help with anything else?"*

Then he did a radio check and was off again.

Before Ethan could take three steps, his radio crackled.

It was Mercedes. *"Ethan, you copy?"*

He pressed the transmitter. "Go ahead."

The radio spit out a burst of static. *"I need you to pull these parts!"*

Before he could respond, his email pinged. Shaye-Shaye. *Subject line: YES!*

He squeezed the radio again. "Mercedes, send me a list. I'll go pull them."

Ethan's email binged again. Shaye-Shaye: "*Why'd my transaction turn red?"*

Before he could respond, Mercedes crackled across the radio again. *"What's your twenty? I'm not at a computer."*

The rest of the cycle passed in a rush of activity. Thrumming air-trawlers, shuffling feet, and the crackling radio melted together into numbing white noise. The place was bustling. Assembly lines clattered, drones zipped with sharp, programmed bursts, and the air was thick with dust.

It took three hours, but Mercedes finally found the missing scanners. They were inside a locker, shoved underneath the drone command tower, half-buried behind papers and stray parts in loose totes.

How'd they get there? No one knew.

Ethan decided to blame it on B-shift. He'd been fiddling with one of the scanners since second break, but he couldn't find the setting. It wasn't complicated, just a cache that needed clearing, but figuring out how had taken him hours.

By the end of the cycle, Jim's parts were stacked in front of plating, but the trash had started to reek. Banana peels, leaky coffee cups, and mystery leftovers were mixed with balled-up papers and chip bags, forming a small mountain of filth. Ethan pushed one last button on the scanner. Just as the screen flashed blue indicating success, he heard the familiar shuffle of boots behind him. He set the scanner down, feeling a small flicker of accomplishment that already felt hollow.

Ike, a man stooped with age, his face chiseled from stone, walked up and held out a large card. "You got a second?" His voice was softer than usual. Ethan knew immediately something was wrong. "We're passing this around for Stan's family. He passed last night."

Ethan froze. "Stan," he asked, and the name came out strangled. "The trashman?"

Ike nodded and held out a card. Handwritten condolences from two dozen coworkers were already crowded together on its surface. "Security did a wellness check on him at lunch. Found him still in his bunk, stone dead. I heard they think he had a heart attack in his sleep." He shook his head.

Ike nodded grimly. "Old age and spotty gravity," the greybeard added. "Stan lived in Sector Six. The gravity has been cutting out over there for a few seconds at a time. Doesn't do much for pacemakers."

Ethan handed him the card back. "Well, I hope Stan's grilling in Heaven right now."

Ike took the card and moved on, asking others to sign, and the usual noises of the ship returned. Ethan stood there for a moment longer, staring at the trash he'd just bagged. The warehouse had emptied out by the time he returned; the lights flickered as some of the systems, sensing that no one was nearby, powered down.

Ethan went to his computer desk just long enough to grab his things as the last few stragglers filed out toward the exit. He fell into step behind Barry and Shaye-Shaye as they made their way toward the time clock. This giant ship, the warehouse, his routine—it all felt like it might chew him up, the way it ground on, cycle after cycle.

Shaye-Shaye slowed her pace, her well-worn sneakers shuffling on the floor, and glanced over her shoulder. "So, Ethan, what are you and Rose eating for dinner? Still sticking with that healthy stuff?" Her voice carried a familiar, maternal quality that made even mundane topics feel warm.

She was a sturdy woman with soft, greying hair pulled back into a bun, a few silver strands escaping to frame her face. Her eyes were calm, her skin lightly weathered by years of long shifts. Shaye-Shaye carried nothing but a light jacket folded neatly in her crossed arms; Barry served as her pack mule, toting both of their lunch boxes and water bottles.

Ethan shrugged. "I'm not sure how healthy *Marry Me Chicken* is, but probably not." He offered her a tired smile and slumped further. "That stuff is a lot of work. I'll probably just have a liquid dinner tonight."

Shaye-Shaye wasn't amused. "Ethan, you need more than alcohol." She scolded.

He shot back. "Orange juice is healthy. Lots of vitamin C." He added, "What are you two having?"

Barry answered. "Pizza."

Shaye-Shaye nodded. "Barry ordered a large meat lovers. You should order one; those are easy! You can pick it up on the way home."

Barry nodded. "*The Big Banjo*, bro. It's the best."

Ethan badged his way through the final door. Together, they filtered out onto the platform to wait for the trams. For twelve hours, he was free. If you could call it that.

Something had been weighing on his mind all cycle, whether or not to tell anyone what he suspected. Now, there wasn't much time left to make up his mind.

Ethan cleared his throat and lowered his voice. "You know that special project we did for Jim today?"

Shaye-Shaye nodded. "Yeah, that was a lot of gold!" she said, her eyes widening at the memory.

Ethan nodded, his expression grim. "Yeah, it was." He explained quickly, his words tumbling out in a breathless whisper. "I used to work for Katarina. She was my boss when I was in distribution; before she went over to maintenance, she told me once that they coat these special TT panels in a tritium bath; that's why they glow. If you shoot electricity through tritium a certain way, it creates artificial gravity. I racked them once when I first started here. Those panels dry for a cycle, and then they're ready to be installed…*outside* the hull.

"Jim said engineering needed them to fix the gravity bubble. But they aren't going to send a bunch of engineers out on the hull to change out the bad ones. I think there's going to be another round-up soon."

Shaye-Shaye stiffened. "Why wouldn't they send them? They have the most training!"

Ethan's anxiety spiked. "Because there aren't enough of them to spare. You know how long it takes to train an engineer? Years." He held up two fingers. "How long to get a yellow vest? A couple of weeks."

She protested, a tremor in her voice. "But then who would run everything?"

Ethan shook his head sadly. "When they rebuilt the SM-Racks, they didn't replace the old team they sent to Delta with real people. Instead, they brought in those drones that barely work to do the job. That's what they'll do to us, too."

Shaye-Shayne turned a shade paler. "Barry, you're almost out of time!" She hissed, "You can't miss another cycle!"

Barry went green.

Ethan nodded grimly. "I don't think any of us can."

The tram arrived with a hiss and a shudder. Ethan let Barry and Shaye-Shaye climb on first, then followed, his hands tight on the rail.

The doors hissed shut. The tram lurched forward.

Ethan stared at his reflection in the dark glass and tried not to picture the hull.

CHAPTER 5
Six Business Cycles

Ethan shuffled in and all but collapsed in his chair. His porthole was waiting for him, but he paid little attention to the stars. Instead, he reached for the remote. The tube came to life with a bright flash of light. Soon, Rose would be home, and then she would commandeer it for an episode of *90 Cycles*. Love would force him to watch the RTS network turn long-distance relationships into bite-sized, televised dramas.

Until then, he could watch reruns of the big tournament. Ethan poked at the interface, keying in his search slowly and methodically. *Kraven wins with fame*. Enter.

The tube considered this for a second. *IS THIS ETHAN?* The words flashed on the screen in neon blues and greens over the picture of a cartoonish goblin wearing a tuxedo. The account icon gave a little wave.

Ethan sighed. His thumb typed back. *Yes*.

Hi Ethan! Based on your search history, I think you want to watch xXxKravenxXx win the 32nd Time Traveler Pro Tour. Is that correct?

Ethan sighed again. *Yes*.

OK! Let me show you what I've found! The goblin danced on screen as videos loaded. Seconds later, he scrolled down to the first one. The game was twenty-two minutes and nineteen seconds long. If he got lucky, very lucky, he could finish the game before Rose got home. The preview clip played on a loop, showing the competitors as they drew their opening hands.

All four players held a three-card hand. The screen was divided into quarters, each square showing the player's cards in full view.

Only Kraven drew *Nepo Baby.*

Ethan felt himself lean forward as Kraven's cursor immediately selected it and pressed enter.

Just as the video began to play, he heard the muted click-clack of Rose's boots outside the door, followed by the sharp release of pressure as it hissed open. A familiar mix of lavender and something faintly singed reached him before she did.

Ethan's thumb hovered over the pause button, caught between the game and greeting his wife properly. He smiled automatically and pushed the button. So much for that.

"Hey, baby, I'm home!" Rose's voice was bright but undercut with fatigue. She kicked the door shut behind her with practiced ease, then tossed her bag onto the counter. "Did you miss me, or were you too busy watching sweaty nerds play pretend?"

He pushed himself up and clutched his chest with mock drama. "Shots fired."

She pointed at the tube. "Am I wrong?"

Ethan wrapped his arms around her and kissed her cheek. "Never ever," he agreed. "How was your cycle?"

Rose returned the kiss. "Just a hellish mix of boring and frustrating." Then she pulled away and crossed the room to grab the remote, plopping down on the couch. "I've been looking forward to the new episode of *90 Cycles*! Lavender and Mickey are going to go at it! She took five thousand credits he gave her for a wedding dress and spent it on a butt lift!"

Ethan whistled. "Yeah. That will do it."

Rose grinned. "That's not even the best part! The five thousand wasn't enough. So her ex-boyfriend, who actually lives in her ship, Mike, also gave her a few thousand credits."

Ethan shook his head. "Yeah, that will *definitely* do it." He chuckled. "Want a drink?"

Rose nodded enthusiastically. "Please! I can't wait to see the look on Mickey's face when she tells him. Here we go!" A bright, bubbly title screen swallowed the Pro Tour. Oversaturated letters flashed.

"90 CYCLES—NEW EPISODE LOADING… "

A peppy announcer's voice chimed in. *"Welcome back, Cycle-Heads! This time, Mickey is in for a big surprise, and Lavender has some explaining to do!"* A musical number blared with gusto alongside the show's opening montage.

It was a sound Ethan would be tormented with in Hell. At least he was watching it with an angel for now. Sure, she was covered in tattoos of cow skulls and thorny cacti, without wings or a halo, but an angel nonetheless. He made their drinks and returned to the couch.

Rose beamed. "Thanks, babe!" She had already settled into her favorite spot in the middle of the couch. "This episode is trending all over *Knock-Knock* right now. Basically, she puts all that butt in his lap, and that's how she convinces him to get over it."

Ethan just shook his head and sipped his drink, his eyes drifting toward the porthole. He could feel his whole body sink into his chair. Part of him wondered if he could feel roots sprouting, too. As if his body was made of wood.

"Oh, babe! I think we have some popcorn in the pantry! Will you check?"

Ethan opened his eyes. He hadn't even realized they were closed, but they were, and everything inside of him groaned as he mustered the will to stand back up. Rose had a knack for waiting until he had just gotten comfortable to ask for something. But he didn't mind. There were worse problems to have. "Sure thing, sweetheart."

Sure enough, a bag of popcorn sat in the pantry. He tossed it in the microwave and pressed the button. There were so many buttons in his life, so many buttons. Sometimes, that's all it felt like life amounted to: just a whole bunch of buttons and the people who pressed them.

Rose called out. "No slushie today?"

Ethan shook his head from the kitchen. "Didn't feel like crushing the ice."

When the kernels fell silent, he tossed the popcorn into a pink plastic bowl. Not just any pink, either. This specific shade was trademarked. *Pink-a-licious*, by Pink Karsmashian, another celebrity Rose adored.

Ethan set the bowl down in front of her and crash-landed back in his chair. He took another sip of his drink, a big one. Ethan savored the burn, enjoying the last tangy dregs from the bottom of the glass.

"Babe! You forgot the salt!"

He smiled again. "I'm going straight to the bad place for that one."

Rose winked at him. "The big guy upstairs will forgive you if you hurry!"

A small huff escaped him. Thankfully, his joints still held plenty of spongy cartilage, and his rump still had just enough bounce left in it. With herculean effort, he gritted his teeth, summoned some inner strength, and clawed his way back to his feet. Like Rocky Balboa after fifteen grueling rounds with Apollo Creed, he rose to his full height and fetched the salt.

Rose beamed again. "Thanks!" She swiped it from him and promptly proceeded to make it snow on the popcorn, that was the only word for it. "Scoot over!" she added. "You're not made of glass!"

He took another sip, this one even bigger than the rest. The fiery line it burned going down settled inside his belly and relit his pilot light. Then he divided the rest of the bottle between their two glasses, added a little lemon juice to each, and stirred them with a spoon. As he was putting the bottle back, a sound on the tube made him turn and knock his drink over.

Rose's eyes stayed glued to the screen. "Careful, babe!" she said, eyes still on the screen. "Did you see that? The ex-boyfriend lives just two apartments over from Lavender! Mickey's been paying for her room, too. He has no idea about the other man!"

Ethan closed his eyes. He thought about puppies and rainbows, anything other than how annoyed he was, how he just wanted to sit down. Then he brought Rose her drink, started looking for the broom, and cleared his throat. "Poor Mickey."

Rose shook her head. "Don't feel bad for him! We don't like Mickey! He sent private pictures of Lavender to his ex-wife to make her jealous!"

Ethan made a face. "I mean, that's not cool," he said as he swept up the broken glass. "But does it justify her cheating on the guy and using him for his credits?"

Rose raised a finger in Lavender's defense. "We don't know that she cheated! She says she didn't, and that's good enough for me. I'm Team Lavender!"

Ethan dumped the broken glass into the trash and returned the broom to its spot. "Is that so? I guess all you hoes have to stick together. Is that it?"

"Dang!" Rose's jaw dropped, but her eyes widened with amusement. "That is not it, and I am not a hoe! Neither is Lavender. We are ladies, thank you very much!"

"Right." He winked at her. "Whatever you say, babe."

Rose shot him a look full of mock warning. "Don't make me press this pause button. I will get up off this couch." She took a sip of her drink, made a face, then got all serious again and set it down; you know, to play tough. "Don't test me," she finished.

Ethan took the bait with a smile. "And what are you going to do, Hoe?"

Rose shrieked and jumped up at once. "That's it! I'm going to get you this time, old man!"

She ran him around the kitchen in circles, tickling, pinching, and giggling. Ethan let her chase him all the way into their room, where she finally managed to tackle him onto the bed. Somehow, he found the energy to do more than lay there like a starfish. In no time, they got all tangled up together under the sheets and did a lot more than just tickle.

Ethan lay in bed. "I love being newly approved."

Rose grinned. "Soak it all in, Big Boy. Enjoy it while you can. That's what I'm doing!" With a bounce, she hopped off the bed, grabbed a towel, wiped off, and tossed it at Ethan's head.

Her silhouette slipped into a pair of jeans. "Don't expect it to be like this forever. Once the baby arrives, I'll be too busy changing diapers and getting puked on to accommodate you."

Feeling completely exhausted, Ethan remained planted in the center of the bed, lying in a puddle of sweat and other mystery fluids. He was too tired to care about the dampness. Ethan wasn't even really there right now.

Rose asked, "Do you want to skip *90 Cycles* and go get something to eat?"

Ethan answered, "Sure." Truthfully, he didn't know what he had agreed to, but it didn't matter. At that moment, he would have agreed to anything.

"Me too. What are you hungry for?"

Crap. He could tell by her tone that it was a question, which meant he needed to answer something. But what? He managed, "You know, I'm not sure."

Rose pulled a shirt on. "That popcorn hit the spot, but my tummy is still grumbling. I need something…more. Something I don't have to cook."

The lightbulb clicked on in Ethan's head. "How does pizza sound?"

Rose cooed at the idea. "We could pick one up from the Caf. Put a shirt on, babe!" she added, throwing more clothes at Ethan. "Hurry, before they're all gone!"

Ethan puffed. "Hurry is my middle name, babe."

He put on a pair of camouflage leggings and a black t-shirt featuring a cartoon wizard holding two watermelon-sized crystal balls. Thunderous yellow letters read: *MANA IS STORED IN THE BALLS.* His left sock was orange with black tiger stripes. His right sock? Yellow with black leopard spots. He finished the outfit with a pair of slides. Now, he just needed to find his hat.

As Ethan left the room to do just that, he found Rose waiting for him in a blue floral print shirt to go with her blue jeans, ready to go. He wasn't half as awake as she was. His spirit was willing to walk down to the Caf, but the flesh was weak. Yawning, Ethan rubbed his eyes.

Rose teased, "Come on, slowpoke. You act like I'm dragging you on a spacewalk."

"Feels like it," Ethan mumbled. "I swear, I feel like I'm running on fumes."

Rose grinned. "You'll thank me once we get a hot slice of pizza in your belly."

That was debatable, but Ethan followed her anyway, too groggy to do much more than try to keep up. Rose blazed a trail down the hallway.

A dull roar surrounded them as they walked: hissing air vents, thrumming artificial gravity, and a cacophony of voices all trying to talk over one another. C-Shift was over, and the halls were busy with crew members heading to the cafeteria or relaxing outside their quarters. Ethan shuffled along, rubbing a livid bruise the shuttle door had given him on his arm. Worse, a combination of sweaty, chafing thighs and running around had rubbed him raw.

The familiar aroma of recycled air and fresh bread drifted through the vents as they approached. The Caf was a spacious, open area with rows of metal tables bolted to the floor. The ceiling arched high above, lined with soft sodium lights. A constant hum of conversation filled the space, blending with the clatter of trays and scuffing shoes. Crew members lined up along the near wall, waiting to pick up a tray and their options at the buffet. A long viewport stretched across the far wall, offering a view of the endless stars, though most people were too busy eating to notice them.

Rose half-shouted, "You get the table; I'll grab the pizza."

Ethan chose one closest to the window. As he waited for Rose, the stars kept him company. They shone brightly, coldly, and distantly, like hearts on social media. Delta was barely visible, just a tiny speck of technology whose interior and running lights he strained to see.

Would it be better there? He would earn more per hour for doing the exact same job. So why not? It's better to take a guaranteed pay per hour than a false promise for two.

He pondered an old Earth saying: the grass isn't always greener over the next hill. His father had told him that the grass is greenest where you water it, but maybe a bunch of goat herders made that saying up. What did the people of Earth know about living on a spaceship? No matter how much you water irradiated soil, nothing grows there. Sometimes, you have to move on.

Rose didn't make him wait long. "What are you thinking about?" She set a slice of pizza down on the table in front of him. "*Time Traveler*?"

Ethan shook his head.

Rose sat down. "Oh no, was your pay still messed up?" The look on Ethan's face told her everything she needed to know. She pouted sympathetically. "What happened?"

Ethan rubbed his face. "I went and talked to Jim." He just shook his head.

Rose prodded. "And?"

Ethan shook his head again.

"Tell me!" Rose insisted. "What did he say?"

"He asked me a couple of questions and told me I was the guy they wanted for the job." Ethan shrugged, picking up his pizza and inspecting it.

Rose shrugged back. "So? Why are you upset then?"

He set the pizza down, untouched. "It was pretty much the same old story. Told me it was taking a while because so many people applied." Ethan rolled his eyes and looked straight at Rose. "It sounded good, but I didn't really buy it. I *wanted* to believe him, but I don't think he was being completely honest."

Rose took a bite of her slice. "What do you mean?"

"It's hard to explain, I just don't think that's really what's going on. The whole thing felt like a sham. All Jim really wanted was for me to pull those special gold panels and get them to plating."

Rose nearly choked on her food. "Wait, didn't you tell me once those go on the outside of the ship?"

He nodded. "I… I think there's going to be another round-up soon, Rose. Maybe even by the next cycle, I don't know." He gave her a worried look. "I do know those panels will be ready for installation by the next cycle."

Rose grabbed his hand and squeezed it. "Hey. Don't worry, we always use our vacation points or perfect attendance. Our time is fine. Eat," she urged.

Ethan shook his head. "I think my semaglutide shot hasn't worn off yet."

Rose squeezed his fingers again supportively. "Well, mine has." She took another bite, chewed, and pushed a foam cup with a plastic lid at him. "At least drink something. I got fizzy water, pink flavor."

"Your favorite." He smiled at her. "I'm glad they have it this time."

Rose nodded and took another bite. "I know, right? Last time all they had was red and blue. I need pink. I crave it!"

Ethan released her hand. "Maybe you're pregnant." He dared to hope.

"Maybe," she agreed happily. "But I think it's just period cravings. Well, how about I wrap this up, we'll go grab one more for the road, and then take it back to our room? Does that sound good? Come on."

She pushed herself up and grabbed a couple of paper napkins from the dispenser on the table. "You've been with bitches who have had a period before. Do you get bloated and gassy when you're on your period? I've only had like two, and that was years ago. All I really remember was freaking out when I saw the little glob of blood in my underwear."

Ethan hung his head. "I don't know," he mumbled. "My brain's not working right now."

Rose smacked him playfully. "Obviously, you didn't pay much attention when you were with those hoes, but you're going to pay attention to me." She winked at him.

By some last miracle from God, he managed to push himself back onto his feet once more. "It's not exactly something I want to talk about while you're eating," Ethan said, "but I know there's something called period diarrhea. How's that little butt been feeling?"

Rose bit her bottom lip. "I have been going to the bathroom a lot. It's always so peaceful being on the toilet, until it's time to flush. Then I always worry that it's not going to work again. At least when we're home."

Ethan snorted. "The ten-step reminder plaque doesn't bring you comfort?" he teased her. "I can't wait for the next cycle when you're the one who finally clogs the toilet. Remember when you told me ladies can't do that?"

Rose finished wrapping up his pizza. "I told you hoes don't get cold, too. Get enough to drink in me, and I say all kinds of things."

They slipped back into the pizza line, waiting behind half a dozen other crew members chatting while they waited. The Caf smelled like melted cheese and marinara sauce here, which was normally a comforting aroma, but it made his stomach twist into knots now. Rose skipped the plates and grabbed a fresh, triangular slice of cheese pizza for the ride home, tossing Ethan a smirk.

Her sarcasm and sympathy blended into a single tone. "You're looking a little green. Come on, Big Boy, you brave astronaut you; let's get you home."

They made their way toward the exit, and somehow, the ribbed hallway stretching ahead seemed even longer on the way back. The familiar hum of the ship's systems in the background accompanied them every step of the way. Portholes along the walls showed the endless black of space, dotted with distant stars.

He pointed at one, wincing as he took a step. "I never get sick of the view."

Rose said, "You were born to be on the bridge crew, babe."

Ethan moped. "Doesn't feel like it. Not when I'm getting shortchanged like this." An undercurrent of anger ran through his words.

"Oh, come on," Rose said, trying to be supportive. "All sorts of bad things happened to Queen Elizabeth, right? All those people in *Time Traveler* went through it. You got this."

"Yeah, well, something tells me Jim isn't going to get executed for betraying me. That's what happened to Robert Devereux when he betrayed Queen Elizabeth. Only somehow, I'm Devereux, and instead of getting my head chopped off, I'm going to be sent out again."

Rose reached over and squeezed his fingers again. "Hey, come on, that's not going to happen. Our time is fine. I know you're worried, but you're going to be OK. You'll see."

Ethan winced. He felt like he was beating a dead horse. He didn't really know much about horses, but Ethan was pretty sure the phrase meant *wasting time*. "I just wish they would pay me what they said they would. At least tell me you're not; if you're not going to, don't lie to me!"

Rose squeezed his hand harder. "Babe. You're yelling."

Ethan blinked. "Sorry. I don't hear as well since—"

Rose interrupted. "Ever since you worked around those loud machines." She smiled as their fingers laced together, delicately balancing the pizza in her free hand. "While you were on the Beta, I know. Just…take a deep breath."

He hung his head. "Sorry. To hear myself talk, I have to raise my voice, so I don't realize how loud I'm really yelling."

"I know," Rose said, jerking her head toward their compartment. "Help me with the door."

Ethan reached out and pressed his badge against the scanner. A soft beep sounded, and the door slid open with a hiss of pressurized air. The sterile blue-white glow of the monitors welcomed them inside. Rose stepped in first, setting the pizza down on the small table in front of the couch. The smell of greasy, melted cheese filled the room, making Ethan's stomach growl despite his lingering frustration. He followed her in, closing the door behind them with another hiss.

"Do you want to talk about it more?" Rose asked, watching him pensively as he rubbed his face at the question.

Ethan exhaled deeply, shaking his head. "Not really. I'm just tired of asking for what I'm owed. It feels like begging now." He slumped into his chair, staring at the porthole. "I'm never going to see these credits, and I feel so…disposable. It just sucks."

Rose sat beside him on the couch, letting her fingers brush his forearm. "I get it, but you're not disposable, Ethan. You know that, right?"

He let out a dry chuckle. "Try telling that to Jim."

"I'd rather tell you," she said, nudging him lightly. "Because what he thinks doesn't matter half as much to me as what you do."

For a moment, he simply allowed himself to sit in the quiet, feeling the warmth of her next to him. The steady hum of the ship, which usually reminded him of how trapped he felt, seemed less suffocating for a moment. Rose shifted and reached for the pizza. "Here," she said, pushing a piece toward him. "Take at least one bite before it gets completely cold. Nothing fixes a crap cycle like carbs."

Ethan snorted but still took a slice, the soft crust folding between his fingers. "I'm just going to throw it up later."

She grinned. "It's worth it."

Ethan took a bite and chewed in peaceful silence, the weight in his chest easing just a bit as he swallowed. "All right, maybe you're onto something."

Rose's smile broadened. "Told you." She cleared her throat. "Listen, babe, I get how you feel—I really do. When I asked for a raise, Jim told me he didn't have a magic button he could press to give me any more credits."

Ethan's lips pressed into a thin, grim line. "Yeah, I remember. We're both getting shafted."

Rose gently rubbed his arm, "Without a drop of lube," and gave him a small pat. "Jim never actually told me he was going to pay me more, though. He just expects me to do all this extra work just because. You should call Whiskey."

Ethan shook his head and put the pizza down. "I heard they aren't taking our calls anymore—too many complaints."

Rose squeezed his arm. "Ethan, have you tried?" She looked at him. "You should try. If nothing else, it will make you feel better. Want to use my tablet? Wait right here; I'll go get it for you."

Ethan took another bite, chewing slowly, as he stared out the porthole. Maybe things weren't fair. Maybe Jim was never going to make things right. The frustration was still there, simmering beneath the surface, but at least, in this moment, he didn't have to bear it alone.

Rose returned a moment later. "Here." She pushed the tablet into his lap. "The hotline is saved right here. Call them," she urged again. "If nothing else, maybe they can give you the closure you need."

Ethan stared at the tablet in his lap, his fingers resting on its edges but making no move to lift it. The hotline number was right there, a single tap away, but the thought of calling made his stomach clench. What was the point? If they weren't taking calls anymore, all he'd get was an automated response or some apathetic rep telling him there was nothing they could do. And if they did answer, then what? Another useless promise? Another hollow assurance that they'd "look into it"?

He exhaled through his nose, his grip tightening around the device, and swallowed. Staring out the porthole at the stars streaking past, he felt the hum of the ship press in around him. That same feeling of being trapped returned. Finally, he reached out. Every second felt like a minute. He pressed his thumb against the screen. The number glowed. It began to ring.

Rose squeezed his shoulder in support. "Don't hang up. I'm going to go make the bed while you talk to them."

On the third ring, Ethan began to wonder if the hotline was still available around the clock. Then a man with a heavy accent picked up on the other end. Ethan tried to place it. Maybe the Indian ship?

"Hello, thank you for calling Whiskey's ethics department. My name is Singh. Please be aware this call is being monitored and recorded for quality and training purposes. Are you calling to report an issue or follow up on an existing case?"

The soft blue glow of the wall screen flickered. A new alert pulsed in the corner:

System notice - maintenance alert

Zone heating at 67% efficiency

Gravity strength at 99% efficiency

Maintenance notified. No action required.

Ethan ripped his eyes away from the screen. "I…I'm calling to report an issue."

The sound of muted office chatter preceded Singh's response. *"What's your location and clock number?"*

"Foxtrot. AM178J8"

"Please identify the person engaged in the problematic behaviour."

"Well, Singh, I guess that would be my supervisor, Jim. He handles my payroll."

Singh sounded relieved. *"It's a pay issue? Let me transfer you to Foxtrot's HR—"*

Ethan cut him off. "No, please, I tried talking to my HR representative already, and she couldn't really help me. Said it was hearsay. That's why I'm calling you."

Singh sighed. Ethan heard the rapid clack of keys. *"When did this start?"*

"Last November. I checked my pay this cycle around 10:00 and it was wrong again. Jim told me he would pay me 22 credits an hour, but I'm still getting 20. It's been months."

"And I take it you want back pay for the credits you didn't receive?"

"I want what I was promised."

"Understood. Alright, Sir. Your report is filed. Please give us six business cycles to investigate your claim. I need a passcode for the follow-up."

Ethan stood up and crossed the room. "Ugh…hold on." He minimized the alert and kept clicking. "Let me pull up my notes…ready? 867-530-9999."

Singh tried his hardest to enunciate every number as he repeated them back, and then it was over. He hung up, saved the note, and closed his eyes in his chair.

His complaint was officially filed. Ethan exhaled, waiting for the relief to come, for the frustration to abate now that he had done something about it, but that didn't happen. He had gone through all the motions, followed the right steps, and… yet the same helplessness still gnawed at the edges of his thoughts. He was still waiting to feel better when Rose's voice drifted from the other room, calling his name.

Ethan just had to get up one more time, that's all. Then he could sink into a bed freshly made with care and finally rest. His inner thighs could start to heal under an inch of salve. All he had to do was get up. One. More. Time.

Ethan braced himself, like Atlas preparing to shoulder the weight of the heavens, and slowly began to put weight on his feet. The transition was arduous, full of peril and joint pain; his achy muscles protested every inch of the way. Once, the cushions nearly devoured him. It was only by the narrowest of margins that Ethan escaped the chair alive.

He wondered if this was how Lazarus felt when he rose again. His t-shirt was a far cry from a linen burial shroud, and his limbs weren't bound, but he shambled nonetheless, toward his room—practically a cave. One made of aluminum, not limestone, but still a cave. His impatient siren was calling out to him in a loud voice, telling him to come to bed. Nothing would stop him from answering that call.

Rose was waiting for him when he finally arrived, lounging in her usual sleepwear—an oversized t-shirt and nothing else. Ethan smiled when he saw it. Across the chest, a pair of flaming cards was emblazoned alongside the words: *Smokin' Aces.*

She patted the bed. "Come on, come on. Don't forget to lock the door."

Ethan flipped her a thumbs-up but didn't say anything.

Rose frowned. "Babe, what's up? What did the guy say?"

He sighed, rubbing his temples. "Well… Singh filed my complaint." He shook his head, switched off the light, and crawled into bed beside her.

"So why the long face?"

Ethan exhaled sharply, adjusting his pillow like it was part of the problem. "They told me to call back in a week."

Rose tilted her head. "Okay? So call them back in a week. What's the big deal?"

CHAPTER 6
The Gravity of the Situation

Another cycle, another credit. The same old drudgery. Ethan scanned the manifest in his hands. In big, bold black font, it read: ***1255725. Assembly, Valve Body—Hydro***. Beneath that was a barcode, and below that, the quantity: forty-two.

But how?

Ethan scrutinized the skid, circling it and tallying the red totes stacked chest-high. Maybe the total was forty-two? No. There were fifty-six. Nine totes per row, six rows deep—that was fifty-four. Two more balanced on top made fifty-six.

Per tote, then? Maybe they meant forty-two per tote? Impossible. He knew the standard count: fifty-one. Three layers of seventeen—no foam, only dividers. The two extras on top broke the pattern: one held twenty-one, the other thirteen. Someone could have combined them, but no one had.

Now, Ethan was no mathematician. Far from it. But no matter how many times he calculated, the sum was the same: twenty-eight hundred and ninety parts. Whichever way he sliced it, forty-two simply refused to appear. He tapped a few buttons on his scan gun and checked the stock in BCT. It matched the paperwork, of course. Ethan exhaled slowly.

Then came the clomp of boots. A familiar voice cut in. "Something wrong?"

Ethan glanced up and passed Buck the manifest. "Maybe they mean the skid weighs forty-two tons."

Buck looked down at the sticker. He kept his graying hair in a tight buzz cut, and his radio hung from his belt like a sheriff's pistol. Buck let out a low chuckle as he looked at it. "That joke was so dry I might have to go get some lotion!"

Ethan remained unmoved. "How did they let this through?"

Buck unholstered his own scan gun with alacrity, training its red beams on Ethan's chest from the hip. "Maybe they got in a shootout!"

"I need more coffee."

Buck grinned. "Let's go get some. I just made a fresh pot."

The break room smelled faintly of burnt plastic and hazelnut. A vending machine buzzed in the corner, its refrigeration unit clicking like a dying beetle. Overhead, the PA system squawked, *"Eggplant, to the back dock,"* as they entered.

Buck stopped in front of the coffee pot, glaring at the empty glass carafe like it had personally wronged him.

"Thought you said you just made a fresh pot," Ethan said flatly.

Buck scratched the back of his neck. "I *thought* I did." They both stood in silence for a moment, the empty pot staring back.

Ethan exhaled. "I'll make more," he offered, reaching for the filter.

"Suit yourself," Buck said, retreating like a man dodging responsibility.

Ethan dumped the old grounds, rinsed the carafe with little enthusiasm, and started a new brew. The aroma of coffee beans soon filled the room. He leaned against the counter with a sigh that felt weightier than the skid full of valve bodies.

"They ever fix James's BCT account?"

Buck sucked air through his teeth.

"So, no."

"Yeah, still throws an 821 error," Buck said. "Sometimes it logs the transaction twice. Sometimes, not at all."

"Terrific," Ethan muttered dryly. "How long now?"

Buck snorted. "Months."

The coffee sputtered to life behind them.

"You know this whole manifest thing isn't just a one-off, right?" Ethan said.

Buck scratched his chin. "Yeah. I've sent two back already."

Ethan watched the life-giving, caffeinated brown water steam out. "The whole system is rotting like pitting rust in a panel," he said.

Buck shot him a look. "That's a little dramatic."

Ethan scowled. "I'm tired of writing emails to three different people, begging someone to fix it."

Buck winced. "Do the keys on your keyboard hurt your soft fingers?" He clutched his chest. "Is that it?"

Ethan scowled, ignoring the remark. "If I send it to just one, they'll say I should've copied the other two. If I send it to all of them, they'll collectively ignore it. It shouldn't be like this."

The coffee finished brewing with a final hiss. "Smells like burnt optimism," Buck said, filling his cup. He raised it in a toast. "To a cycle where everything works the way it should."

"May it come soon," Ethan added, raising his cup.

Buck laughed softly. "Cheers."

They clinked cups. Ethan took a sip and grimaced. "That tastes like a bad omen."

Buck just shook his head and took another long sip. "You've been playing too much *Time Traveler*."

Ethan met his gaze. "Impossible. I guess I'm going to go write those emails now. What are you going to do?"

Buck tried to look serious. "Don't get mad."

"I knew it was a bad omen."

Buck tried not to grin. "You know those panels you spent all cycle pulling?"

"The TT panels?"

"Yep." Buck took another sip.

"All eight hundred and sixty-seven of them?"

Buck gave a slow nod. "Yes sir! Katarina can't get the plating line to work. So, we have to put them back in stock until she gets it fixed."

Ethan took another sip, considering this. Maybe there wasn't going to be a roundup after all? At least, not right away. He felt his blood pressure begin to settle and leaned into his cup. "Well," he decided, "at least Jim won't be scheduling another safety meeting about tether protocols for spacewalks. So the rework is actually good news."

Buck agreed with revved-up enthusiasm. "That's the spirit! And don't worry—we're storing them all in one place this time. That's progress, baby!"

Ethan asked a simple question. "Where?"

Buck's answer wasn't so straightforward. "I'll figure that out while you write your emails."

His radio crackled to life with a cough of static. Mercedes's voice came through. *"Buck Pebbles, what's your location?"*

Buck drained his coffee in one swallow. "Change of plans. You figure it out while I help her." He thumbed his radio, already heading out the door. "Where do you need me?"

Then he was gone.

Ethan refilled his cup before following in Buck's wake. Where, oh where, could he put those parts? They came twelve to a box, weighed close to twenty pounds, and there were seventy-odd of them. Cradling his cup on the walk back, Ethan kept his eyes high, scanning for a gap in the Curved-Isle. No such luck.

Ethan was halfway through a mental game of Tetris when he heard a shout and turned to see a skinny guy waving him over from behind a stack of boxes. He was in his late twenties, with a thin goatee and short dreadlocks peeking out from beneath a faded black beanie, and he was leaning on a pallet jack like it owed him something.

"Just the man I wanted to see!"

Ethan reflexively took a sip of coffee, keeping his head on a swivel. "What's up, buddy? Do you need help with something?" he asked, scanning the area.

Vinny nodded. "Yeah, Buck sent me up here." He gestured to his right, toward the rows of pallets lined up on the back dock. "I'm supposed to grab a skid, but … I don't know which one."

Ethan slid to a stop. "Well, let's go take a look. Ours usually have pink or yellow stickers somewhere."

"I know, but I didn't see any stickers."

Ethan sighed. "At all? That's not good."

It took a string of unspeakable language and about ten minutes, but eventually, Ethan and Vinny found the manifests. They were all five, folded up together and cocooned in thick plastic wrap, on a single skid.

Vinny squinted at the stack. "Five pages? That can't be right. There's no way that many parts fit on one skid."

Ethan took a long sip of coffee and scowled.

"Uh- oh," Vinny laughed. "I *know* that look. Bad omen."

Ethan nodded, took another sip just to confirm it, then nodded again. "Definitely not good."

He held the pages up and compared the list to the topmost totes peeking above the plastic, then checked the inventory with his scan gun. There had to be some rhyme or reason to this. Were the numbers sequential? Was it organized by material type? No matter how he stared at the papers in his hands, meaning eluded him.

Vinny, meanwhile, ran his pallet jack into a nearby skid and started cranking. "Let me get this out of the way." Vinny jerked his thumb over his shoulder. "I don't know why Eggplant didn't set it over there, out of the way."

Ethan glanced up. Eggplant sat hunched over a terminal, his balding head nearly touching the monitor, and his fingers hammered away at the keys furiously. A mix of shaky letters, crude symbols, and faded glyphs crawled up his neck, down his arms, and over his fingers. They were the kind of tattoos you don't get sitting in a chair.

"How old is he?" Vinny asked. "I can never decide if he's my age or your age."

Ethan blinked. "That's a funny way of calling me old."

"No, no!" Vinny laughed. "That's not what I meant. I swear."

"Sure." Ethan cleared his throat in a dramatic display of mock offense. "To answer your question, I don't know. He never says, and I've never asked. But I think he's a little older than me."

"He's a real keyboard warrior," Vinny grunted as he tugged on the skid. Even jacked up, the skid was still heavy. Irritation had started to creep into his voice. "I wish he'd stop typing and bring that pallet jack over here and help out."

"James would help us if we asked. Let's not bother him now, though."

Vinny made a face. "If you say so."

"He would, "Ethan insisted. "Earlier, he set two skids up by the desks for me. I didn't ask him. He didn't have to. You know what I mean? James isn't a bad guy. He's just...sassy."

"Well, he wants to be sassy, and then runs off to write emails the second someone claps back. You know he snatched a pen from Lavion?"

"Wait? What did you say?"

"I know, right? He snatched a pen out of—"

Ethan shook his head. "No, before that."

Vinny paused. "I said he gets all sassy and—"

"Runs off," Ethan finished for him.

An idea clicked inside his head. "So this is a row — that means this was the *first* one unloaded, which means it had to be the *last* one put on the ship." He pointed.

Vinny shrugged. "So?"

Ethan tapped the manifest. "I bet the loaders at Delta forgot to put the manifests on the pallets. That's why they stuck them all on the last one like this — someone realized and ran over there real quick. And if that's true … then the pages probably came out of the printer in order — this order."

He handed Vinny a paper. "See if this manifest matches that skid. I'll check this one."

Vinny blinked. "How did you guess that?"

Ethan shrugged. "They manifested the skids one at a time. Pulled the orders, printed the sheets, and then forgot to slap them on as they wrapped the skids. Just a good, old - fashioned human error."

He clapped Vinny on the back, pointed at the skids he needed to take, and then he was off again with another sip. He should have had his email sent by now. The TT panels were waiting for him on a skid when he made it back. Five minutes into powering up the computer, whispering sweet nothings to the hard drive's RAM, trying to coax it into pulling up his email, Shaye-Shaye waved him over from her desk.

She called, "Ethan, you got a minute?"

He didn't really, but he nodded anyway, pushing his safety glasses back into place and falling in step behind her. She led him around to a section of the aft deck and pointed. One of the clamps on the overhead pipes had come loose, and without the right tension, the pipes hissed every time the gravity feed cycled. It wasn't dangerous, not yet, just mostly irritating. The sound it made was loud and sharp, almost like a bell, a chirp that sounded every few seconds.

Ethan craned his neck as he looked at it. "We'll have to call maintenance."

Shaye-Shaye winced as the pipe chirped again. "I hope they hurry. Do you think it will fall?"

Ethan shook his head. "I hope not. As far behind as the maintenance department is, it might be a while, though. I'll write Katarina an email."

Shaye-Shaye simply shook her head. "This place is falling apart," she muttered, leaning on a rack, sweat glistening on her neck.

Ethan merely grunted and nodded. "Let's notify maintenance."

By the time he got back to his computer, the panels hadn't moved. No one had touched them. No one would.

He bent to heft a box, grappling with its unwieldy bulk, struggling with the unexpected weight, and clipped his shin on the edge of the pallet. He cursed under his breath. Was that another gravity surge?

Ethan carried it back to the desk, plopped it down, then called maintenance while signing into his account. Then he squinted at the numbers on the box and began typing them in. Logging them took longer than it should have. The boxes were slightly crushed from before, which didn't help. Were gravity fluctuations to blame?

By the time he logged the second box, sweat was plastering his shirt to his back. He checked his wristwatch. Half the cycle was gone, and he still hadn't taken a break. By the time he finished the last one, it was nearly lunch, and everything still felt heavier than it should.

The horn blared minutes later—lunchtime. He set the last box down and rolled his shoulder with a soft groan. The sweat under his collar had gone cold, plastering his shirt to his spine. With a sigh, he pushed himself away from the desk and trudged toward the break room, weighing his options between chocolate bars. Did he want almonds or peanuts? Such decisions.

The vending machine stood at the far end, humming softly in the recirculated air, its glass front smeared with a haze of fingerprints. Rows of neatly arranged snacks gleamed under flickering LEDs. Ethan fished in his pocket for his keycard and swiped it over the reader. A green light pulsed.

Slot C5: chocolate bar, with peanuts. Dense, cheap, slightly bitter. He keyed in the code and watched the machine creak into motion. The auger turned once, twice—then paused.

"Come on," he muttered.

The bar teetered.

One more turn and it fell, thudding into the tray with a satisfying clunk.

He grabbed it, tore the wrapper open without turning around, and took a bite. The chocolate dissolved over his tongue as he chewed. He popped the lid off his coffee and dunked the bar a few times, then took another bite.

His boots thudded dully on the floor as he walked back to his desk. The window framed the ship's warehouses—rows of metal racks bursting with boxes of various sizes, and beyond them, a glimpse of stars through the reinforced glass. He sat down, logged into his account, and pulled up his IM window.

User: EthanWilco_37

Status: Available

Open Chat: ***MaggieRose_26***

He stared at the blinking cursor for a second, unsure what to say. Then he typed: *"You survive the morning?"* Followed by a GIF: a bleary-eyed cat drinking coffee on a loop.

A few seconds passed. Then:

MaggieRose_26 is typing…

"Barely. I just had to clear a bunch of errors in Bay 3. They didn't confirm anything, again. I swear I'm going to scream." She sent him a GIF back: a red kettle whistling with steam.

Ethan smiled faintly. He took another bite of the chocolate and leaned back in his chair.

"Classic. Go get ' em! Haha." He followed up her kettle GIF with a boxing reel of Dyson Miller throwing a punch.

Her reply came faster this time.

"This is me writing emails today." She sent him a GIF of a cowboy drawing his pistol.

He chuckled softly.

"I believe you." He paused, then added: *"What do you want to do after work?"* There was a longer pause. He imagined her sitting in her cubicle, brows furrowed as she stared at the screen.

"Idk. Why?"

Ethan hesitated, thumb hovering over the keyboard as he chose his words.

"Just thought we could get some takeout. Maybe watch a movie?"

Another pause.

"Yeah. I'd like that. Your shot must be wearing off."

Ethan smiled again. He looked out the window at the faint glimmer of stars. For a second, the ship didn't feel quite so broken.

"Yeah, must be." He took another bite, chewed, and sent her a GIF of a chubby boy eating chocolate cake. *"Break's almost over. Gotta get back to it. Love you."*

MaggieRose_26 is typing…

"Love you too, babe. GL!"

Ethan stared at the message for a second longer than he meant to. Then the warehouse swallowed him again.

CHAPTER 7
Sector Six

Work passed in a blur. Delta disgorged a bellyache of parts, Ethan and the team stowed them, and he complained every step of the way. Everything with Eggplant's name on it came in with a no-stock status and an 821 error—all nine of them. He wanted to send them back up there, but Buck wouldn't let him, so he compromised by firing off emails instead. Fussing was all he could really do, so he wrote nine separate messages—one for every error—just to raise as much hell as possible.

New message. He tagged everyone in it—Buck, Jim, the whole roster—and typed.

Hello. We the unwilling, led by the unknowing, are doing the impossible for the ungrateful. We have done so much, for so long, for so little, we are now eminently qualified to do anything with nothing forever.

That said, it would be a miracle if we could get James' account fixed.

Against his better judgment, he hit send on number ten, and his IMs chimed back at once. A blue pop-up flickered. The computer hesitated, then pulled up a message from Gigi.

GigiBrazier_43:

Can you tell me who I can talk to? I need to move some stock out of 300, but I'm restricted over here at Delta.

EthanWilco_37 is typing...

Sure, I can move stock out of there. Send me a list of what you need moved and where.

GigiBrazier_43 is typing...

Thanks. I need you to pull 1274525-TT. Twelve of them.

Ethan blinked. Dash TT? Those were the artificial gravity arrays. BCT confirmed there were twelve of them, but they weren't in the 300 zone. At least, not in the conventional sense. They were in a restricted part of 300, called Engineering Hold.

EthanWilco_37:

Engineering has them. Let me go walk over there and talk to them. Brb.

Ethan's boots struck the concrete with a dull thud. He walked the same paths every cycle, but it had been a while since he had made the trek to quality. The humming drones and the ever-present stink of dust and sweat were his constant companions. His eyes scanned for hazards, but only in the absent way a man does when his mind is light-years away. He knew every sound, every worn patch on the floor, and most of the people here. There would be another rotation soon, of course, as the younger generation started plastering over the cracks of an aging workforce, and he'd have plenty of new names to learn.

His paycheck was 1,438 credits. That was before ship and corporate taxes, before insurance. The number was intended to mean something. It was supposed to be a reward for picking up a couple cycles of overtime, covering the slack when half the department called off, and reconciling all the bins on the ten aisle. Instead, he felt like a setup with no punchline.

He hung a left as he approached the UB-lines, past the desks, nodding to Darnell, ensconced at his workstation typing away at the computer array in his typical yellow vest and orange bandanna, a coffee in one hand. Ethan noticed a fresh tattoo wrapped around his arm as he walked by.

An eagle with wide, sweeping wings was now inked into his biceps, still raw and gleaming. Everyone knew what an Eagle was, because it was America's mascot, and everyone knew what had happened to them.

"Hey," Ethan said, easing up. "Nice tattoo."

"Thanks! I've been flying Six for ten years now." He rotated his arm so Ethan could get a better look at it.

"Congratulations. You ought to meet Rose and me down at the Caf some time. I'll buy you a drink, celebrate. I gotta run right now."

"Sounds good, E."

The factory was loud this cycle, but somewhere inside his head, Ethan's thoughts were louder. 2-bits an hour. 24-bits a cycle. 80-bits a check. The arithmetic gnawed at him.

The walk to the quality lab took six minutes at a clip. He went past the mezzanine, past the print room, down the well-worn, painted walkway. Ethan made it there in five and a half. A new record. Then he rapped on the door and stepped inside.

The air here was cooler, still. The hum of the AC and the fluorescent lights made a different kind of din—sterile, controlled. The lab was all glass cabinets, steel tables, and meticulously labeled bins. There were torque wrenches beside digital calipers, hardness testers next to 3D scanners. It all felt orderly in a way the rest of the factory refused to be. Ethan liked that.

"Hey."

Mister O was hunched at the computer desk, typing away at something. He glanced at him, then flitted back to his screen. He had his hair slicked back with some kind of wax and his black vest hung off the back of his chair. Ethan couldn't help but notice he typed with his gloves still on.

"Hey. What's up?"

Ethan nodded. "I got a message from a girl at Delta. She wants me to transfer some parts BCT says you have."

He adjusted his glasses. "What's the part number?"

Ethan told him and together they regarded the screen. "See what I mean?"

He nodded. "Yeah. That's above my weight class."

Ethan thought about the raise he got last quarter. Half a lousy credit. The explanation had been the flagship's favorite flavor: "Budgetary constraints." Same explanation for why they cut paid perfect attendance bonuses.

Ethan wasn't stupid. He knew what they paid the new hires—he broke in most of them. He'd been here almost a decade, and some greenhorn kid was starting at three credits less than his rate. Three credits was a signal. Everyone's replaceable.

"Right. So what now? I need to send someone an email?"

Mister O nodded. "Fox-Engineering. Someone will circle back to you next cycle."

Always tomorrow with this place. Ethan stood up and arched his back. His shoulders burned from lifting boxes all cycle, but there was still plenty more to do.

"Alright, well I'd better get back to it then. Thanks."

Ethan stepped back into the cacophony. The factory didn't care what he was thinking. It kept going—drills screeched, boxes clattered, and the overhead lights hummed nonstop. Somewhere behind him, someone dropped a metal bracket and swore loud enough to pierce the din.

He walked the path in reverse; past Darnell, still at his desk, sipping his drink like he hoped it might transform into something stronger. Ethan nodded again, and the old man gave him the same weary smile.

Back at his station, the monitor was still glowering. The message from Gigi sat there waiting, bright and cheerful like this was just a routine favor between friends.

GigiBrazier_43:

You get the okay?

Ethan sat down and cracked his knuckles.

EthanWilco_37:

Can't do it. Run it through Mister O.

He hit send. There was a brief pause before the typing bubble appeared again.

GigiBrazier_43 is typing…

GigiBrazier_43:

You can move them with LXR6. I'll email him and let him know.

Ethan stared at the message. His jaw tightened. Did he even have clearance for that program? It pulled up when he typed in the code.

EthanWilco_37:

I'm not comfortable doing that. I've never had anyone ask me to circumvent process like this.

Another pause. Another bubble.

GigiBrazier_43:

All you have to do is type in the part, the quantity, the origin, and the destination. Under special characters, type "B" because they're blocked. Quality won't care because the parts are right here. Someone just forgot to log it.

Ethan frowned. His hands hovered over the keyboard, but his fingers stayed frozen. He could do it. It'd take ten seconds. No paperwork, no hassle. Gigi would get her stock, and Ethan wouldn't hear about it again.

But he'd also be the one left holding the bag if something went wrong, so to speak, been there, done that. Suddenly everyone's pointing fingers and it's, *"Well, what employee number is attached to the transaction?"*

He stared at the screen like he was waiting for it to flinch.

EthanWilco_37:

I can't do that. Sorry.

This time the response came swifter.

GigiBrazier_43:

I understand, but I need some help here. I've been chasing someone all cycle. No one else is available.

He leaned back in his chair and pressed his palms against his eyes. The hum of the factory was in his bones now. Same as the pay stub still crammed in his back pocket. Same as the ache in his spine.

He typed slowly this time, each keystroke deliberate.

EthanWilco_37:

Let me make a phone call.

He reached for the desk phone, punched in extension 48866, and waited as it rang. A moment later, Rose picked up. She sounded just as drained as he felt.

"Technical support. This is Rose speaking. How can I help you?"

"Hey babe, it's Ethan."

"Oh hey, Sweetie. What's going on?"

"Gigi messaged me on Teams."

"Oh! How is she?"

She wants me to move something out of quality hold, but I can't get a hold of anyone at Quality to sign off. She says the parts are at Delta, and she's not taking no for an answer."

"That's not like her."

"Yeah, I know what you mean."

Ethan heard her typing furiously.

"Yeah, okay—I see the parts. She wants them out of quality? Why's she coming to you?"

"Apparently, no one else is around. Told me to use LRX6."

"They use that at warehouse 770. You're probably not provisioned for it, though. If you do, you'll trip an error. She should know that. What's the part number?"

Ethan rattled it off.

More typing followed.

"You'd have to flip them from 300 to 350, then to 315... but hold on. Your parameters aren't set, and the system will spit out a 21. Only quality or the lead on the back dock should handle those transfers."

"Got it. I'll go grab James and have him do it. Thanks, babe."

"No problem—hey, before you go. Pasta tonight?"

He smiled. "Sounds good to me. Venos?"

"Yes! You read my mind."

"Alright. See you soon. Love you."

"Love you too."

She hung up.

He set the phone back in its cradle and stared at the screen a moment longer. Outside his little station, the factory kept churning. Someone shouted something over the noise, and a forklift bleeped in the distance. Ethan stood up, arched his back, and grabbed the next bin. No one was coming to save him, but dinner was pasta, and that was something.

Ethan wiped his hands on his pants and started the long walk across the factory floor. The overhead lights buzzed, drones flitted around, semi-present and barely-aware, humming as they passed him by. He ducked under one hovering in the walkway, then threaded through pallets of shrink-wrapped parts stacked up on the back dock. Eggplant was right where he left him, hunched over his keyboard, at the desk squeezed between the bays. The way he sat there typing away made him look a little like a human question mark.

"James," Ethan said, stopping beside him.

Eggplant didn't look up. "What?"

"I need you to IM Gigi and transfer this part to Zone-15."

At that, Eggplant stopped typing. He leaned back slightly, scratching at the faded purple tattoo that was his namesake inked across the side of his neck.

"What part?" he asked flatly.

Ethan flicked it to him on his tablet. "That one. Gigi says it's at Delta, and I'm not authorized to transfer to that zone. So, you have to do it."

Eggplant looked at it on his monitor, squinting over the rim of his glasses. "OK. Click. Click. Done. Is that all?"

"That's all I got."

Eggplant winked at Ethan. "Are you sure? You're always giving me such a hard time. And right here at the end of the cycle, too."

"You wish, James." Ethan smirked. "Don't start with me."

"Alright. I'll spare you—this time."

Ethan lingered a moment, then tapped the edge of the desk. "Thanks, man. I gotta get back to it."

Eggplant didn't answer right away, but he lifted a hand halfway off the keyboard in a dismissive half-wave before going right back to typing like a man possessed. "OK. I gotta finish this email too! See you next cycle."

Ethan rubbed his eyes and looked at the clock near the ceiling. The short hand had somehow jumped ahead several hours without him noticing. Somewhere on the floor, an air trawler beeped in reverse, but it felt distant, like this was all just a memory already. He sighed and started to go back for his things. Most of the crew had already left by the time he reached the door. Ethan walked away through the empty room, his footsteps echoing a little louder now. The factory was quieter. Still noisy, but the volume didn't feel the same. There were just a few stragglers like him heading for the time clock.

The tram felt unusually shaky as Ethan rode home. Maybe the ship's gravity grid was malfunctioning again. He dropped his hat as an experiment. At least it didn't float. He picked it up and dropped it again, still uncertain.

"What are you doing?"

Ethan looked up. "Barry? Didn't expect to see you here. I was just testing the gravity."

The big man snorted and adjusted his thick black glasses higher up the bridge of his nose. "Oh, OK. Well, me and Shaggy are going to play *Bot Hunter* at his place. He's going to show me how to beat the Analyst."

"Oh ok. Who's the Analyst? Some evil robot?"

Barry gave a slow nod. "Basically. Analyst isn't really evil, it's just…you ever see that one old movie from Earth? There's this robot named Hal in it, and Analyst is kind of like Hal."

Ethan shook his head, frowning. "Nah, don't think so. I love those old scifi movies though. What's it called?"

Barry grinned. "Man, I can't remember. Space something—Space Odyssey, something like that." He fiddled with his backwards ball cap excitedly, the gesture almost manic. The tan hat was still sweat-soaked. "Hal is the AI on the ship that goes crazy because it has conflicting programming—it doesn't want to be shut off. Analyst is kinda like that."

"Space Odyssey, huh? "I'll have to see if I can find it."

"Yeah, man. Check it out. I think it was 2001: A Space Odyssey, but I'm not sure." Barry laughed. Ethan shoved the hat back onto his head. "Where is Shaggy this cycle anyway? The tram rocked again, hard enough to make a few overhead lights flicker momentarily. When it did, the darkness was so absolute that Ethan couldn't see his hand in front of his face.

"It's his birthcycle, so he took the shift off." Barry settled into the empty seat beside him. "This place is a wreck," he added, gesturing toward the lights.

"I *feel* wrecked," Ethan muttered. "The factory was insane. Rose finally got her pink keyboard back, thank god."

Barry chuckled. "She hasn't shut up about that thing."

"Nope. She practically floated home on a cloud." Ethan smiled faintly, then leaned his head back against the window. The glass was blessedly cool against his skin. "It feels later than it is," he added.

"Gravity's denser at night. That's why you can barely keep your eyes open." Barry said it dead-serious, like he was explaining the fundamentals of plumbing. Ethan squinted at him, trying to gauge if he was joking. It was hard to say.

Ethan couldn't help but laugh.

The tram jolted again, its pace slackening as it neared the next stop. A soft *ding* rang overhead, followed by a garbled voice announcing the stop. The car was half-empty now, just a few scattered workers slumped in their seats, their heads nodding along with the rocking tram.

Barry stood up and stretched, his back cracking audibly. "This is me. You wanna head over? We'll show you the ropes."

Ethan gave a tired shake of his head. Every part of him screamed to go home, collapse face-first into his mattress, and not move until tomorrow. "I appreciate the offer, but I think I'm going to pass. Rose and I are headed to Venos."

Barry's eyebrows lifted. "Venos? Damn, man. That's fancy."

Ethan managed a weary grin. "Yeah, well, you know how she is about that place."

"That sounds nice. Venos isn't cheap, man."

"I know," Ethan said, scrubbing his eyes with the heels of his hands. "Believe it."

The tram hissed to a full stop. The doors groaned open on their hinges. Barry stepped out, walking backward a few steps to face the tram. "Alright Ethan, rest easy."

"You too," Ethan called to his retreating back.

The doors slid shut, and the tram lurched forward, even emptier than before. Ethan let his head fall back against the window with a soft thunk. Venos. He still almost couldn't believe he'd agreed. He wasn't even sure he had clothes nice enough for a place like that.

Then the tram gave another jolt, even harder this time. Hard enough to send his hat sliding down over his eyes. He gave a soft chuckle, adjusted it, and tried to stay awake. Just a little longer.

The rhythmic clatter of the tram tracks melted into a low, steady hum, like a lullaby for the exhausted. Ethan let his eyes slide shut again, just for a second. The tram kept swaying. He barely registered it.

When the intercom binged again, he jerked upright.

"Now approaching Sector Six. Please ensure all personal belongings are with you before disembarking."

The tram was now nearly empty. An old man near the front snored softly into his coat, while a maintenance drone buzzed lazily down the aisle, sweeping up scraps of litter. Ethan blinked at the windows, his vision bleary. The station lights outside flickered past in streams of neon and gold, reflecting off the dull bulkheads in little restless star patterns. This wasn't his stop, not by a long shot.

"Ah, crap," he muttered, sitting up straight. His hat tipped forward again, threatening to fall into his lap. He pushed it back impatiently, scrambled to his feet, and tried to get a better look at the scrolling map above the doors.

The tram dinged again, decelerating into the station. Pale yellow letters glowed faintly above the exit, spelling out his mistake in stark, blinking technicolor. Sector Six. The doors hissed open with a reluctant sigh. For a second, Ethan considered sitting back down.

The tram emitted a warning beep. *"Doors closing."*

There was barely time to think. Ethan grabbed his hat, stumbled down the aisle, and hurled himself through the doors just as they started to slide shut. They caught the back of his vest on the way out, but he squeezed by just in time. He stumbled onto the platform, his heart hammering against his ribs. The tram pulled away without him, its lights dwindling into the darkness before twisting around the corner.

The platform was utterly deserted. Not a single living soul to ask for directions.

"Great," he muttered, zipping his vest up tighter against the chill. "An hour for the next tram."

Something clicked behind him.

Ethan turned just in time to see a loose bolt drift upward off the platform a few inches. It hovered there for half a second, then fell back down with a metallic clink. He just stared at it.

"...Okay."

Ethan waited a long minute. Nothing else made a move to float, so he finally risked it.

Sector Six was cold. Ethan could see his breath pluming as he fidgeted on the platform and pulled his vest tighter around himself. He started walking, hands jammed in his vest pockets, shoulders hunched against the stale, dusty air, with no clear destination. It would be faster just to make his way home from here.

His every step echoed, and it wasn't long before he realized just how deserted this part of Foxtrot really was. Once, Sector Six had been lively, full of people, small shops, and homes. Now entire corridors were welded shut. Heavy bulkheads were covered in peeling hazard tape and faded warning stencils.

Ethan quickened his pace.

He made it two blocks down only to find that Main Street was sealed off with a thick steel gate lowered across it. He cursed under his breath and considered going back to wait on the tram, but the thought of Rose worrying about him stopped him. He needed to find a working phone, if nothing else.

Ethan looked around, weighing his options. He hesitated for a moment, then ducked down a side street. He'd have to cut through the alley, he decided. But if he did, he should be able to get around the block. The metal walls pressed in close. Exposed wiring hung in spiderwebs from open panels all around. Somewhere above, unseen, a pipe hissed slowly, joined by the rhythmic drip of liquid somewhere in the darkness. Maybe water, but the air smelled like coolant, making it impossible to tell.

He took a left at the end of the passage, and cursed again. Blocked there, too. Somewhere deeper in the ship, something let out a low groan. It was a long, low, mechanical noise that emanated from nowhere and everywhere at once—and it didn't sound good. He told himself it was nothing, just an echo bouncing through the hull, but his imagination didn't quite believe it.

Ethan weighed his options, chewing the inside of his cheek. He could crawl through a random, cracked maintenance tunnel gaping open at the bottom of the wall, but that wasn't exactly high on his list of intelligent moves. Especially not when he didn't know what was seeping through the pipes. Reluctantly, he sighed, turned, and retraced his steps. Every step was heavy with thoughts of Rose alone, checking the time, chewing her lip.

"Just a little longer," he muttered, as if she could hear him.

The side corridors felt even tighter as he made his way back to Main Street. A loose floor grate caught under his boot; the hollow sound it made as it clattered down the alley was downright eerie. His fingers itched to pull out his radio and call someone—anyone—but he could already imagine how that would sound. Especially since he wasn't even technically supposed to be in here.

Where to go next?

The maintenance lighting here barely worked, an unhelpful inconvenience in a place already thick with them. Every third panel overhead buzzed, flickered, or simply gave up. Every few seconds, a warning light strobed a soft red pulse, the only real illumination in the corridor.

As Ethan stood there, looking for another way around the barrier, he caught sight of movement close by. A figure—just a glimpse—someone in a filthy yellow vest slipped into the shadows.

"Hey!" Ethan called out, his pace quickening. "Hey, hold up!"

No answer.

He jogged a few steps, and when he reached the spot, he noticed a door, but it had already shut with a soft hydraulic hiss. No sign of whoever it was. No footprints. No wet marks. Just a door sealed from the other side and a maintenance terminal flashing an error message in looping red text.

"Hey!" His fingers curled into a fist. He took a step forward and started beating on the door. "Can you hear me? Hello?!"

An intercom crackled back, its speaker distorted. *"What do you want?"*

"Missed my stop," Ethan said, rubbing the back of his neck nervously. "I didn't want to wait for the tram to come back around. The last time I was here, everything wasn't sealed off."

The intercom grunted in response. *"You'd better go back. This ain't no place to wander."*

"I would, but I don't want to worry my wife. Do you have a comm I can use?"

"No! Go back and wait for the tram!"

Ethan cleared his throat, his nerves fraying. "Please? I need to call my wife!"

"Around these parts," the intercom buzzed with static, *"there aren't any."*

A pause stretched out, broken only by the low throb of the strobe and the distant creak of settling metal. Then, with a sudden click and hiss, pneumatic lines released as the magnetic seal disengaged with a soft snap. The door split down the center, and slid open.

A woman stood half-shrouded in the red glow of the strobe light. She wore a patched-up denim jacket, the shadows clinging to her head and shoulders.

"Ethan!" A familiar voice yelled. "Is that you? I couldn't tell, my camera feed is spotty. Come on before you let out all the heat!"

Ethan exhaled a sigh of relief. "Mercedes, you scared the hell out of me!"

As she led him inside, he asked, "What happened here?"

"It used to be a good place to live," she answered, her voice bitter. "But all kinds of things went wrong. The gravity has been fluctuating lately. Sometimes it gets lighter, sometimes it gets heavier."

"Geez," Ethan said, fiddling with his hat. "By how much?"

Mercedes shrugged, her shoulders disappearing into her jacket. "I don't know. Too much."

The farther they walked, the less the corridors resembled anything he recognized. Familiar signs were absent or mismatched. One hallway had been stripped bare, no wall panels, no conduit coverings, just open ribs of steel and dark, exposed cables snaking out of the walls. He passed an old vending machine rusted into the bulkhead, its screen cracked, its shelves picked clean. Somehow, the blinking interface still offered a rice cake for twelve credits.

"This is... this is worse than terrible," Ethan muttered, his eyes scanning the wreckage. "I had no idea it had gotten this bad. How can you live like this?"

"Honestly, this place runs off spliced wires and duct tape at this point. This ain't nothing new. There were still nice parts a few years ago, but now it's all like this. People find a way. Not like I can afford to go anywhere else," she added, her irritation surfacing. "I still owe on my pod."

Finally, they reached the old lift—dented, scarred, but still humming quietly. Mercedes slapped the call button. "If it jams," she said, "don't panic. Just kick it. Works for me."

The doors opened with a groan of protest, and Ethan stepped inside. "Thanks," he said.

"You're welcome. Now that you owe me, you can pay me back with another batch of that smoked cheese dip. Like that one you brought for our pot luck last month."

He laughed as the doors slid shut between them. "You got it!"

The lift delivered him down. For a moment, he was convinced it might stop halfway and strand him there, but it didn't. As the lift hummed down, he noticed the soft flicker of a red dot from the ceiling camera turn toward him. Anxiety made the hairs on his neck stand up.

It was a relatively short walk home after that. His legs ached, and his nerves were frayed. His eyes kept drifting to every security camera he passed, wondering if the red dots had always followed him like that or if this was something new. Wondering who was on the other side.

Outside his door, one of the lights was dead. The other flickered like it had a short. The keypad lagged as he tapped in his code. The door finally hissed open with a dry, sluggish sound. Warmth met him immediately—but not much. The heater was on but struggling. A small, flickering yellow triangle glowed in the corner of the computer monitor, demanding attention.

System notice - maintenance alert

Zone heating at 60% efficiency.

Gravity strength at 99% efficiency.

Maintenance notified. No action required.

Status: Green.

He let the words sit for a long few seconds. Read them twice. Then a third time. Finally, his eyes moved on, drifting around the room.

Rose's boots were by the wall. Her vest hung with her badge. A half-finished glass of orange juice sat on the counter, its melting ice settled into a thin layer of slush. She had written a quick note on a sticky note and stuck it to the air fryer.

Don't wake me, Nerd.

Too tired for Venos.

Love you.

Ethan allowed himself a tiny smile.

He kicked off his boots, peeled off his vest, and collapsed into the chair beside the window. The stars outside still looked the same—cold, bright, indifferent. They offered no answers. He let the silence settle over him and took off his hat, holding it in his lap. Somewhere behind his eyes, the flickering strobes of Sector Six still pulsed, refusing to fade completely.

CHAPTER 8
Until Further Notice

The path to the Butterfly Palace curved upward in a spiral, featuring soft, green carpeted steps and AI-artist airbrushed walls painted by drones to recreate the rainforests of Earth. For once, it wasn't crowded. Just the excited voices of visitors, many with children, and the bright white light clearly illuminating the entrance.

Ethan looked at Rose. She wasn't exactly smiling, but the tension around her eyes had eased, and she was walking a little slower than usual. Her hand brushed along the textured wall as they moved.

"You know they grow vines right into the structure," she said. "I looked it up."

"That's cool," Ethan said. "That must be why it's so humid in here," he added, as a mister went off.

Rose nodded. "Yeah. It only gets warmer the closer we get to the actual garden." She tapped the door panel. It slid open with a quiet hiss.

Even wetter, warm humidity spilled out like breath as they approached the terrarium. The floor became softer near the door, paved with something springy that looked like moss. Overhead, more simulated sunlight shone down through a glass dome in golden beams, cutting through a fine mist that hovered in the upper canopy and sparkled in the light.

The first set of doors led them into a controlled room, then real butterflies appeared. They fluttered among flowering bushes, drifted in slow, looping circles at all heights—too many to count. Their wings shimmered with golds, deep blues, and iridescent greens—a full rainbow of colors—as they moved from flower to flower. For a moment, he wondered if this was what it really felt like to stand outside on Earth.

"Wow," Ethan said, because there was nothing else to say.

Rose reached out and caught his hand, gently. "I know you didn't want to come here," she said. "But... I'm glad you did."

He didn't answer immediately, just stared out at the living kaleidoscope of motion and color. A nectar dispenser drone handed them a pair of artificial flowers to carry.

When the drone handed them over, it chirped. *"Please remain in marked walkways."*

Seconds after Rose received hers, a pink butterfly landed on it, and she froze.

Ethan observed the butterfly extend its thin straw-like tongue into the flower's transparent, fluid-filled stem and sighed. "I've been feeling as if I'm made of bricks, as if every step requires more effort than it should."

Rose nodded. "Me too. That's how I knew we needed to go on a little vacation."

They walked slowly, winding along a path bordered by bamboo stalks and an artificial feeding station. Children laughed around them. A drone whirled past. Ethan could almost pretend it was a bird flying by.

Then a butterfly landed on his hat. He froze, smiling, wordlessly trying to catch Rose's eye.

She whispered, "You ever think…maybe we were supposed to live in places like this?"

Ethan looked at her, then around them. "Yeah, I guess. But…if Earth was perfect, people wouldn't have gone to Mars. Right?"

She laughed under her breath. "I guess I'm trying to say…I don't think domes and ships were ever part of nature's plan."

"We know how nature's plan worked out for the dinosaurs. Just saying."

Rose rolled her eyes at him.

They kept walking past a pond filled with dozens of fat, golden fish, all fighting each other over pellets kids tossed. An automated display explained how pumps recycled the water, cleaning it for the fish while also feeding the many plants here in the process. They sat on a bench beneath a curved glass arch and watched them for a while. The normal sounds of the ship were absent here; no groaning steel, no echoing footfalls, or hissing valves. Just the whisper of hundreds of tiny, paper-thin wings.

Ethan closed his eyes. For a moment, everything felt weightless. He didn't realize how badly he needed this peace until he entered it. The glass dome arched high overhead, shaped in a way that didn't seem industrial or militaristic. It felt organic, like a bubble of Earth trapped in space, beneath the stars. Walkways wove through hanging vines and leafy plants, and fluttering all around them were hundreds of butterflies.

Rose smiled as he stopped walking. "They're heavier than air," she whispered, pointing, watching one land on a star-shaped lily. "But they still fly. That's wild."

Ethan nodded. "Literally and figuratively." His legs were sore from walking all week, and his back ached from bending over boxes, but here, it didn't matter. There was something pleasant about the air. It was still, fragrant, and pure, unlike the factory. "I don't want to return to mud huts, but… this is nice."

Rose nodded. "Really makes me miss MBA Park."

"Yeah. Good ole' Mars Base Alpha. If we can just get to Ceres and back alive, we'll be able to afford a place with a view of it."

"You think?"

"I hope." He confessed. "They say almost thirty percent of it is ice. What's the going rate on water lately?"

Rose answered quietly. "Sixty two credits a gallon."

"I don't know how much we will actually manage to bring back, but we get a bonus when we return—ten percent of the total hall. Foxtrot might be a junker, but its cargo hold is pretty big."

Rose smiled and squeezed his hand. "Big enough to make us all dreamers, right babe? Even if we are going to split that ten percent in two thousand different ways."

"Right." He smiled back at her. "If we can just get to Ceres and back alive…" Ethan glanced up at the arching dome above them. "We'll be hauling so much ice, people back on MBA will be drinking it for years. And us? We won't ever have to do anything we don't want to ever again. That's the plan anyway."

She squeezed his hand again. "Sounds good to me."

They ventured further in, following the bubbling sound of water. A pond shimmered next to a spraying stone fountain ahead. Children pointed up at the swirling flock of butterflies and laughed. For the first time in weeks, Ethan felt the muscles in his shoulders finally loosen.

Then the gravity shifted.

At first, it was subtle. For half a heartbeat, Ethan's stomach rose weightlessly, then his guts slammed back down. *Splat*—a butterfly hit the ground beside him. Another dropped into the pond with a *kerplunk* a split-second later, and was quickly eaten. Dozens more fell. Hundreds of them. The air filled with soft, papery thumps.

Rose gasped. Children began crying. A worker in a green jumpsuit stumbled, grabbing the railing. The overhead lights flickered, and the filtration hum hiccupped.

"Rose—" Ethan grabbed her hand sluggishly, suddenly finding it hard to move.

The butterflies lay on the floor, their bodies broken. A few buzzed weakly, but most didn't move at all. People were shouting now. A man near the entrance slipped and slammed into the glass wall, stunned.

Ethan looked up. There had been no announcement, or warning. Just weight. Raw, terrible weight. Then it stopped. Just like that.

The artificial sun resumed its warm glow. The misting system hissed back on. But no one moved. The butterflies were all dead, and the room was quieter than before, that strange quiet where no one knows what to do. He crouched as if to pick one up, then stopped, unsure if he should.

Rose also knelt beside one of the fallen butterflies. Her fingers trembled, and the shimmer in her eyes faded. Ethan reached for her shoulder, but she didn't flinch or look up.

"We should go," he said, quietly.

She nodded once and stood up. Her face became blank, the way it did when she didn't want him to see her hurt. As they walked back down the winding path, a pair of crew in bright yellow moved past them in a rush. One held a tablet, the other a containment case. Neither looked at each other. A net hung from the belt of the taller one.

"Do you think it was a malfunction?" Rose asked, voice low. "Or—?"

Ethan didn't respond. He was watching the small boy from earlier, still clutching his mother's leg, tears streaking down his cheeks. The mother mouthed silent words to him, a protective lie. "Just a system glitching, sweetie. Just for a few seconds. Everything's okay now."

The doors hissed open behind them. Cool, sterile corridor air swept in.

"I don't know what to think anymore. The ship is supposed to be stable," Ethan muttered. "But this doesn't feel very stable does it?"

Rose bit her lip. "They also said we had two years' redundancy on all rations." Rose's voice was calm, but there was something under it stretched as tight as piano wire. "Then they started giving us appetite-suppression shots."

They walked in silence for a while together after that. The colorful spiral of the corridor no longer felt cheerful. It felt exposed, vulnerable, as if things could fall on them at any moment.

Rose scowled. "Why did this have to happen? We were having such a good time. I was just about to get you to take a picture with me by that fountain."

"Let's try not to let it ruin our cycle. It took almost three hours to get all the way out here."

Rose nodded. "Yeah, you're right. I'm not ready to take the tram back. They have a low-gravity pool. I'd say we could go for a swim, except, I don't want to drown if there's another gravity surge. So, how about a movie?"

Ethan agreed, chuckling nervously. "Movie it is."

The theater was half-full. An old Earth film flickered against the curved wall. It was one of those silent, black-and-white movies, something about a runaway train. It was meant to be a classic. Rose chuckled at the outdated tech and curled under Ethan's arm. The film rattled toward its climax, but Rose wasn't watching. She was eavesdropping on the people around them.

"...it was an AI glitch, barely four seconds long..."

"...the ship was hit by debris, and the impact made the gravity recalibrate..."

"...they're calling it a noncritical anomaly..."

The murmurs were soft, but each word felt as sharp as broken glass. Rose rested her head against Ethan's shoulder. She didn't want to talk about it, but she couldn't stop her stomach from knotting.

She whispered, "I wonder if they ever knew."

Ethan glanced at her. "What do you mean?"

"When they hit the ground. Whether they knew something was wrong before it happened."

Ethan pulled her closer.

She sat up slightly; the screen's flicker caught the edge of her face. "This movie isn't working for me. Let's get out of here. I want some food."

They slipped out the side door. The corridor beyond hummed with low light, soft music, and the faint scent of lemon cleaner. A camera shifted in the corner with a nearly silent motorized whirr, tracking them.

"What do you want to eat?" Ethan asked, trying to stay casual.

Rose sighed. "I don't know, but that popcorn was burned. And they only gave me a single packet of salt."

Ethan teased, "The nerve."

Rose didn't smile. "It's not funny, Ethan. You *know* how much I love salt." She ran a hand through her hair and added, "And they were slower than that Eggplant getting it to me."

Ethan raised an eyebrow. "Old Eggplant's making you wait?"

She nodded hard. "I confronted him last cycle. Took him *forever* to count a bin, like an hour and a half, so I asked him about it. And it was *amazing*. Like I had this authority I've never had before." She grinned. "He mumbled something about a faulty lift, and five minutes later? He shows up with the count. Can you imagine?"

Ethan chuckled, slightly uneasy. "Oh, Eggplant. That tattoo on his neck is quite something."

Rose shot him a look. "He's got to advertise some way." They exchanged a grin, and then she shrugged. "I've got to work with him again next cycle, and Eggplant and I are *not* going to be friends first thing in the cycle." She threw her hands up. "I know he's going to try to steal my keyboard again.

"And did you know he lost some pallets, so now I'm supposed to find them? I'm in tech support. Why is it my job? Does Jim think I own a hat I can reach into and pull a rabbit out of? Only, the rabbit would be a bunch of TT parts, and the hat is my…"

Ethan cut in laughing. "OK, OK. Tell me how you really feel." His eyes flicked toward the camera in the corner. In a world with a two-to-one person-to-camera ratio, someone was always watching. He wondered, once more, who was on the other end.

Rose caught his glance and traced it, then forced a smile. "We'll figure it out."

"Right," Ethan said, then more quietly, glancing toward another camera. "You should be more careful how you talk about that stuff in public."

Rose's smile faded. "I know. I know. "

Ethan waited until they were around the corner, hidden behind the vending bay, before speaking again. "You heard what happened to Asher, right? After he complained about the medbay delay?"

Rose stared at the floor.

"They said he was 'redirected for psychological realignment.'"

"Two-week sentence," Rose muttered. "Except it's been three. That's just the way it is in paradise."

Ethan put his arm around her shoulder, supportive. "As far as I'm concerned, you're a tech-support superhero. You have got this."

"Thanks, babe." Then, under her breath, she added, "Don't fine me, bro."

They both looked up at the same time at the blinking red light of the camera overhead.

Ethan kissed her head. "We'll be all right," he promised, more hopeful than certain. "Want to take the train to Vitos?"

She nodded. "Yeah, that still sounds good. Why didn't we go last cycle? You took forever to get home," she added.

Ethan adjusted his hat. "Sorry about that. I fell asleep on the train and overshot my stop."

Rose smiled. A small one. The kind you give someone when everything's on fire, and yet it's fine.

The train to Venos was half-empty, typical for this late in the cycle. Rose pressed her forehead to the window, watching streaks of light blurring past. The hum of the maglev line was almost soothing, broken only by the occasional *thud* of track magnets snapping into place.

Ethan slouched beside her, legs stretched out, his cap tugged low. He glanced over. "You've gone quiet."

Rose smirked. "Eggplant."

Ethan groaned. "Oh no. What did he do now?"

She turned toward him, eyes bright. "Apparently, they pulled him off airlift detail because he kept hitting too many things." A pause. "Like… how do you even do that? There's *nothing there.* "

Ethan snorted. "He's got a real gift."

"They put him on Zambino duty instead. You know, water cart, floor polisher, that whole glamorous gig." He nodded. "Go on." "Well, it lasted *one shift*. He's zooming around the techlab like he owns the place, and then the left wheel falls off. Just *thunk*! Gone. The whole cart tipped over, and water spilled everywhere. They had to call a full safety sweep."

Ethan burst out laughing. "No. Way."

"I swear! And get this, rumor is D-shift crashed the Zambino last week racing it against an air trawler."

"You're making that up."

"I *wish*! Eggplant told me himself. Said he was *trying* to keep it under the speed limit."

"Is there even a speed limit on a Zambino?"

"Apparently. He goes, 'I was goin' one mile an hour, I swear,' and I said, 'Eggplant, *the wheel fell off*.' Did you even inspect it first?"

Ethan leaned back, smirking. "You love this."

"No. I love the *stories*. Working with Eggplant is like inhabiting a sitcom, but I'm not mourning the finale. I haven't even told you the best part."

"Oh no. There's more?"

"He'd already dumped the water tank *twice* before the wheel detached. First time, he overfilled it, didn't know there was a fill line. The pump lost suction, and greywater flooded the floor."

Ethan blinked. "Okay, but how did he manage it *again*?"

She rolled her eyes. "He said no one told him what he did wrong, so he just... repeated himself."

"Wow."

The train decelerated as the automated voice announced the stop. Rose stretched.

"Alright. Let's go inflict some Alfredo on ourselves."

Vitos thrummed, its neon sign spelling the restaurant's name in lascivious red letters bright as Sirius. The dinner rush was in full swing. A-shift was off, trying to decompress over a meal. Rose led the way, threading through a corridor of noodle joints and synth-meat carts until they reached a secluded diner wedged between two holo-ad boards. Plenty of cleaner bots and delivery drones were still laboring, further clogging the thoroughfare.

"Alfredo Heaven," Ethan said, gesturing at the building. "That's what they should have called it."

"That would have been a good one," Rose agreed, pushing the door open. "So would Pasta Palace. This place is the best."

Inside: hardwood floors, white walls, black furniture, and a glowing menu screen embedded in each table. They slid into a back booth, tucked beneath a languidly spinning fan.

A server-bot wheeled over, mid-spiel. "Welcome to Vito's. May I take your order?"

Rose tapped a steaming plate on the display. "Two of those. And water."

"Same."

"Affirmative." The bot spun away.

Ethan leaned forward. "So, about Eggplant—"

"Later," she interrupted. "You notice the guy by the window?"

Ethan glanced over. An old man sat alone, no food, no drink, wearing tinted glasses, a black ball cap, and an olive tracksuit, staring at a sleek grey tablet. "Yeah. What about him?"

"He was on the train. Our car."

"You sure?"

Rose nodded slowly. "Didn't think much of it then. But now... I think he's tailing us."

Ethan's expression shifted, subtle, but his shoulders tightened. "You think he's tailing us?" He repeated. "Really?"

"Maybe it's a coincidence."

The server-bot returned. Neither reached for their plates. From the window booth, the old man in the olive tracksuit glanced up at them, then snapped back to his tablet.

Ethan watched him while he ate. The Alfredo was surprisingly good, distracting, at least for a minute. Rose picked at hers, eyes flicking to the old man every few bites.

"He hasn't ordered anything," she muttered. "Isn't that too on the nose? He's wearing security green. The one color an undercover officer wouldn't wear."

"Maybe he's just some guy waiting for divine Alfredo inspiration," Ethan said, half-joking. He watched him, too.

Then the old man in the olive tracksuit stood.

Rose's elbow inched toward the table's edge.

Ethan straightened.

The old man didn't rush. He walked past them toward the bathroom. As he passed, he looked directly at them. Not a glance, a solid look. Just long enough for Ethan to notice something in the lens frames.

Rose's fork clattered from her fingers.

The old man didn't stop. He reached the bathroom and disappeared inside.

Ethan stared after him, then leaned in. "Did you see that?" he hissed. "His glasses?"

Rose whispered, voice low. "Recording us."

Ethan stood. "Yep," he said, decided.

Rose's face tightened. "Where are you going?"

Ethan adjusted his hat. "In there."

Rose protested: "Babe, no. Let's just go."

Ethan was already moving. He didn't hear the rest. As Rose called after him, he marched into the bathroom.

The lights flickered once. It wasn't much: two sinks, one mirror, a urinal, a stall. Cold tile. Recycled air smelling of feet.

The old man was already at the sink, washing his hands as if nothing was wrong. Big for an old-timer, broad shoulders, little gut. He took care of himself.

Ethan let the door shut behind him, soft *click*.

"Hey," Ethan said, voice low, serious as a heart attack. "I know you filmed me and my wife."

No response.

The old man turned off the water. Sixty, maybe older. He took his time drying his hands on the dispenser towel. His voice was smooth, sweet, honey off the comb. "I don't know what you're talking about."

Ethan scowled. "Why were you recording us?" He stepped closer, fingers curling, blood pressure spiking. "We saw you."

The old man met his gaze in the mirror. Ethan stared at the tiny black dots embedded in the tinted lens. Nothing.

"I can see them right now," Ethan burst. "I know what you're doing!" He pointed at the glasses. "Stop recording us!"

A pause.

The old man remained unfazed. Calm. He turned and locked eyes with Ethan.

"You didn't see a damn thing."

The old man in the olive tracksuit stared at him. Ethan could see his own fear reflected in those black mirrored sunglasses. That scar he could see it, too. Filament thin, stretching unnaturally long. Had a razor made it?

"Have a nice cycle, Ethan."

Ethan stood there, fists clenched, knuckles bloodless.

How did he know his name?

The old man tossed the used paper towel into the trash and walked right past him.

Rose was already on her feet when Ethan emerged a moment later. She raked her gaze over him, scanning for signs of a struggle.

"What happened?" Her voice was taut as a wire.

"He knew my name," Ethan said.

Rose snatched her coat. "We need to go."

They left the diner without further comment and plunged back into the cacophony and neon. The hallway of food carts thrummed with life, but Ethan scanned every face now. No tracksuit guy. Not yet.

They turned a corner, moving fast, and reached the main corridor. Ethan halted. A camera was mounted above them. Watching.

They kept moving fast, keeping their heads down, trying to dissolve into the crowd. Venos faded quickly behind them, replaced by a cylindrical street, echoing announcements, and a scattering of passersby. Down on the lower platform, it was quieter. A cleaner bot wheeled past, humming to itself but that was about it.

Rose and Ethan found a spot around the corner, out of sight of the main hallway. Rose leaned against the wall, arms folded. Ethan stood close as well, eyes raking every passerby as if expecting recognition.

"Okay," Rose said, voice low. "We're definitely being watched."

"Yeah. He knew my name," Ethan said again, more to himself than to her. "Didn't show a badge, didn't make a threat. Just said it like he knew exactly who I was. Creeped me out. " He added with a shiver.

Rose rubbed her temples. "This can't be because of what I did."

He nodded. "He got here too fast. We must have been on surveillance for a while."

"You sure?"

He sighed. "It's gotta be Sector Six."

Rose shot him a sharp look. "What were you doing in Sector Six?"

"I fell asleep on the train last cycle and tried to cut through there to get home. Remember?" He adjusted his hat nervously.

"Half that place is sealed off now. I swear I saw a camera swivel after me when I got off an elevator there."

Rose took his hand. "Let's get out of here before our tram pass is revoked."

They left without another word, never looking back.

Ethan counted camera stations all the way to the platform. Most cycles, he never noticed them. This time: fifty-six.

CHAPTER 9
The Coffee Maker

The tram hummed and coughed down the track, rocking a half-dozen pallid passengers beneath sterile, stuttering light. Outside the windows, the vacuous black of space pressed close, broken only by scattered points of starlight. Ethan stared into it as if it might yield answers. None came.

Rose sat beside him, shoulder to shoulder, the warmth of her body deadened by scratchy synthetic fabric. She took a slow breath, sniffed her shirt collar with a wince, then leaned back and exhaled through her nose.

"Remember that guy who kept calling the hotline because he swore the meat machine was haunted?" she asked, her voice arid.

Ethan blinked. "Didn't you say he thought it was blinking Morse code?"

She nodded. "Yeah. He called again on the last shift. I told him it was just a diagnostic LED, but he didn't believe me. So I told him I booked an exorcism for Thursday."

He turned toward her, brows arched. "You didn't."

A thin smile played on her lips. "Did I? Or am I rehearsing a comedy special? You tell me, Camera Men." She tossed a quick, mirthless grin at the fisheye lens mounted in the ceiling.

The tram slipped into a maintenance tunnel. For a second, the lights guttered. Both of them tensed, just a flicker, but neither spoke. The moment passed.

"It's dumb," Ethan said finally, his voice dropping, "but I keep thinking about that camera by the door. Like... what if someone's watching us right now, just bored? We're just two tired nobodies riding home."

Rose shrugged. "Of course someone's watching. That's the whole point. You behave better under surveillance." She glanced at him, sideways. "You know they watch us have sex, right?"

Her smile was faint, cold, half a joke. Half not. She looked back up at the black bulb in the center of the tram, unblinking, ceaseless.

"That's just a rumor," Ethan muttered. "They don't actually do that."

She arched an eyebrow but didn't push it. "I got another manifesto submitted as a work request," she said. "Some tirade about how the corporation targets 'vocal workers' and how we need to unionize."

He blinked. "That's... brave."

"I flagged it for mental health. Second one this month." Her voice went flat. "System flagged me too, for looking at it too long. 'Abnormal viewing pattern.' So maybe the guy was right. Maybe that's why they're watching us."

The tram began to slow. Outside, the familiar lights of Sector Four came into view. The exposed wires, flaking paint, and gouged walls made it look like a bomb had gone off in there.

Ethan rubbed at his temples. "Maybe, babe. I don't know." He leaned in, dropping his voice to a near-whisper. "I think they're going to send people out to fix the gravity. And part of me thinks... they're deciding who."

Rose met his gaze. For a long beat, neither of them spoke.

Then she asked, "Still glad it's the weekend?" Her smile was small again, but this time it reached her eyes.

"Surveillance beats warehouse duty by about an inch," Ethan said. "What about you?"

"No calls. No tickets. No one asking me why the air smells funny or if a bot is flirting with them." She leaned back again, her voice softening. "What more could a gal ask for?"

The tram doors opened with a hiss, exhaling a gust of cold, recycled air. They stepped off together.

"Who asked if a bot was flirting?" Ethan said.

Rose shot him an amused look. "Kale. He wanted me to do a reverse image search for him. I didn't even need to, it was Lavender from *90 Cycles*."

Ethan blinked. Then snorted. "Kale Chairman?"

She nodded, grinning now. "I know, right? He asked me to check anyway, like I haven't seen six seasons. And I love the confidence. Seriously. It's wild, you've seen her!"

Ethan grinned. "Hope is a dangerous thing."

Their boots echoed down the corridor, the walls buzzing faintly with the ship's systems. Overhead, the lights flickered in that faint, uneven rhythm Ethan had stopped noticing. Now, every flicker caught his eye.

Rose shook her head. "If we go somewhere with this man and she pulls up, I'll eat every word, but until then, he's in denial.

I told this man to get some confidence and the guy went to the moon."

Sector Four was quiet. There were fewer bodies in the halls, but the silence still felt watched. Everything did.

They reached Unit 402, ten feet wide, twenty-seven feet long, plus a bedroom. A rounded hatch, pale gray and smudged with fingerprints. Rose pressed her wrist to the panel, and the door thudded open with the usual half-second delay. Everyone else knew it was lag from outdated firmware they refused to patch.

Inside, the room was a tight rectangle of brushed metal and faded faux-fabric walls. Bunk, desk, wall screen, storage. One porthole, usually open. A strip of programmable LEDs glowed a dull gold along the ceiling. A faint scent of detergent and stale air clung to everything.

Rose stepped in first and immediately peeled off her boots with a groan. "My feet are plotting to unionize."

Ethan followed, unzipping his jacket. "Let them. Might negotiate better conditions than us."

She flopped onto the couch, in the truest sense of the word, face-first into the cushions. "I'd kill for an actual cotton blanket. Like, soft ones. Remember cotton?"

Ethan tossed his boots toward the wall and missed the shelf. "I never had one. Just saw them on a screen."

"I had a blend," she said into the pillow. "It was better than this scrub-brush polyplastic crap. It makes my thighs sweat."

He chuckled, sitting beside her. "Want me to grab you a blanket off the bed?"

She turned her head just enough to see him and nodded. "I'm going to submit a ticket."

"You'll have to flag your own account."

"I already did. Three times. If I go missing, it's because I tried to unionize my couch."

He laughed harder than he should've. It was more relief than mirth. Relief to still be able to laugh at all.

He stood, stretched, cricked his neck, then walked to the bedroom and fetched the blanket. On the way back, he crossed to the wall screen and flicked it on. A loop of sponsored nature footage began to play—synthetic birds, synthetic rivers, synthetic forests. Soothing, scripted wilderness that never did anything too exhilarating, never got too dark.

"Do you want music or quiet?" he asked.

"Surprise me. Just not the fusion station."

He paused. "What about *Raining in Tokyo*?"

He switched it to the ambient, quiet lofi. Soft and sluggish. Something that felt almost, vaguely, like the world before.

Rose rolled over onto her back. "You really think they're simulating who goes outside?"

"I think the system tracks our vitals, our sleep, our macros, our blink rate, if they could read our minds, they would. So yeah. I think the system picks."

"God. That's so much worse than I thought." She stared up at the ceiling. "What if we're past the threshold already?"

"You'll be fine, babe," he said, sitting beside her again. "They won't send you out. You got approval to get pregnant."

She reached over and laced her fingers through his, then bit her lip. His hands were callused, warm, tangible. For a few seconds, neither of them spoke. The ambient whisper of the music blended with the hum of the artificial gravity.

Then, barely louder than the music, Rose asked, "What would you do if we didn't have to live like this anymore?"

He didn't answer immediately.

Finally, he said, "Sleep late. Get real cotton sheets. Take you on a tour of Earth."

She smiled, eyes still fixed on the ceiling.

"Good answer," she said. "I'd get drunk in the sun. Naked. Feel the wind on my skin."

They lay there, hands clasped, surrounded by metal, recycled air, and silence.

Rose whispered, "What if I don't get pregnant?"

Ethan squeezed her hand. "Don't say that. You will."

"What if I don't?" she repeated.

Ethan's jaw clenched, but he didn't let go of her hand.

"You will," he said again, softer this time.

Rose didn't answer immediately. Her eyes stayed fixed on the ceiling, on nothing, on something. The synthetic rain fell in a perfect looping pattern. In the corner, a vent clanked once, then settled. A silence opened between them. Not angry. Not cold. Just dense.

Ethan didn't speak for a long while.

Then, without looking at her, he said, "I don't care if we have to grow a baby in a hydroponic tub, I'll make it happen. Even if I have to steal it from Myrtle."

That coaxed a soft smile out of her. Fragile, but there.

"She might kill you if you do," she whispered, pulling off her shirt. "We better just have sex."

He brushed a strand of hair from her face. The lofi track looped again. Outside the porthole, the view drifted as the ship made another correction. Rose closed her eyes and leaned into Ethan's kisses.

They held each other closely, tangled on the couch, the blanket draped haphazardly over their legs.

Rose pressed her forehead to Ethan's collarbone, listening to the slow rhythm of his breath and the soft murmur of synthesized rain from the wall screen.

Ethan woke first. He always had.

Rose liked to burrow under the covers and steal every last second of sleep.

Meanwhile, Ethan's body had become so calibrated to the ship's artificial work-rest cycle that his eyes simply opened, on cue, at the same hour every morning, even on off-cycles.

He sat up slowly, pushing the duvet aside. Beside him, Rose murmured something garbled and flopped onto her stomach, one foot escaping the blanket fortress she'd built in her sleep. Ethan smiled.

He padded into the tiny galley, still rubbing his eyes, and started the coffee. The machine coughed a warning, something about calcium buildup, but he ignored it. Half the systems on Foxtrot grumbled before obeying, just to let you know they were trying.

While the coffee brewed, he opened the freezer. One bag of dehydrated hash browns. One vacuum-sealed burrito. And bingo, one cinnamon pastry that had definitely been someone else's at some point, but had been in the freezer for over a week now. That made it fair game.

He popped it in the reheater and leaned back against the counter, waiting. The cabin was still dim. Their makeshift window screen let in the softest edge of the hallway's artificial glow, like dawn filtering through frosted glass.

From the bedroom, Rose groaned. "Is that *cinnamon* I smell?"

"You bet your sweet butt it is," Ethan called back.

"You didn't even ask if I wanted it."

"You were dead to the world."

"I'm perpetually asleep."

Ethan grinned and pulled the pastry out, steam curling from its center like a soul escaping.

"Split it?"

There was a pause. Then the shuffle of blankets. "I guess."

Minutes later, they were both at the island in the middle of their kitchen. One cup of coffee, one can of Blue Bolt, one pastry cut into slightly uneven halves, and a packet of shelf-stable creamer that Ethan had ripped open with his teeth.

Rose looked better with caffeine in her system—more awake, less Medusa. She poked at the pastry, then looked at Ethan as she sipped her energy drink.

"Hey, remember that bizarre manifesto I was telling you about?"

Ethan raised an eyebrow. "The one about unionizing the couch?"

She nodded. "That one."

"Yeah. What about it?"

They both sipped in unison.

"I mean, it's probably nothing," Rose said. "But ugh… well, do you know who the 'Analyst' is?"

"Sure," Ethan said with a nod. "It's a video game character."

She shot him a look but smirked, rolling her eyes. "I knew I was asking the right man."

He gave a small bow. "Thank you, thank you. Apparently, it's a notoriously difficult level in *Bot Hunter*."

She slanted him a glance. "The manifesto said: Beware the Analyst. Over and over. They must be young."

The lights were dim. Not broken but dim. A deliberate choice. Rose had learned to override the defaults, bathing their quarters in a soft amber glow. Ethan thought it made the room feel warmer, though the temperature setting hadn't changed.

"Do you ever think about just leaving?" Rose asked.

She sat cross-legged on the floor, folding laundry into tidy stacks while she ate. The vent's air stirred the fabric edges, and her bangs framed her face in layered halos. Ethan sprawled on the couch, watching her instead of the rerun of *90 Cycles* flickering on the screen behind her.

"Leaving?" he echoed. "Like leaving Foxtrot?"

"Yeah," she said. "Just pack up and transfer. Start fresh somewhere else."

Ethan chuckled. "Babe, you say that every time."

Rose flung a rolled-up sock at his chest. "Because I mean it. Come on, don't you ever think about it? There are other ships. Better ones. Some even have real windows."

"These are real windows," Ethan drawled. "They just don't open."

She rolled her eyes and folded a pair of cargo pants. "You know what I mean."

He did. And she wasn't wrong. There were other ships that were bigger, newer. Some orbited Mars instead of ghosting through deep space. But Foxtrot was home.

"I don't know," he said after a pause. "I think about it occasionally, but it's not that easy."

"It is that easy," she countered. "You're capable. People like you. You could transfer. So why don't you?"

Ethan didn't answer immediately. He shifted on the couch, exhaling slowly. The vent's hum filled the silence.

"I think…" he began slowly, "I stay because I know what to expect. Foxtrot might be falling apart, but I'm committed. Have you heard the saying, 'The grass is greenest where you water it'?"

Rose paused, looking at him, waiting.

"What I'm trying to say is… I used to want more, you know," Ethan continued. "Back before the mines. I thought maybe I'd end up planetside. Fixing ships… maybe writing a little fiction."

"You wanted to be a writer?" Rose asked, surprised.

"I wanted to be more than a man counting bins," he said, half-laughing. "Saving credits for a functional dryer. After Beta and the asteroid mine, I needed something solid, no pun intended. Reliable. Foxtrot… well, it's a mess, but it's my mess, and I'm tired of starting over. Plus, I worked much harder on Beta for fewer credits."

Rose was quiet a moment. Then she stood, walked over, and sat beside him, resting her head against his shoulder.

"I never knew you wanted to write," she said softly.

"I still think about it now and then," Ethan admitted. "A little horror story called *How Not to Die in Space*. Part One: Don't Work on Beta."

She chuckled. "You'd sell a million easily."

Ethan smiled, but his eyes remained on the ceiling. "I guess I stay because I'm scared," he said. "Of leaving. Of starting over. Of things becoming worse. It's not brave, but it's true."

Rose shifted beside him, her fingers toying absently with the hem of her oversized T-shirt. She always stole the softest ones.

"You're not the only one who's scared," she said, so quietly it was nearly a whisper. "I talk big about transferring, but I don't know if I'd actually go through with it."

Ethan tilted his head. "Really?"

Rose nodded. "Delta sounds better in theory, but I don't know. Gigi's heading some department now, but it's weird."

Ethan frowned. "Weird how?"

She hesitated. "Gigi says things like 'Affirmative' when I message her now." Rose's voice went flat as she mimicked the phrasing. "No emojis. No typos. Just… corporate speak."

The couch creaked as Ethan sat up straighter. He rubbed the back of his neck, brow furrowed. "I admit… that sounds off."

"Exactly."

She trailed into silence.

He squeezed her hand. "All we have to do is stick it out, mine a lot of ice, and make it back in one piece. Then we'll have all the time we want together.

"I've made peace with not becoming whoever I thought I'd be. I don't need to be important or remembered. I want to be with you. With Aspen or Celeste or whoever comes next.

"I think we can have a decent little life together if we can make this Foxtrot job work."

Rose blinked away tears, then leaned in and kissed him, a long, soft moment. The kind that said *I love you* and *I hope you're right.* When she pulled back, her voice was thick. "Promise me something?"

"What, babe?"

She smiled, stood, and stretched. "No more serious topics for a while. You're being a real tearjerker!"

Ethan stayed on the couch, watching her walk to the small galley. Rose opened a cupboard and grabbed the chipped green bottle of Firesauce. "You want some hot sauce? Three shakes only," she warned. "Any more and you'll regret it."

Ethan leaned back, arms behind his head. "I'm a grown man, Rose. I can handle four."

"You say that now, but I'm not cleaning the bathroom twice in a single cycle."

He snorted. "Fair enough."

She tossed the bottle toward him. He caught it one-handed and gave his breakfast plate a generous splash.

The cinnamon pastry was long gone, but he'd scrounged up a leftover protein biscuit and a single-serving tub of mystery eggs, pale yellow, unsettlingly glossy. He drowned them in hot sauce and convinced himself it made them taste better.

Just as he took a bite, the coffee maker let out a series of clicks, wheezed, and then fell silent.

Ethan eyed it with suspicion.

The red light blinked at him. Once. Twice. And then, nothing.

"You have got to be kidding me."

Rose poked her head out of the galley. "What?"

"The coffee maker just died."

She leaned against the counter wearing a half-grin. "Did it die, or did it just get tired of being abused?"

"Same thing," Ethan grumbled, rising and tapping the side of the unit. "I descaled it last week."

Rose gave him a skeptical look. "You poured vinegar into it and forgot to rinse it out."

"Cleaning is a subjective experience."

He pressed a few buttons. Nothing. Held down the power. Nothing. Finally, he unplugged it, waited five seconds, and plugged it back in.

Still nothing.

"Okay," Ethan muttered. "So maybe it is dying."

"Just let it go," Rose said. "We'll file another maintenance ticket."

He groaned. "That's three this month. The dryer, the vent rattle, and now the coffee maker."

She raised her can. "This is why I drink Blue Bolt."

Ethan reluctantly abandoned the coffee maker and joined her at the galley counter, where they polished off the rest of the eggs and protein crumbs in companionable silence. Just as he started wiping down the table, a knock came at the door.

Ethan and Rose exchanged a glance.

"Maintenance?" she guessed. Ethan shrugged. "Who else would knock?"

He crossed the room and pressed the manual open. The door slid back. Sure enough, there he was: the red-vested, steel-bearded maintenance guy from a few cycles ago. The one who looked like a grizzled Mickey. Same grimy clipboard, same hooded eyes, same faint smell of heat-warped plastic.

"402?" he asked flatly. "Yeah," Ethan replied. "The coffee maker," Rose called out from the kitchen. "But that just died. Perfect timing."

"Terrific." The maintenance guy grunted. "Yeah, that's not on the list. I'm supposed to do appliances today."

He stepped inside without waiting for an invitation.

Ethan sidestepped as the man shouldered past him, tools jingling on his belt.

"You got a name?" Ethan tried.

The guy didn't look up. "The name's Buzz."

He crouched beside the coffee machine and pried off the back panel. Ethan winced at the grinding sound it made.

"You're just going to start with that one?" Ethan asked. "What about the dryer?"

"This one's easier. The dryer's probably toast. Your model's in the replacement queue."

Ethan opened his mouth to ask what that meant exactly, but Rose gave him the look. So instead, he just stood there while Buzz fiddled with the insides of the coffee maker, muttering and poking wires with something that looked like a dentist's pick.

Then, just as suddenly, Buzz stopped and held something up: a tiny chip, circular, almost like a SIM card, charred around the edges. He squinted at it, then at the inside of the machine, then slowly at Ethan.

"This is weird." Buzz blinked. He rolled it between his fingers, still squinting. "Really weird."

"How weird?" Ethan pressed.

"This isn't supposed to be part of a coffee maker. It records audio."

Rose stepped forward. "Wait, are you saying our coffee maker has been bugged?"

Buzz shrugged. "Definitely. This thing's older than both of us." He tapped the machine affectionately. "But this isn't," he added, brandishing the chip. "Who knows how long it's been in there."

"Great." Ethan rubbed the back of his neck. "But it's dead now?"

"Dead and toasted," Buzz confirmed, rising to his feet. "Power surge fried it. I'll need to log this." He slipped the chip into a sealed evidence bag with a barcode. "You'll have to get another coffee maker too, by the way. The whole unit is fried."

Rose looked at Ethan. He looked at her. They both looked at the maintenance man.

He scratched his beard and stepped toward the door. "We'll have to reschedule the dryer. I'll send you an email. Now, if you'll excuse me. "

Just like that, he was gone into the hallway. The door hissed closed behind him.

Ethan exhaled. "Did we just discover a spy chip in our coffee maker?"

Rose blinked. "I don't know, but I feel way more awake than I did five minutes ago. We were this close to getting our dryer fixed!" She let out a sound straight out of Godzilla in 1963, then stormed into the kitchen to make a drink.

"We're out of vodka," Ethan said quietly.

Rose promptly started breathing atomic fire. It came out as a torrent of unrepeatable words that roasted the spy bug, the maintenance man, the man in glasses, and the entire security department. She had practically incinerated all of Foxtrot before she stopped to take a breath.

Rose finally finished scorching her foes and collapsed onto the couch, her hair askew and one sock halfway off.

Ethan sat down beside her. "So," he said, "on a scale of one to ten, how bad is this?"

She groaned into her hands. "If someone's been eavesdropping on everything we say..."

Ethan winced. "Even the karaoke night."

"And your so-called philosophical monologues," she added.

"Hey, I was being profound. I hope our spy was listening to that."

"It was about whether aliens are real," she reminded him.

"They are," he muttered defensively.

They sat in silence for a moment, the weight of the discovery settling between them like a third roommate with terrible hygiene.

"I can't believe we got bugged," Rose said finally. "Don't they have to disclose stuff like this?"

"Apparently not," Ethan said quietly.

Rose looked up. "You know some pervert listened to us fooling around on the couch. That's so disgusting!" She narrowed her eyes. "We need to check everything. The oven, the fridge, the wall panels, hell, even the showerhead. If someone's listening to us on the toilet, I swear I'll lose my mind."

Ethan raised a hand and scratched his head. "How many could there possibly be?"

Rose pried loose the vent cover. Something inside blinked red.

They found three more bugs. One was behind the wall-mounted utensil rack. Another was inside the vent housing. And a third had been delicately lodged in the corner of the light fixture, disguised as a speck of dust.

Rose held them up in her palm like dead insects. "I take it back. I want to torch the whole room."

Ethan scowled. "This looks undeniably deliberate."

Rose stared at the tiny chips. "But why us? We're nobodies."

Ethan glanced toward the door, his voice low. "That's what everyone says before they get arrested."

"Okay, well, this is real life, not a thriller."

"Is it, though?"

A knock at the door made them both flinch.

Rose nearly sent the bugs flying.

Ethan slowly stood up. "Maybe it's Buzz coming back."

He crossed the room and opened the door. Only it wasn't Buzz.

The knock came again, softer this time, not the hammer blows of security.

Ethan cracked the door open a few inches.

Barry stood there in a rumpled hoodie and compression socks, balancing a six-pack of synthbrew in one hand and a battered game controller in the other. He smiled.

"Hey, man." It was one of those big sheepish grins, like he knew he was interrupting but did it anyway. "Didn't mean to bother you two. We were about to fire up *Bot Hunter.* Couch co-op. Really old-school."

Ethan blinked. "Is that the one with the evil robot, Analyst?"

"Yeah. A few of the guys from B-shift are over. Thought I'd check and see if you wanted to play." He looked past Ethan, over his shoulder, into the unit, and his eyes lingered on the open vent, then went back to Ethan like nothing had happened.

Rose appeared then, bugs held tightly in her clenched fist. "Sounds tempting. But we're busy."

Barry gave a theatrical wince. "Busy-Busy."

His eyes flicked to her clenched fist for just a beat, and then he smirked a little knowingly. "Signal is trash over at my place, but we don't mind. It's nice to be able to talk without…you know. Oh, and hey." His tone shifted just a hair, still friendly but also excited. "Did you hear? The butterflies died at the palace last cycle. Another gravity surge."

Ethan's fingers tightened slightly on the doorframe. "We were there."

“That must have been something to see.” Barry’s words were normal enough, but the excitement in his eyes wasn’t. “People are saying it was a glitch,” he added, almost offhandedly. “It’s crazy what can happen in 4.2 seconds.”

Ethan didn’t respond.

Barry’s smile returned, wide, harmless, and genuine. “Anyway, door’s open if you change your mind.”

He walked off down the corridor. When Ethan closed the door, Rose looked at him.

“What was that?”

Ethan shook his head. “4.2 is oddly specific. He really wants us to come over.”

Rose made a face. “We’re not going to play video games. We’re going to the security department,” she decided, planting her hand on her hip. “They have some explaining to do.”

CHAPTER 10
Secret Squirrel

A few minutes later, they were walking toward Sector Seven, Security, Ethan carrying a Ziploc pouch of defunct surveillance chips like he was peddling contraband. Rose marched two paces ahead with the rigidity normally reserved for job interviews and war crimes tribunals.

"I'm just saying," Ethan muttered, "we could still turn around, claim we found nothing, and feign paranoia."

Rose didn't slow. "We are paranoid. That doesn't make us wrong."

"I prefer being wrong about this kind of thing," Ethan said. "Wrong means we weren't bugged."

"Ethan, I looked up one of those chips. Standard serial code. You know what that means?"

"That we're headed outside for unauthorized possession of corporate property?"

She shot him a look over her shoulder. "It means they were manufactured within the last year, when they switched to this numeral." She pointed. "We've occupied that room for two years.

This was unequivocally meant to spy on us, but why? We're not even interesting."

Ethan tried for a joke. "Hey, I'm moderately interesting."

They reached the security department: two thick doors with reinforced plating, a blank monitor above them, and a solitary wall camera that pivoted as they approached. Rose stabbed the call button. Nothing. She pressed again, holding. The speaker buzzed and crackled. "State your business."

"We're here to report unauthorized surveillance devices," Rose said, crisp and direct.

A long pause. Then: Click. The door opened.

Inside, the reception area was needlessly intimidating. Ethan and Rose took in gray steel walls, flickering overhead lights, a reception desk fashioned from what looked like leftover cargo ramp plating, and a sole security officer behind it, staring at a terminal with the patience of a cadaver.

Rose stepped forward. "We found these in our apartment." She extended the pouch.

The officer didn't blink. Only stared at the bag, then at them. "Name and unit?"

"Ethan and Rose Parks. Four-oh-two."

Still nothing. Then the officer double-tapped the console and said, "Wait here."

Rose exhaled slowly as they sat on the room's only chairs: barely more than slightly warped metal stools bolted to the floor. A solitary framed sign on the wall read: **PLEASE REMAIN CALM DURING INCIDENT REPORTING.**

"Reassuring," Ethan whispered.

After a few minutes, a different voice said, "Mr. and Mrs. Parks?"

They looked up. Ethan knew that voice. Recognized it at once, even though he'd heard it just once before.

A man blocked the doorway. Broad shoulders, late fifties, olive security uniform straining over his shoulders. Silver-gray hair cropped short. A faint scar tracked across his jaw, disappearing beneath his collar. His ID tag read: **M. MARROW. INVESTIGATIONS**.

"Unauthorized, huh." The old man nearly chuckled. "This way."

It was the old man from Venos, the one with cameras in his sunglasses. Ethan was too shocked to speak. For once, Rose was also speechless. They made eye contact but said nothing.

Marrow led them down a narrow hall into a small, windowless interview room that was clean, less threatening than the lobby, but hardly comfortable. One table. Three chairs. A camera in the corner. Spartan, but the old man swept in like it was his living room.

Marrow dropped into the chair, leaned back, and gave a broad wave for them to sit. Then he plucked the bag from Rose, glanced inside, and set it on the table.

"Okay, ground rules," he said, voice booming like a PA system. "This conversation, right now, is top-shelf restricted. If you breathe a word of this to anyone, I'll be so far down your neck you'll think I'm your new husband."

He didn't wait for a nod.

Marrow added, "I'll save you the song and dance. Yes, I bugged you."

Ethan blinked. "Why?"

"Well," Marrow said, with rehearsed polish, "for security purposes, way back when gravity first started acting up."

Rose exploded. "How long ago exactly, and why didn't you tell us? You can't just plant bugs in our living room and keep quiet!"

"Actually, I can. Covered under investigation," Marrow said, dropping his voice to something serious. "TT panels are walking off the racks, and they don't come with legs installed.

He looked at Ethan. "You've been handling those panels lately, so…" He let the sentence trail off and held eye contact.

Rose folded her arms across her chest. "Ethan wouldn't—"

Marrow wagged a finger. "I'm not accusing anyone just yet. Merely collecting data." The old man held both hands up in mock surrender. "I listened to a few auto-flagged recordings, mostly. Don't worry."

He smiled, but it wasn't a nice look, eyes cutting to Rose. "Intimate audio is filtered out by the AI," the old man added coldly. "As long as you don't say something that triggers the safety protocol."

Rose raised her eyebrows. "Excuse me?"

Marrow slid the bugs aside, ignoring her outburst. "Since you're now aware of the investigation, that changes things." He slapped a data slate on the table. "The department is investigating every warehouse worker, because gravity is failing. People are dying because of it. Those panels are how we fix this, but someone is making sure that doesn't happen."

He leaned forward, bluster gone for a beat. "So here's the deal. I need you to play Secret Squirrel. Just observe. I'll come to you discreetly."

Ethan froze. "And if we say no?"

Marrow spread his arms as if delivering a sermon. "Then you go back to Four-oh-two, hug your pillows, and pray this mystery solves itself without you, before something bad happens again. Everyone wants to talk about the damn butterflies, but did you know a baby girl died? Six months old," he said quietly. "She went into cardiac arrest when the gravity coughed."

He glanced at Rose, his expression softening for a half-second. "I know it's unsettling, but until further notice, that's where we are. And that's why this investigation is so important."

Ethan scratched his head. "Are you sure this isn't just bad data? People routinely forget to confirm their transactions. How do you know it's intentional?"

Marrow clicked his tongue, leaned forward, and retrieved a ceramic coffee mug from his desk. Ethan couldn't help but notice the bright red A01 logo on the side. "The errors are too...specific. Same shift. Mostly from the 'Bent' aisle. But," he slapped his palms on the table, making them both flinch, "I hope you can help me determine exactly that."

The old man stood and swept the door open. "Mr. and Mrs. Parks?"

Ethan and Rose stiffened.

Marrow's tone turned warm and sweet again, saccharine as honey on a blade. "Have a nice cycle."

They exited the room, and the door hissed shut immediately behind them.

Rose looked at Ethan. "That didn't go how I thought it would."

Ethan didn't answer right away. "No," he agreed. "It didn't."

"I can't believe these people broke into our home and now they want us to work for them."

Ethan tucked the empty bag into his jacket pocket. The hallway felt colder than before and quieter, too. "They didn't ask," he said after a moment. "They just… assumed we'd do it."

Rose gave a sharp exhale, somewhere between a scoff and a laugh. "Not even a threat. Just that smile. That *'this is where we are'* nonsense."

They passed two custodial drones scrubbing the floor near the admin wing, their brushes hissing in tight circles. One lifted its optical sensor as they walked by. Or maybe it didn't. It was hard to tell anymore.

"I don't like this," she said. "They didn't even try to defend it. Like bugging us was standard procedure."

"Maybe it is," Ethan muttered.

Rose stopped walking. He turned to see her standing in the middle of the corridor, arms folded, brows drawn tight.

"You're not actually considering helping them, are you?"

Ethan hesitated. "I don't want to. But... what if someone is stealing those panels?"

"You think we're going to fix that?" Rose asked. "You and me? We can't even stop a coffee maker from dying."

"That's not the point."

She waited.

He rubbed the back of his neck, lowering his voice. "If we say no, we get watched harder. We become suspicious by default. But if we say yes... maybe we don't get sent outside. Quid pro quo, right?"

Rose looked at him for a long moment, then turned and started walking again. "I hate that you're probably right."

They walked the rest of the way in silence.

When they reached their unit, Ethan opened the door and stepped inside. The place felt smaller now. More cramped. Like the walls had crept closer while they were gone.

He looked at the vent. The coffee machine. The faint scuff mark on the floor where Buzz had stood.

Rose dropped her bag on the counter, then slumped onto the couch.

"I hate this," she mumbled into a cushion.

Ethan sat beside her, staring at nothing. "I know."

A long pause.

Then she lifted her head. "Whatever you decide, tell me. No secrets. No lies. Deal?"

He looked at her. Nodded slowly. "OK, babe. I promise."

The coffee maker was gone. The vent still hung crooked.

Ethan stood in front of the fridge, staring at the same half-empty shelves he'd seen a dozen times this week, hoping something new would appear. It didn't.

"Why does it feel like we've been gone for cycles?" he asked, reaching for the last protein bar.

Rose leaned on the kitchen counter, scrolling absently through channels. "Because our entire apartment was a crime scene and nobody told us."

He bit into the bar and winced. "Tastes like betrayal."

She didn't laugh.

The silence stretched again.

Rose finally broke the silence. "We have to work next cycle."

"I know."

She scrolled another moment, then set the remote down. "Do you think we're being watched right now?"

"I think we always have been."

Rose didn't respond right away. She just began slowly sorting through clothes, looking for a clean vest. "You sure you want to go back to work like nothing happened?"

He shrugged. "What choice do we have?"

Rose shrugged and kept digging. "Nothing here is clean. What should I wash for you?"

"I don't care," Ethan said, gesturing to the ceiling. "That light's flickering now."

She groaned. "We're absolutely cursed."

He smiled faintly, walked over, and kissed her forehead. "I love you, babe. We're going to get through this."

It was easy to say now. But after everything that had happened, Ethan knew it would be far harder to repeat to himself when he tried to sleep later.

The room hummed softly around them.

His familiar chair sat where it always had. The porthole still framed the same scattered stars, distant, indifferent.

The light flickered once more.

Ethan didn't look up.

CHAPTER 11
Business as Usual

Work didn't suck quite bad enough that Ethan forgot he was being watched. Could it have sucked a golf ball through a garden hose? Easily. Probably could've stripped the chrome off a trailer hitch, too but Ethan hardly cared anymore. Most cycles, stepping into eighteen skids would've erased anything from his mind. This time, it barely coaxed him to sip his coffee.

Instead, he paced around shelving boxes, tallying cameras as he went, muttering a bad word or two when the scan gun inevitably gave out. He tried to distract himself with a fantasy Rose, topless, making popcorn. Even that fell flat.

Once again, his pay was short, and he couldn't shake that. In fact, it clung to him. Another eighty credits gone hasta nunca and he was being watched; and someone was hiding the TT panels. That sucked, too.

Not that he believed the missing panels weren't just another casualty of incompetence. Most things back here ended up that way. So why was Marrow so confident someone was stealing them? If they had caught someone on camera, they'd be in custody already, and there'd be no active investigation. Ethan thought to himself, "Do they want a scapegoat?"

He scanned the next bin. Error. Second try. Error. Time to purge the cache again. "Thank God for *90 Cycles*," he muttered, shaking it like a broken magic wand. Third attempt beep. Success.

He slid the box onto the shelf and moved on. Eighteen skids made a long stretch of racking, dimly lit wherever the sensors had died. Someone had affixed a picture of a cat to one of the vertical support beams. Another beam held a post-it with "*YOU GOT THIS*," written in optimistic handwriting, now brown and curling at the edges.

Ethan stopped in front of bin MS1111D6. A single, lonely box sat in the middle of the dusty walkway. Just lying there like it belonged, completely out of place. The label had been peeled off and reapplied at a slight angle. That wasn't unusual. People got lazy. Stickers curled. But this one hadn't curled. It looked brand new. He scanned it again. The manifest flashed on his scanner, logged three cycles ago, tagged for rerouting to Engineering.

Ethan frowned. Engineering had been sealed for structural reinforcement the past month. He knew that because he'd tried to deliver a crate there two weeks ago and gotten reamed over it. He tapped for the details:

Movement: 146289479

User ID: AM00A01

Quantity: 20

Time: 13:45

Product #: 1274525-TT

Description: Panel, Exterior

"Cool," he said aloud, as if that would make it less suspicious. He glanced over his shoulder. No one visible was watching. At least, not obviously. He considered reporting it, maybe sending a discreet ping to his supervisor. But what could he say? "Hey, this box smells like a trap." Instead, he stepped past it. Then doubled back five minutes later and scanned it again, squirreling away the manifest to his personal archive. Just in case.

Barry was loading crates onto a motor pallet near the wall. Ethan ambled over, pretending to re-check his checklist. "Hey," he said offhandedly, "you ever see TT panels routed out of Engineering?" Barry blinked. "That zone's sealed, isn't it?" "Supposed to be," Ethan said. "But I saw a crate logged for delivery there. AM00A01. Looks… off."

Barry shrugged, tugging his gloves. "Honestly? I wouldn't be surprised. The routing's been busted since the last update. Last week I got a bin marked for 7311. We don't even have a 7311." Ethan offered a weak laugh. "So, you know why that box is just sitting there?" Barry shook his head. "Nah. I've been over on Bent putting up some totes. You want me to stow it for you?"

Ethan considered it. "Yeah," he said finally. "Make sure you log the transfer. Let me know if you need a hand. Okay? It's one of those priority boxes Buck was on about in the meeting." Barry tilted his backwards ballcap. "Got it. "He wiped the sweat off his face and added, "I'll have Momma do it."

Before Ethan could take another sip of his coffee, Buck materialized, shooting finger pistols at them both as he stepped out of one of the aisles. He made a show of blowing smoke off his pointer finger as he holstered the imaginary gun and approached. "What's up, guys? Murdering these boxes like a couple of psychos, I see." Barry just grinned. "Yes, sir." Buck gave him a good-natured punch in the arm. "Hell yeah, you are. After you ritualistically dismember your next box victim, what then, Barry? When will you stop? You monster! "

Barry glanced at the clock on the wall. "Not a minute before five, boss" Buck smirked, then wheeled on Ethan. "Speaking of monsters, I've got a job for you, E." Ethan lifted an eyebrow. "Yeah? There's a load sitting in Receiving with your name on it. Real Frankenstein job misc parts, no pack list, half the barcodes look like someone scribbled them with a crayon. Management wants it sorted, inventoried, and logged by the end of shift." He patted Ethan's shoulder as if this were a gift. "Figured you'd enjoy the chaos."

Ethan sighed. "Sounds like a nightmare dressed as a dream." Oh, it is," Buck said cheerfully, already turning aside. Ethan sighed deeper. "I can't wait to go home and watch *Time Traveler.*" Buck nodded. "Yeah, great game. I can't play it anymore because I logged in for one quick round, and then all of a sudden I'd been playing for thirty hours straight, and Security was running a welfare check on me."

Barry chuckled. Ethan just shook his head. "What was your best run?" Buck's eyes went as bright as neon when he answered. "Probably the one where I got to draft Colossal Biosciences and T-Rex. It was legendary." Ethan nodded. "Love Colossal; such a fun card." Buck agreed. "Super fun. Not worth getting sent to the mines over, though."

Buck shot him with finger pistols once more. "Alright, brochachos, I'll let you get back to the fine work you do."

Ethan slung the last sip of lukewarm coffee into a nearby trash chute and ambled toward Receiving. The walk wasn't far, but the closer he came, the more the drone of industrial fans and conveyor belts swelled. He scanned his badge at the checkpoint, and the door sighed open. Inside, Receiving unspooled in its usual chaos: overhead lights flickering like they were powered by hesitant electricity, a few loose crates jammed against walls.

The Frankenstein cart was inescapable. It crouched in the middle of the bay like a grievance—a patchwork of different containers zip-strapped together, top-heavy and tilting left like it had opinions. Stickers from at least four zones. No pack list. Two barcodes scrawled in Sharpie. One label simply said, "FRAGILE??"

Ethan circled it slowly, hands on hips. "Where to start," he murmured, then unclipped his scan gun. First barcode, dead. He tried again. Error. A third scan bleeped with success, but the data that populated his scanner didn't match the label.

Item: Washer, Structural Reinforcement

Qty: 150

Zone: 7300

ID Logged by: AM00A01

Timestamp: [all zeroes]

Ethan frowned. There was that number again, paired with a weird timestamp. His stomach cinched instinctively. Something was wrong.

He moved to the next crate. No barcode at all. He tried scanning the label instead. No response. He wiped the dust off with his sleeve and tried a manual entry. The tablet spat a red error message for his trouble. He probed around the side of the crate until he found a screw bolt that had been sheared clean off. Another had been substituted with a zip tie.

One of the side bins was sealed with duct tape, shiny, new duct tape, decidedly not warehouse issue. Ethan peeled it back, heart drumming an odd rhythm, and lifted the lid. Inside lay two long, flat panels swathed in anti-static sheeting.

1274525-TT. Exterior panels. Naturally.

"Of course," Ethan breathed.

He looked around. No one else in sight. He re-sealed the lid and backed away slowly, as if the box might bite. He took two steps back, opened his camera app, and captured four photos: one of the barcode mismatch, one of the error message, and two of the TT panels nesting inside. Then he closed the crate, reapplied the tape, and wheeled the whole apparatus out of Receiving.

He was damp with sweat by the time he made it back to his part of the warehouse. Before he could get the skid parked and the jack out, he sensed a nearness. Moments later, he felt, more than heard, Shaggy materialize behind him.

The rail-thin gamer cleared his throat softly to be acknowledged. "What ya got there, boss?" His voice was arid and amused.

Ethan scowled bleakly. "An End-Boss."

Shaggy chuckled. A faint smile twitched at the corner of his mouth. "Have you played *Bot Hunter* yet? It's got some good ones."

Ethan shook his head. "So I've heard, but no. I've been grinding the same game for years now. It's hard enough to find time for it."

Shaggy just nodded. "Hey, chief, I get it. The tragedy of man is that circumstances change but he does not. You talkin' about the *Time Traveler*?"

Now it was Ethan's turn to concede with a nod.

Shaggy pushed his glasses up his nose absently as he examined the cart. From the way his eyebrows climbed, it was clear, quite the formidable beast indeed. Terrifyingly so. He pushed his glasses up his nose again, with more vigor this time. "That's your favorite thing to talk about. I drafted this pile once, with Jesus, Elvis, and some K-Pop Superstars."

Ethan smiled as he tallied one of the boxes on the cart. "Talk about a gospel band."

Shaggy nodded emphatically. "It worked," he said flatly.

"I didn't know you were into it."

Shaggy nodded again. "I watch more than I play."

"Honestly, same."

"Barry and I could play with you. I'm heading over to his place to play *Bot Hunter* after work. You know where he lives, right?"

Ethan gave a short nod.

The rest of the cycle went by in a blur before the bell rang for the end of the shift. Ethan gave the Frankenstein cart a final once-over, then handed off his scanner to a passing D-shifter. "Do me a favor," he said. "Enjoy yourself."

The tech nodded, a little confused. Ethan didn't explain. He just punched out.

The buzz of the warehouse faded as he left, supplanted by the low thrum of walkers in the hallway to the tram platform. The air outside the factory was cool and still faintly chemical, like the filter had forgotten how to strain solvents.

By the time he stepped through the door back home, the smell of popcorn was already in the air, butter and salt, welcoming him like an old habit.

"Hey, babe," Rose called from the kitchen. "How was the salt mine?"

"Glorious," Ethan said, kicking off his boots. "My first cycle as a spy for the security department, I nearly got eaten by a monster cart, and was treated to the pleasure of cataloging zero-barcode parts by hand."

"Oof." She popped a piece of popcorn into her mouth. "Where are your stress levels?"

"Elevated. Dangerously close to requiring emergency relief."

Rose grinned. "That grim, huh?"

"Worse. But Shaggy invited me to play cards at Barry's. They're doing *Bot Hunter*, but we're gonna slide in a game of *Time Traveler*, too."

She leaned against the counter, arms crossed, still smiling. "And you want me there?"

"You always pull the best cards," he said, walking over to pilfer a handful of popcorn.

Rose rolled her eyes. "Fine, but you have to let me draft the Plague Doctor if I go."

"You always draft that ghoulish bastard."

"Well, I know how to close a timeline with that card."

"The last time you had it, you vaporized the timeline."

"Exactly, and I would have won, but you assassinated my Plague Doctor before he saw everyone die." Rose stuck out her tongue at Ethan.

He smiled. "You really would have if I hadn't sniped it. So, do you want to go?"

"I know you do…so, I suppose. One game."

They exchanged a look, tired, amused, deeply familiar. Then Rose pushed the half-empty bowl away and turned toward the den. She said, "I guess I should put a bra on then."

"That's the spirit." He followed her into the room, fingers already twitching to shuffle the deck.

She poked a finger at him in warning. "Don't get too excited. If you keep me up all night at Barry's, I'm gonna want to go to bed when we get back home. Bed-bed," she added for emphasis. "Capisce?"

"Yes ma'am." He gave a lazy salute.

Barry's room is dim, lit mostly by the flickering glow of the wall screen and a single overhead light that buzzes faintly. Music plays in the background, *Conspiracy by Yung Gravity*, loud enough to needle Ethan's ears as he steps in behind Rose. The rapper's flow is as smooth as still water. *"I've been known to pull, baby, it's Yung Gravity."*

Barry's place is smaller than Ethan's, though far less cluttered. Shaye-Shaye had scooped up all the laundry that used to litter the corners of his home, and there were no dishes in the sink, either. Barry sat on the couch beside Shaggy, nursing a half-eaten plate of nachos and grinning like a kid when they stepped in. Barry pointed at the screen. "Shoot him! Shoot him! Shoot, Hey, what's up, guys! We weren't sure you'd come."

That's when Shaye-Shaye appeared out of the back. "Want some goo?" She laughed a beat too loud and wrung her hands. "Barry says the tube cheese is good, he's on his second plate, but I'm not brave enough to try it." Rose wrinkled her nose. "Neither am I."

Ethan smiled apologetically. "My shot hasn't worn off yet. You gonna play *Time Traveler* with us, Shaye-Shaye?" She shook her head. "Me? No." She tucked a strand of greying hair behind her ear and lingered by the stove. "That stuff's for you kids. I'm too old."

Shaggy paused the game, his eyes darting toward the big man for reassurance. For his part, Barry turned up the music another notch and shot Ethan and Rose an apologetic look. "Can't be too careful." Ethan frowned. Barry kept fidgeting with his plate. There was something in the way everyone moved, a coiled stillness like they were tense. Rose voiced what he was thinking. "Of what?"

Shaggy set the controller down and stood. His voice was barely louder than the music as he spoke. "You ever wonder how we keep 'losing' TT panels?" Ethan stood up a little straighter. "Not really. But I'm starting now." Shaggy pushed his glasses up the bridge of his nose. "They aren't accidents." He waited until Ethan met his eyes, then he just smiled, a small, thin smile.

Barry cut in, excitement cracking his voice. "We've been working with the Delta Union." They all looked at Ethan and Rose now, small, hopeful smiles with no humor in them, nervous but also hopeful, expectant even. Barry reached for the volume knob and clicked it up another notch. Now bass thumped through the floor panels. Then he fidgeted with his cap and elaborated: "We've been trying to bring you in for a while, because…well, you could really help us."

Shaye-Shaye added, "And you're right! What you said at the train station, you were right. We've been thinking the same thing." Rose looked alarmed. "Bring us into what, exactly?" Shaye-Shaye went right to the point. "The Foxtrot Union. We're hiding the panels on purpose, until we get to Ceres."

Ethan just stared at her. For a moment, the whole room seemed to tilt forward a few degrees. "Foxtrot doesn't have a union. We're not allowed." Fear rang plain in the older woman's voice now. "Not openly, not yet. But you said it yourself!" She shivered as she spoke, jabbing a finger at Ethan. "There's not enough engineers, they are going to send us out there! And it's not safe! If you tear your suit somehow and lose pressure, nitrogen bubbles start to form in your blood, and then—" Ethan finished her sentence, flat. "You die."

Shaggy nodded. "Man, you're exactly right," he said. "Corporate won't care. HR will just file some paperwork. So we're doing something about it, starting a union, whether corporate likes it or not." Barry added quickly, "We're not doing anything crazy. Just…slowing things down, that's all. Blame the scanners, blame the other shifts, blame the kitters, but we're hiding the TT panels by not transferring them so we don't get sent out yet. We'll be orbiting Ceres in a few more cycles, and once we're there, we can fix the ship safely, with help from the rest of the fleet."

Shaye-Shaye cut in. "We won't haul as much ice…but you can't make money when you're dead. And we have a plan for that." Shaggy pushed his glasses up the bridge of his nose again. "Corporate is back on Mars. Safe. Who are they to say Delta can have a union and Foxtrot can't? We're out here risking our lives. We should be in charge."

Ethan didn't say anything. Rose bit her lip. "What are you going to do when you get caught?" Shaye-Shaye didn't miss a beat. "Get sent out, of course. And sooner than if we'd never tried to stall things." Ethan shook his head. "Shaye-Shaye, you never miss a cycle. They aren't going to send you—" She interrupted. "No. But they will send Barry. I can't let that happen. When you're a parent, you'll understand."

Barry tossed his plate in the trash and took his hat off, holding it in both hands. "Look, we're eventually going to go outside and fix this. All we're doing is trying to control the when and the how. They always preach safety first, but remember when they were rebuilding the warehouse? Remember how they wanted us to work under that construction? No hard hats. Safety just stood there and watched. Powerless, bro."

Ethan nodded, almost too nervous to budge. Almost. "You're not wrong." He could feel the weight of their eyes boring into him. "But…" Shaggy stepped forward. "But what?" Ethan exploded. "But this can't work! Three people can't stop the system, not even with help from the Delta Union." He hissed, "Security is probably listening to all of this right now."

The skinny youth smiled. "There's a lot more than just the three of us. Believe it or not, we've known we're bugged for weeks. That's why we have the music cranked. As long as we keep it casual, no shouting, the AI thinks we're talking about *Bot Hunter*, so our conversations don't get flagged."

Rose cocked a laminated eyebrow at him. "How can you possibly know that?" Shaggy shrugged. "I studied AI models in college. Routine is a real-life superpower." Before she could ask what he meant by that, he elaborated quickly: "We meet with different people to 'play video games' a few times a week and listen to loud music. Basically, it tricks the AI into ignoring us."

Rose shook her head in disbelief. "So you're just pretending to be a nerd? My mind's blown."

Shaggy smiled. "Oh no, that's entirely real. It's why this is all so convincing. The AI has no reason to suspect we're secretly talking about something else."

Rose hissed, her voice brittle with dread. "You can't know that."

The music swelled. Barry snatched up his controller and resumed mashing buttons, plunging back into the game. Shaye-Shaye cracked another joke about nacho goo, and Shaggy laughed just a beat too loud, too bright.

Ethan didn't laugh. He didn't so much as twitch.The sandy-haired beanpole sat down on the couch again, seized the other controller, and jumped back into the game. "Look, in about twenty minutes, if you sit down and eat some nachos, the AI will log it as a mild case of food poisoning, and you can go back to your regular life as though none of this ever happened.

"If you want to do that, I completely understand. I know all of this is shocking, but try not to panic. Say nothing about this, and it will be like it never happened."

Ethan shook his head. His shoulders had turned to blocks of stone. "Shaggy, what if the gravity fails before we get there? If your plan works, it probably will. Then more people like Mr. Stan will die."

Shaggy didn't blink. "People were always going to die. We can't stop that. The calculated risk remains that this ends up killing fewer people overall."

Rose gasped, clamping her hands over her mouth. "Oh my God. It's you." The words came muffled through her fingers. "You're the one writing the crazy work orders."

Shaggy grinned slow, unbothered, the grin of someone who has been waiting for this moment for a long time. "Never was anything great achieved without danger?" He tapped the side of his head once, lightly. "Machiavelli gets called paranoid, but he was just paying attention."

Rose shook her head. "Shaggy, it looked like a..."

She shook her head again and lowered her voice. "Anybody who reads that is getting flagged. That's exactly what it looked like. "

Shaggy looked back at the game and shrugged. Not a careless gesture, because he was that confident. "Basically, it said we're too far out now to be replaced, so if an issue becomes mission critical, Amoogle will be forced to negotiate directly with us. And we can demand better safety procedures and hazard pay if we form a union."

He was so calm. So certain. Explaining everything in the same measured tone Ethan's childhood math teacher had used for fractions. "I uploaded the message using a public library computer, on the guest account, with a USB that I stole."

Ethan looked at him sharply. "One of our flash drives? From the office?"

Shaggy shook his head. His eyes flicked briefly to him sharp, measuring, but the smile returned at once, easy and thin. "I'm sneakier than that." He leaned back, elbows hooked over the chair, his posture loose, almost careless. His fingers tapped an idle rhythm on his thigh: calm, patient, as though he'd already planned for this exact question.

"Look," he said, no longer meeting Ethan's eyes, watching the paused game instead. "Do you know how the AI thinks about us?" He clicked his tongue. "We're numbers. Percentages. Our messages are just noise unless we give the system a reason to look more closely."

He gestured vaguely at the ceiling, toward the cameras hunched in the corners. "But the moment someone starts saying the wrong words in the wrong place?" He let the silence finish the sentence for him.

Ethan felt Rose stir beside him.

Shaggy shrugged. "I make sure the system never has time to focus on what we're doing." Now he finally looked at Ethan. Still smiling, but the smile didn't quite reach his eyes.

Ethan shook his head. "I want to believe you—"

"Well, guy, I want to tell you more, but I need to know something first. Are you in? This is an 'in-or-out' kind of situation, and if you don't want to be in, I can't tell you any of the fun stuff."

Rose clenched her fist, nails cutting into her palms. "You're putting me in a really tough spot, Shaggy. I like you guys. I don't want to report you, but I have to."

Shaggy kept shooting robots alongside Barry. "Well hold on...why?"

Rose shook her head. "Because if we come clean, we'll be safe. I haven't hidden anything, and neither has Ethan, but if we don't tell them," she hissed, spelling out the obvious, "they'll send us outside."

Shaggy looked up, no longer smiling. "I don't have to tell you that if you snitch, Security is going to dig through your records, your messages, your shift logs and they'll investigate everything. You really think someone looking for anything won't find something? Nothing on either one of you?"

Rose looked away from the screen and pressed a hand to her stomach. Her face tightened. Ethan couldn't tell if it was the situation or the reek of melted tube-cheese.

She murmured, "Ethan found a bug in our coffee maker last cycle, and we turned it over to Security. They have us reporting to them now."

Shaggy just shrugged, his thumb tapping the trigger twice before he spoke. Another spray of digital fire. "Yeah, same thing happened to me. They called me in when I found mine." His voice was mild, almost bored. "I answered their questions. Smiled. Went back to work. You know how it goes. "

The flames on the screen died out as his character reloaded. His next words came more softly.

"We've been at this for a while." He flicked his eyes toward them once, like a card player checking who's bluffing. "What you're saying is actually good news. Security still doesn't know anything."

He went back to the game, but his voice stayed soft. Steady as a pulse.

"You know how this place works." Shaggy didn't look up from the screen as another blast of flames lit up the room. "No one is going to save us out here. We're going to have to do it ourselves." He added, matter-of-factly, "That's all this is."

Rose blinked and looked at Ethan, then back at Shaggy, Barry, and Shaye-Shaye in turn.

"I... I don't know if I believe you," Rose whispered. "I won't report you, but we can't be a part of this." Her voice faltered. "We've got too much to lose now. I missed my period two weeks ago. "

Ethan jerked his head toward her. "What? "

Shaye-Shaye's eyes widened. "Have you taken a pregnancy test yet? "

Rose shook her head: no.

The old woman threw up her hands. "Why not?"

She turned to Ethan. "Because I'm scared. Right now I feel nauseous. I want to throw up in the sanctity of my own home, so we're leaving." Then Rose grabbed Ethan by the hand without another word and pulled him out of the room.

Ethan looked back once. Barry and Shaggy didn't turn the music down or stop playing video games; Shaye-Shaye just closed the door.

CHAPTER 12
Processing...

Silence wasn't so peaceful anymore. It pressed against Ethan's skull like the vacuum of space, airless, oppressive, inexorable.

He sat in his chair, staring at the stars through the porthole, idly flipping through his cat book as if the glossy pages might offer an escape hatch.

Though only a few feet separated him from Rose, the distance between them felt galactic, cold, expanding, indifferent.

SYSTEM NOTICE. MAINTENANCE ALERT

Zone heating at sixty percent efficiency

Gravity strength at ninety-seven percent efficiency

Air filter expired.

Carbon monoxide detector expired.

Smoke alarm expired.

Maintenance notified. No action required.

STATUS: GREEN

Ethan cleared his throat and gestured at the monitor. "I weighed myself. Lost five pounds, thanks to the gravity shift."

"Mhm." Rose didn't look up. "Same difference. "

The silence stretched again, thicker this time, viscous and greasy, like too much butter on bread that had already gone stale.

She pointed the remote at the tube and thumbed the power button without another word.

"90 CYCLES. NEW EPISODE LOADING…"

A peppy announcer's voice sliced in. *"Welcome back, Cycle-heads! This time, Mickey takes on the other couples, and things get more than a little volatile at the tell-all!"* A musical number blared with gusto alongside the show's opening montage.

Ethan sighed and rubbed his face. He tried to turn his brain off, to unburden himself of reality's weight and submerge into the show's manufactured absurdity.

Letting the glowing screen wash over him did little to anesthetize him from his own problems.

They barely even looked like people anymore. Since the last episode, Lavender had undergone more surgery. Now she looked less like a woman and more like a *Nok-Nok* filter crossed with a bargain-bin mannequin.

Meanwhile, Mickey was balder, fatter, slouching and frowning with the permanence of carved wood. It was quite unfortunate that his shirt and hat were both white, because the combination made him look like a hospital curtain someone had forgotten to draw.

Ethan watched his slushie sloshing, trying to gauge how much lighter the glass had become. The dishwasher had clouded the surface too much to show his reflection.

He shifted in his chair. It creaked strangely, like something inside had misaligned, and for a moment, he felt just a little too light, as if his stomach had forgotten which way was down.

Rose curled deeper into the couch without a word, the blanket tucked to her chin like makeshift armor.

Her face seemed especially pale in the screen's flicker, and she hadn't touched her drink once.

"Is there something wrong with that one? Want me to fix you another one?" Ethan asked, already half out of his chair.

The tube's glow flickered slightly, just enough to be irksome, not enough to report to maintenance. As if that would do any good anyway.

"No." Her voice was a flatline.

"Right," he muttered, lowering himself back into the chair. "Probably not enough orange juice anyway."

The canned laughter from the tube erupted, too loud, then cut off mid-cackle. The audio stumbled to catch up a second later.

Ethan rubbed his thumb along the side of his glass, tracing the condensation like a worry bead. "Mickey and Lavender fighting again?"

"Yep." Pop went the syllable, hollow as a dead channel.

"Of course."

Onscreen, Lavender was crying. Or attempting to. Her face barely moved. Mickey hurled a cup across the studio and stormed offstage. The camera lingered on the splay pattern.

"I think that was scripted," Ethan said, his voice flat as the gravity leak.

Rose offered nothing.

Silence again. Thicker. Clammier. More alive than either of them. The stars through the porthole were static pricks of cold light, staring back with the patience of eons.

He tried again. "You about ready to turn in?"

"No." She didn't even blink.

Ethan nodded, then caught himself. "Yeah. Me neither."

The tube cut to a clip montage: *Best Fights of the Season.* Lavender slapped a girl named Rose, one of Mickey's many off-the-books girlfriends.

"That looked like it hurt," Ethan said, the ghost of a smile tugging at his mouth.

Still nothing from Rose. Her fingers twitched beneath the blanket, but she didn't utter a sound. Ethan didn't either, not for a long while.

He stared at the tube, pretending the silence wasn't flaying his insides raw.

Onscreen, a producer's voice drifted over the footage. "Mickey, do you think she ever truly loved you?"

"Well," Mickey said, turning slowly toward the camera. His eyes looked excavated. "I guess it doesn't really matter anymore."

Then the monitor pinged again, sharp as a needle.

SYSTEM NOTICE. MAINTENANCE ALERT

Zone heating at sixty percent efficiency

Gravity strength at ninety-four percent efficiency

Air filter expired.

Carbon monoxide detector expired.

Smoke alarm expired.

Water temperature sensor offline.

System attempting reboot.

PROCESSING… PLEASE WAIT…

Rose squinted at the alert. "How bad has it actually gotten?"

Ethan sat back, watching the stars. "Looks like it froze, which means … the hot water might be getting ready to give out."

Rose's jaw clenched so hard he thought he heard a tooth creak, but she said nothing else.

On the screen, Lavender was shrieking at Mickey. There were fireworks. Or CGI stand-ins for fireworks. It was hard to tell. Then the credits crawled upward like a sigh.

Ethan reached for the remote out of habit.

Rose swatted his hand away. "Leave it," she said. "Nothing else is better."

Ethan slouched deeper into his chair, his hand hovering over the glass again before retreating. He wasn't thirsty anymore. He wasn't much of anything.

The room buzzed faintly, like something in the wall was misfiring, or maybe just exhausted from pretending to function.

Then the lights dimmed. Not all the way. Just a flicker, a blink like a tired eye refusing to close fully.

He sat up straighter. "You saw that, right?"

Rose didn't look away from the screen. "Just a surge. It happens." She pulled the blanket a little tighter around her legs, cinching it like a tourniquet.

The credits ended then. A looping promo crawled across the screen: *"Stay tuned for bonus content! Behind the scenes with Lavender as she tells all!"*

The screen froze for a second, glitched, then repeated the line with a mechanical stammer.

"Be. Behind … the scenes … with … Lav. Lav. Lav. Lav …"

Ethan snatched the remote. Pressed the power button.

Nothing.

He hit it again. Then held it down until his thumb ached.

Still nothing.

The screen kept talking, juddering Lavender's name over and over like a prayer gone wrong.

He stood and walked over to the wall panel, mashing the reset on the entertainment console. The screen blinked black, then blue, then winked out like a dying star.

Another system ping rang out, louder than usual, more insistent.

SYSTEM NOTICE. MAINTENANCE ALERT

Zone heating at sixty percent efficiency

Gravity strength at ninety-four percent efficiency

Air filter expired.

Carbon monoxide detector expired.

Smoke alarm expired.

Water temperature sensor offline.

SEWAGE OVERFLOW RISK

Maintenance notified. BE ALERT.

STATUS: YELLOW

Ethan's gut coiled. He hadn't seen the words "sewage overflow risk" since he worked a mop shift. That had not been a good cycle. That had been the cycle he tried to forget.

He turned to Rose. "So try not to poop at home."

She didn't reply right away. Her eyes were still locked on the glitching screen. Finally, she said, flat as a held breath, "Girls don't poop."

"Oh really," he replied, "come on, Rose. I know they do."

The lights flickered again. This time, they didn't fully come back, but the ambient glow persisted, humming just bright enough to give the impression of effort.

Ethan let out a breath he didn't know he was holding. His slushie glass rattled slightly on the table, not enough to fall, but just enough to register.

Rose closed her eyes and let out a breath. "Nope. We queef out an aroma exactly like vanilla extract, and that's it. Poof, no more constipation. I honestly don't even know why we have a butthole at all."

"I can think of at least one reason."

Rose cracked one eye open. "Disgusting. You wish."

Ethan winked at her and stood up. "What can I say? I guess my mind's having a little 'sewage overflow.'"

Rose offered him a tight, brittle smile. "Where are you going?"

Ethan rubbed the back of his neck and scanned the room for his shoes. They were under the couch. Stooping, he fished them out, and answered her as he wedged his heel into one of the grey slip-ons.

"I'm going to walk down to the store and pick up some batteries, you know, for the carbon monoxide and fire detectors. I'm not sure I can sleep knowing I might asphyxiate if I don't."

Rose bit her lip. "Okay. Babe…listen…"

Ethan went rigid in his tracks.

"I got a job offer from Delta. They want me to be a team lead, but… well, they want me to relocate. I wasn't going to say anything, not with the pregnancy scare, and I didn't want to be away from you. But honestly? I don't like what's happening here. The Security Investigation, the gravity glitches… it's all just getting worse. This ship is breaking down, and I want out, Ethan."

She drew a sudden, sharp breath.

"And if I am pregnant," she hissed, "I need to seize this chance now. They're not going to wait around for an answer forever, and once I start showing, that's it, my shot at a promotion's gone. No one wants to hire a pregnant woman, Ethan."

That felt like a stiff right hand to the nose. Ethan blinked. "That's…huge." He shifted his weight, eyes barely meeting hers. "I wish you had told me about all of this sooner."

"Ethan, I wasn't going to do it without you, but after everything that's happened lately," she stressed, "I just think it would be smartest to leave. While I still can."

"I get it, Rose. I do. Things are bad here. Every cycle it feels like it gets a little bit worse, and I don't want you to get trapped in a bad situation, especially if you've got a way out."

He finally looked at her now.

"But if you're pregnant…where does that leave me? You're going to need someone to take care of you." He tried to smile, but it wouldn't arrive. "And who is going to carry your stuff?"

Her face twitched, half smile, half sob. "You're such an idiot sometimes."

She stood up, put her hands on her hips, then met his eyes with a softer look. "I want you to come with me. As soon as you can. So…submit an application, please. I've been checking. They still have a few lifter positions open."

"Okay. I will." Ethan took a deep breath, then looked back at her. "Have you thought about what happens if I can't get transferred right away? What if you give birth, and I'm still trapped over here?" His voice went soft. "I don't want to become another one of your problems."

Rose didn't answer right away. Her eyes dropped to the floor, then slowly rose back up. She took another step toward him. "If you can't get transferred right away…then I'll wait for you. I'll find a way to come back, if I have to." She looked into his anxious eyes. "Don't ever think I'd trade you for someone else."

They stood there for a moment, the hum of the failing lights flickering above them. Then Rose cleared her throat and added, more softly, "And while you're out…pick up a couple pregnancy tests, would you?"

She forced a smile. "I finally have the guts to pee on one."

Foxtrot's "general store" wasn't far from their section, but Ethan dragged his feet en route, doing his best to turn ten minutes into twenty. The place was tucked behind the rail track, a gauntlet of vending machines that dispensed everything from canned drinks to cleaning products, and, of course, pregnancy tests. Ethan told himself, "No big deal … a totally normal item. Stop sweating. People buy them all the time."

The entrance to the narrow hallway was plastered with flickering neon signs alternating between:

WELCOME SHOPPERS! // THIEVES PAY WITH PTO!

Inside, the air hung faintly with the scent of floor polish and MSG. The aisles were so narrow that two people could not pass without exchanging breath. Shelves sagged under the weight of bulk goods: canned vegetables, vacuum-packed noodles, and synthetic fabrics shrouded in plastic wrap.

Ethan scanned the vending machine's shelves for the tests. There they were. Tucked beside the coffee machine. He tried to be as cool as the other side of the pillow, but inside he felt like he was chewing a habanero. Nervously, he surveyed the aisle as he approached the machine.

"Ethan! My hitta!" He froze mid-stride. Vinny materialized from behind a beetle-cake machine, grinning like the Cheshire Cat. Under one arm, he carried six rolls of toilet tissue; with the other, he crunched a bag of *Jumbo*s.

"Bro, did you come for the low-grav too?" Ethan's fingers curled into a clammy fist. Suddenly, his anxiety spiked. The truth lodged itself in his throat. So he pointed instead. "I need my coffee."

"Hey, didn't you say you were on Beta for a while? My buddy has the hookup on that Keefe they drink over there. None of that cheap chalk powder, either."

Ethan stepped away from the booth and massaged his temple. "I'm good, thanks. Tastes like bad memories now."

Vinny drifted right along beside him. Not literally, but Ethan couldn't help noticing the difference in his own step. He could tell Vinny noticed as well.

"This low gravity is something else. Watch this!" He tossed a *Jumbo* gently upward. The deep-fried beetle hung in the air, offering gravity a pregnant pause while it considered whether it felt like pulling the deep-fried bug down. Before it could make up its mind, Vinny leapt like a superhero and snatched it up. His dreads rebounded as he touched back down a heartbeat later. Still grinning like a madman, he spun around with youthful glee.

"You see that? I got, like, a sixty inch vertical here!"

Ethan shook his head slowly. "The gravity is failing, and you're over here doing high jumps?"

Vinny chuckled at that. "It's called making the best of a bad situation. And just remember this: It's easy to pimp a butterfly, but it's difficult to pimp a wasp."

Ethan just stared at him. "What does that even mean?"

"It means: live a little! But also, in an actual sense, and just between you and me, it means, well … I guess it means you should try it. Because a wasp is the peak of reckless ness!"

Vinny wagged a *Jumbo* at him as if it were a coach's whistle. "You gotta commit, my guy. Look, bend your knees, focus on the float. It's all about the float!"

Ethan rolled his eyes hard. Vinny lofted the *Jumbo* at him. "Your turn!" It hung in the air between them, but Ethan didn't even try. Instead, he reached out and snagged it with his hand, more out of reflex than interest.

"That's cheating," Vinny protested. "You gotta jump for it. That's the whole point!"

Ethan forced a thin smile and devoured the *Jumbo* in one bite. It had a satisfying crunch, and a surprising amount of nacho cheese powder. "Pass." He kept chewing. "I know I look young, but on the inside, I'm actually eighty-seven."

"So dramatic." Vinny shrugged and turned toward the counter himself. "Well, get your coffee, then, with your old ass." He didn't pause for a breath. "You know, that reminds me of this old school cat who always told me as a kid to 'break a leg.' So, I did. And I thought, damn, you know what … this man is crazy. Why would anyone want to do that?"

Ethan shook his head again. "You say the wildest things. "

"Poetry is what I speak."

Ethan promptly rolled his eyes so hard they nearly unscrewed from their sockets. He looked at the canned coffee arrayed in the machine before him. Red and yellow Wonda cans, yellow and orange Fire cans, and prismatic *Boss: Rainbow Edition* cans all stared back at him. They were almost taunting him, as if they knew he didn't actually want any of them. So he simply pressed: A1, then enter.

The vending machine responded with programmed cheer, exuberantly flashing a big neon blue thumbs up, and dispensed a six by four inch can of powdered coffee with a ker thunk. He reached down into the slot by his knees and extracted the can. He turned it over in his hands with mild interest. *White Cat Coffee: Purrr fection.* Even the pun exhausted him.

"White Cat, huh? Didn't take you for a White Cat man."

Ethan shrugged. "Thought I'd try something new."

Vinny nodded slowly. "Bro, I get it. I tried a new show last night, just for the sake of trying it. Right? It's called, *"The Old Wizard's New Wife."* It's about some half man, half demon who's a three-hundred-year-old wizard. He's got a head like a deer skull, horns and all. Right? He looked cool, so I clicked it."

Vinny shook his head in disappointment.

"Let me guess," Ethan said. "You didn't like it?"

"The first episode was whatever. It explained that magic comes from fey creatures most people can't see. Deer Head marries the main character, a fifteen-year-old girl, because she can see them, and he needs an apprentice."

Ethan stowed the coffee in his pocket. "Why did Deer Head marry a teenager if he just needed an apprentice?"

"I don't know. Maybe it explains it later, but I turned it off after the dragon episode. I just wasn't vibing with it. They weren't even dragons, except for one, but it was so old it couldn't move; then it died and turned into a tree."

Vinny laughed. "Yeah! 'C ause it didn't make sense. If you want it to turn into a tree, use a dryad, or a nymph, or something. Don't waste a dragon!"

Ethan shook his head once more.

Vinny held up a finger. "Look, I know it's petty. But it felt wrong. Like a wrestler in a tutu. You can do it, sure, but something about it just ain't right!"

Ethan smirked. "Something ain't right about an old man marrying a high schooler, either."

Vinny grinned wide. "Yeah, well, that's anime for you. I just pretend they're in college. Helps me enjoy the story without getting tripped up by the culture."

"I don't know, bro. I might've given it another episode if somebody threw hands, but nah. It was just some slow burn, slice of life, fantasy romance thing. Felt like watching paint fall in love with drywall."

Vinny tore open another *Jumbo* and pressed on, talking. Ethan only half listened. All he could think about was how much longer he had to keep standing here, nodding along, before Vinny finally bounced off and let him make the purchase in peace. Of course, he didn't do that. Vinny just shook his head and bounced lightly on his heels.

"I think the next episode was about cats, or something."

"I guess you'll never know. "

Vinny laughed. "I guess not! Hey, bro, you got anything going on later? I'm going over to Shaggy's after this. He invited me to play *Bot Hunter*. You wanna come? He says he's got plenty of controllers."

Ethan grimaced. He could feel his palms start to sweat; he turned to wipe them on his pants, nonchalantly, trying not to let Vinny see.

"What, you don't like shoot 'em ups?"

"Nah … not really. Besides, I gotta get back to Rose." He lied. "She's expecting me to cook tonight."

Vinny's dreads bounced again with fresh interest. "What are you going to make?"

Ethan blinked, then coughed into his shirtsleeve. He was trying to buy his brain precious seconds to think. "Chicken. Chicken Alfredo," he added quickly. "It's her favorite."

"Oh, OK. Cool. You better get a basket, bro. That coffee is eating up your pocket. You know where they are, over there?"

Ethan nodded. "Just stopped for the coffee first. Priorities. Am I right?"

Vinny chuckled and leaned against the pregnancy test machine. "You really do love that coffee." He nodded vaguely in the direction of the baskets, nearly sixty feet away. "I bet I can make it in one jump."

God, if only it were just about the coffee. He could feel his anxiety tick upward another notch. Out loud, he added, "There's no way.

I know the gravity is off, but still … you would truly have to be an Olympian, by normal Martian gravity."

Vinny crouched, hugging the toilet paper rolls like a running back. "My hitta 'never tells me what I can't do." He exploded forward with two quick steps, then lifted off. For a single breath he seemed to float, dreads haloing, the *Jumbo* bag still clutched tightly in one hand. Ethan counted floor tiles without meaning to, two, four, six, a dozen feet in the air before Vinny's sneakers kissed the linoleum. Momentum carried him another four feet in a squealing slide, his soles skating on the floor polish. He windmilled, caught himself against a shelf, and bounced up grinning.

"Bro, that was, like, twenty feet, easy. Which is, what, almost half of sixty if you round up?"

A roll of toilet tissue kept rolling, slowly unraveling until it bumped the stack of shopping baskets he had been aiming for and stopped like a lazy cue ball.

Ethan's heart fluttered in his chest. If Vinny had gone two more feet, he'd have slid straight into a vending machine stocked with sandwiches. He forced another smile. "Yeah. Basically."

Vinny dusted off his pants, still grinning like he had just won gold, and tore into another *Jumbo*, never stopping talking. Ethan only half caught him. Every second Vinny lingered felt like someone pressing a finger on a bruise. He shifted his weight, then rubbed his palms against his thighs again, hoping the dampness didn't show.

Ethan gave him a polite chuckle, but his mind wandered. The vending machine across the aisle hummed softly, a row of discreet white boxes resting just below the throat spray and cold medicine. His throat tightened further. Still there. Still waiting.

Then his eyes betrayed him. For just a second, they hovered over the pregnancy tests again, and this time, Vinny followed the glance.

His eyes betrayed him. For just a second, they hovered over the pregnancy tests again, and this time Vinny followed his gaze.

"What, you checking out the cold meds? Bro, you sick or something? You don't have the space sniffles, do you? You know, low gravity can make nasal fluid creep up into your head. Does your face feel puffy? Are your eyes heavy?"

Ethan's throat went dry. "Nah… just looking for mouthwash," he lied again. "You know… so Rose doesn't smell the White Cat on my breath."

Ethan never was very good at lying.

Vinny squinted at him, then started grinning again. "Bro, there ain't no mouthwash in that machine… you ain't lookin' at the baby sticks, are you? Wait… don't tell me…"

Ethan froze. He could feel every muscle in his neck and shoulders tighten into steel girders. A bead of sweat trickled down his spine as his fingers curled into fists at his sides.

Vinny's eyebrows shot up. "Ohhh, you are. You are! Yo, no wonder you're sweating bullets." His joking tone melted into something softer, more genuine as he clapped a hand on Ethan's shoulder. "I was as nervous as a long-tailed cat in a rocking-chair factory when I first found out I was going to be a daddy. You're going to be alright, Bro."

Ethan dry swallowed. His lips moved before the words came. "I don't even know if she's pregnant yet, but…" He trailed off.

Vinny let the silence hang for a beat of the heart. "How late is she?"

Ethan stared at the pregnancy tests, as if the little white boxes would answer for him if he waited long enough. Finally, he licked his lips and spoke. "Two weeks. We've been trying for a while. I want this…I just didn't think I'd be this scared when it happened—if it's even happening."

Vinny looked Ethan in the eyes, a hint of his sly humor returning. "Oh, she's pregnant. Besides, if she wasn't, you wouldn't be sweating bullets. You'd be sweating powder because your little man marched… but not too hard."

He grinned and laughed good naturedly.

Ethan just shook his head and bought a pregnancy test.

"No, you're gonna need more than one. Get you about… ummm, I don't know… ugh, how many times you knocked her off? That many."

Ethan smiled down at his shoes. "All right, I'll buy two." Then he winked at Vinny. "At least while you're standing here."

Vinny laughed and patted his shoulder again. "Alright, I can take a hint. Just get a few. OK? There are evaporation lines and false positives, and all kinds of things can happen."

With that, Vinny went to retrieve his toilet paper. While he did, Ethan simply stood there, staring at the little white box in his hand, rooted to the spot. His fingers tightened around it until his knuckles turned white. Though his body was as still as a mountain, his mind was moving at approximately thirty-six miles per second. Considering the possibilities, he pondered the fragile shape of a future he wasn't sure he was ready for.

He let out a breath he didn't realize he was holding.

And dared to hope.

CHAPTER 13
Five White Boxes

Vinny left, leaving Ethan alone, clutching the tiny, life-altering object he had purchased. Hope lasted nearly four minutes. Ethan bought four more tests just to be safe. He debated buying a sixth, but a voice interrupted his brooding.

"Whatcha got there, Lassie?" Carolina crunched a hot fry, the kind made of compressed, chili-powdered caterpillars, and winked at him. "Dang. Five?" She giggled. "You know…if she can pee that much, she's probably pregnant."

Ethan's eyebrows lifted; he hadn't considered that.

The muscles in his eye sockets turned their dark brown orbs as far as they could manage. Meanwhile, the muscles in his neck and shoulders had hardened past petrification. The combination of high-pressure stress and the scorching temperatures where the insulation actually functioned had transformed him from a man into a diamond block.

Carolina ate another hot fry. "Careful. Squeeze too hard, and you'll break it."

Suddenly Ethan could move again.

He turned fully to face Carolina. Sweat had darkened her yellow button-down shirt, patterned with bright white fractals traced in hair-thin lines. She reached for another hot fry, her fingers nearly as large as Ethan's. With practiced ease, her hand slipped into the bag and pulled out a handful.

"This will be my first child," he said.

She blinked. "Really? I thought you already had one."

He shook his head. "Why would you think that?"

Carolina rolled her eyes and patted her head. Her new weave bounced around her shoulders, those glossy black sheets of 3D-printed hair attached with gourmet glue. The price for being fabulous came as an itchy scalp.

"You know…because you're old," she said.

Ethan cleared his throat. "You make me want a cup of coffee." He tried to compel his body to relax, commanding his heart to beat slower. "What are you even doing over here? Did you come to play around in the low gravity like Vinny?"

Carolina grinned, brushing crumbs from the fractal polygons on her shirt. "Please. I ain't no kid. I got a date."

Ethan blinked. "Really?" he asked.

Carolina cocked her hip immediately. One hand flew down, her arm bending at the elbow to form the point of an isosceles triangle. Her left hand planted on her hip while her right hand came up, and the pointer finger lived up to its name as she fired off.

"What's that supposed to mean?" she demanded.

"Here?" Ethan tried to clarify. "At the General Store? You have a date in this place?" He cocked an eyebrow at her.

"Yeah," she said, popping another hot fry in her mouth defensively. "He's with security. Tall. Kinda loud. Very handsome. We're going to try some of the freaky chip flavors."

Ethan parroted back, "Freaky chip flavors?"

Carolina nodded, pulling out a little brush to groom her wig. "Yeah, like…I want to try these Kimchi ones."

"Got it. Kimchi definitely qualifies," he started.

A booming voice cut through the rest of his words. "Well now, darlin'. I heard someone was lookin' for handsome, and here I am."

Ethan felt his stomach drop. Of course the old man was here. He turned just as Marrow strutted into view, out of uniform but still wearing olive-colored clothes. His boots squeaked far too loudly with each step as he approached. Ethan suspected he had polished them himself.

The off-duty security officer's smile was as broad and bright as the Hercules Supercluster. "Officer Marrow: the law on two legs, keeper of peace, breaker of hearts, and if I may be so bold, your date tonight, Miss Carolina."

She giggled at Ethan, tossing a hot fry into her mouth with delight. Light glinted off her heart-shaped nose rings as the fry hung in the air for a heartbeat too long. She swallowed a moment later and said, "See? I told you."

Ethan scowled, clearly unamused. "And you called me old."

Marrow's voice seemed to echo too loudly, and Ethan couldn't help but notice the blinking camera lights yet again. Watching Marrow watch him, hearing his boisterous, booming voice once more reverberating through the metal tube sucked up his energy like a sponge. Ethan felt eighty years old in that moment, as if his muscles weighed fifty pounds in his neck and a hundred more on each shoulder. His eyes burned, and his heart felt wrinkled, gray, and exhausted.

He just wanted to go home to bed. Sleep. Dream of a better life without all these problems and stay there until they arrived at Ceres. Then perhaps when he opened his eyes again, he would realize that what he had thought was the start of his cycle was actually a false awakening. This was all just another lucid dream turned nightmare, one that he had lost control of, one that had preyed on his fears. In that dream, Rose wasn't really thinking about leaving. Security wasn't bugging his home. He had privacy, and work was paying him what he was owed. Wouldn't that be nice?

But was it too good to be true?

Marrow pointed two thumbs at his chest. "I'm vintage and you're antique. I'm timeless while you're tired. I'm retro but you're 'get off my lawn.' You dig?"

He held up a hand toward Carolina for a high five.

She slapped his palm and giggled again. "He drinks old-man coffee, too. So tell me, how do you two know each other?"

Marrow flashed Ethan a grin. "I know everyone on this ship."

Carolina shot him a look. "That's a lie. You don't know me."

Marrow didn't miss a beat. "I'm working on that right now."

Carolina seemed to like that. "Okay, well, enough picking on Ethan. I'm starving. Let's go get some kimchi and mustard *Jumbos* now, before the line becomes insane. We gotta go all the way back to the med-bay to get any."

Marrow strode by and clapped Ethan's shoulder. Ethan flinched, blinking past the cameras to meet those brown-dwarf-star eyes, their crow's-feet flaring like starbursts, grooves worn deep by smiles that never reached his gaze.

He asked, more quietly, "How's work?"

Ethan scowled. "Fine," he lied.

"Good." Marrow's gaze flicked down for a second and lingered on the little white boxes in Ethan's hands. "You know, back when I was a whipper-snapper, we didn't have pregnancy tests." He winked at Ethan. "If she missed her period, if she looked like she could take a nap standing up, if she wanted something like pickles and ice cream all of a sudden, well, we knew."

Ethan's fingers tightened around the pregnancy tests. He wanted to say something, but the crinkle of the cardboard killed the words in his throat. His wit died. He simply stood there, white-knuckled, watching the two of them walk away, hand in hand.

Time Traveler told its story in fragments, using slivers of flavor text at the bottom of each card. Arranged correctly, they unfolded into a sci-fi epic about the birth of time travel, illustrated with strange, luminous art. Ethan loved that part most. He had lost whole rest cycles inside that world, weighing which hands to keep, practicing different philosophies of play. It wasn't just a game but a doorway to a subculture he loved.

Now the doorway was gone. He hadn't touched the cards in weeks, perhaps months. The clarity they once offered, unbroken cause and effect, timelines snapping into place, now felt slippery. Reality pressed in. Questions swarmed inside his brain, questions he was afraid of, and he felt himself growing rigid again.

So he decided on a massage. Why not? Pregnant or not, the answer would come soon enough. Whatever the tests revealed, he would buy them a little softness, a little quiet time. It was getting late, but it would be worth it. The bathhouses were expensive, sure, but Ethan figured they could float the cost.

They could use a genuine adventure. After that fiasco with the butterflies, the bar for dates was low. Plus, this was something they had never done. Maybe a little spontaneity was the stimulus they both needed right now.

The Duckstaff Bathhouse was one of the oldest parts of Foxtrot. In the beginning, private showers did not exist in every room; those came much later. Astronauts lined up here for their scheduled, segregated showers.

Then Amoogle bought the ship during the "Make Mars Great" push, and credits poured in. Within a few cycles, the public bath transformed into a spa. Massages, facials, aromatherapy, for the right number of credits, you could sweat in scented steam like a Roman senator.

He could picture taking Rose there in his mind's eye. He could almost hear her teasing him about spending all those credits just to smell fancy. Still, it felt like a little light at the end of the tunnel.

Ethan tucked the idea away in his mind. He would tell her when he got back. She would love it because, for once, he would have more to offer than a broken dryer and cheap vodka. What could go wrong?

Then another voice cut through his fantasy.

It was Buck. "Hey, bro. What's up? Didn't expect to see you here."

Ethan pointed down the metal tube across the tram tracks. "I live over there."

Buck offered him another smile and motioned for Ethan to keep up. "Let's walk and talk. Honestly, I was being facetious. I came out here to see you."

In his mind's eye, Ethan took one last look at the bathhouse. He felt steam rising from his ears as that vision faded, replaced by Buck's shadow. He forced a smile and fell into step, marching away from the platform. "Sure thing."

They did not walk far.

Buck fixed him with a paint-peeling glare. "So, we're going to have to work on the way you talk to people at work."

Ethan blinked. "What are you talking about?"

Buck cleared his throat, clearly having rehearsed. "We the unwilling, led by the unknowing, are doing the impossible for the ungrateful. We have done so much, for so long, for so little that we are now qualified to do anything with nothing forever.

"You remember sending that email?"

Ethan nodded nonchalantly. "Mother Teresa said it first."

Buck scowled from beneath his brows and practically hissed. "You need to stop repeating it!"

Ethan lifted his hands in mock surrender, then tugged his hat down. The shorter man topped out at five foot four, but he looked like one of those old Earth creatures, honey badgers, extinct now except for one viral video on server banks across the solar system. With his steely high-and-tight haircut and solid black tracksuit, he even resembled one.

Buck appeared capable of chewing through steel. "I need you to have a can-do, glass-half-full outlook. Build bridges, not walls."

Ethan sighed and adjusted his hat again. "Copy that."

Buck paced as he talked. "Anyway. Look, Shaye-Shaye screwed up the replenishment queues. I need you to go in and work with D-shift. We have to get these panels sent before Jim gets pissed off."

Ethan felt his heart plummet into his gut. "What panels?"

"The TT panels, bro. One minute I'm at the apartment slaying mythic monsters with my kid, grinding out ninety-thousand damage per second; the next, I'm getting told everything is our fault via email on my portable."

Ethan felt something inside him go very still. He licked his lips nervously. "You don't say."

Buck reached into his pocket and pulled out an oval-shaped device of smooth, polished glass, brilliant white. The thing lit up in his hand, seemingly holding a halo of blue light inside itself. As Buck rolled his thumb across its surface, a myriad of lights flared in response. He scrolled through dozens of holographic projections before finally stopping on a file folder, which snapped open with a poke and spat out a mouthful of light a split second later.

Buck swiped aggressively through his shimmering apps with his free hand; the projections flickered in the air before them. A privacy filter on the back shielded the contents from Ethan's eyes. Suddenly, Buck stopped on one all-caps email.

"There it is." He cut his eyes at Ethan. "I live for this, bro. Normally, I'd be all over it with you, but I can't go in now. Sandy and I booked an appointment at Duckstaff ages ago, back when I first hit max level on my main account. It's awesome! We're supposed to go in an hour or so when she gets off work. We have a sitter and everything."

The email title read: **ATTENTION: BUCK PEBBLES—MANDATORY OVERTIME**

Ethan sighed. He did not live for this. "I was just thinking about taking Rose there."

Buck was busy typing. "We've been twice already. You'll love it! I'm putting you down. Try to get there in an hour. Someone has to go in and help them."

Buck shook his head. "I know. It's so weird. Normally, she's perfect, but you know," he said, his voice sharpening, "everyone makes mistakes." He gave Ethan a steely look. "And she's in the med bay. Apparently, she fell and hit her head. Barry's tending her, so I can't send him either."

Ethan shook his head. "You know, if you weren't my buddy, I'd tell you exactly where to shove that portable."

Buck looked up and grinned. "If you weren't my buddy, I wouldn't be hunting you down to cover for me. Sandy will scald me alive if I cancel on her for work."

"You've taken her to the spa twice. How much stress can she have?"

"Operatic levels."

Ethan shook his head again. His jaw cinched, teeth grinding, a dull echo of the knot in his shoulders. In his mind, he was still cocked: safety off, finger on the trigger, ready to loose half a dozen opinions. In reality, he only adjusted his hat again and stared at the tram tracks with a long sigh.

Buck typed, his fingers a blur across the floating keyboard projected in the air. "Don't look like that. I'm only putting you down for half a cycle. You'll get plenty of sleep."

Ethan barked a dry laugh. "Right." He thought of the broken dryer, the pregnancy tests in his pocket, and Rose clamoring to leave for Delta. He might have to cram himself into her suitcase and go too.

A halo of light gilded Buck's face. "Trust me, bro. You'll love it. Sandy swears by the bubbler. She says it's worth the credits alone. You'll love it when you get there."

Ethan smiled bitterly and thought, *"If I ever get there."*

Buck tucked the portable into his pocket and inhaled deeply. "Bro, you're a lifesaver. Thank you." He patted Ethan's arm twice. "So, tell me what you thought of the *Time Traveler* tournament. Pretty sweet, right?"

Ethan smiled. It wasn't a pleasant expression. "Still haven't watched it, but I hear it was sweet. Apparently Kraven won off Fame in one turn."

Buck shot him with finger pistols. "Bang! Bang! Bang! Just like that, bro! He built this infinite loop, played and replayed a Spy until he won. It was epic.

"We had the tournament playing while we ground out mythic loot boxes. I didn't really watch it, but my son nearly botched our legendary run when Kraven went off."

He shook his head again, hands on his hips as he watched the train pull in, and repeated, "Epic. You've got to find the time to watch it, bro."

Ethan's answer was as dry and cold as the Martian deserts. "I'm trying."

Buck patted his arm again. "Try harder. Remember: you're a man. Just go in there and boot that woman off the couch." He winked. "Put her back in the kitchen where she belongs."

"Ah, chauvinism. Didn't consider that."

Buck grinned widely and shot him with another finger pistol. "Works every time. And remember: never take my relationship advice."

He kept talking as he watched people board the train cars. "Anyway, I promised Sandy. I told her flat out: if Jim tries to throw another long shift at me, I'll tell him to go kick rubble."

Ethan laughed a little. "You'd never say that."

Buck laughed too, arms wide. "Yeah, you know me. Captain Corporate." He mimed finger pistols again.

"Anyway," he added, dropping his voice, "Jim's got everyone skating on thin ice, so don't screw this up. We need those panels for engineering."

"Right," Ethan muttered. "Understood."

Buck shrugged, grinning like he'd just offered Ethan front-row seats to the apocalypse. "Captain Corporate," he said again, then leaned closer. "Seriously, though. Last time, I had to make it up to her by getting a mani-pedi with her."

The face he made suggested a fate worse than death.

Ethan forced a laugh. The tram lurched into motion again, coughing a soft metallic sound, and he tucked his hands into his pants, feeling the pregnancy tests like small, cold, square talismans. "Not the mani-pedi."

Buck's smile tightened. "It's not the nails, bro. It's the credits. I don't have a big fancy nursing degree like her, so I work all these extra hours to pay my half of everything. And with our son, and now the new baby... there's always something to pay for. So I go to work, and Sandy's alone at home with the kids."

For once, his mask slipped. Buck put his finger pistols away and slumped. The station around them hummed with its regular energy, but Buck looked deflated. They stood in silence together as the train closed its doors and lurched forward again.

"So yeah," Buck said, relief and embarrassment tangled in his voice. "I owe you." He clapped Ethan's shoulder a third time, eager to seal the deal. "Thank you."

"Don't worry about it, buddy. What's that old Earth cliché about women?"

Buck chuckled. "Can't live with 'em, can't live without 'em!"

"Yeah. That must have been a thing from the start. Why else do you think humans stayed hunter-gatherers so long?"

The tram pulled away, doors sealed, a curl of electricity sparking in its wake. Buck waved once, already typing on his portable again, back in his own small world.

Ethan lingered a moment, listening to the train's fading hum on the tracks. Then he stepped off the platform, crossed the empty rails, and started toward home. He adjusted his hat against the recirculated breeze and kept his head down. A short walk. The pregnancy tests clicked in his pocket every step of the way.

CHAPTER 14
A Thread of Blood

Rose huddled on the couch when Ethan returned, curled tight as a fist, hugging her knees to her chest. She stared at the tube, makeup streaking down her face, utterly silent. The clamor from the show washed over her.

"Welcome back, Cycle-heads! This time, Mickey takes Lavender to a couples resort, and things don't go exactly as planned!"

The lively music hadn't changed, but now it felt different listening to the theme song, seeing the blue glow of the tube spilling onto Rose's melancholy. She didn't look up at Ethan and tried to mask her voice, but failed badly. More than anything, Rose sounded empty.

"Hey, babe."

Ethan asked at once, "What's wrong?"

A single tear gleamed in her eye. "Nothing, really." She gave a dramatic shrug. Her voice trembled, and her fingers dug hard against her knees. "I think..." She swallowed. "I had a miscarriage, a few minutes ago."

Ethan stood there frozen as a statue as she shuddered and began to sob. His knuckles bleached around the door frame. Canned laughter crackled on the show.

The studio audience howled with laughter as Mickey cheered. *"Looks like love's got zero gravity because this relationship's going into orbit!"*

Rose buried her face in her knees. Her shoulders heaved. The words came out muffled. "It just, happened. I went to the bathroom, and…" Her voice fractured. She drifted into silence. "There was blood. And…"

Ethan finally crossed the room, though each step felt awkward and sluggish. He sat on the edge of the couch but didn't reach for her. The physical space between them was small, but emotionally they lay farther apart than the room could contain.

Mickey interjected, *"Nothing to worry about, Lavender. It was just a little accident!"*

Ethan flinched. He grabbed the remote, fumbled with it, and silenced the screen. The blue glow vanished, leaving only the dim lamp light, thick shadows, and the sound of Rose's tears.

What could he say?

Rose looked up and wiped her eyes. She said sharply, "Don't just sit there. Turn it back on."

Ethan blinked, caught off guard. "What?" His brain seemed to buffer.

Rose's lips twisted, releasing neither a sob nor a laugh but some desperate sound between the two. "You cut the show off. Turn it back on!" She buried her face again into her knees, as if retreating from the world could undo what had just happened. "I don't want to sit here in silence."

Ethan licked his lips and pressed the button obediently. Then he opened his mouth, closed it again, but no sound came out. He reached a hand toward her instead, but let it drop halfway, equally useless.

"I don't know what to do," he admitted. The words tasted strange and bitter, as if they were something he wasn't supposed to speak aloud.

Rose turned back toward the tube. "Me either. I feel weird, so let's just watch the show." For a time, silence stretched between them, broken only by the laugh track.

Finally, Ethan cleared his throat. "Did, did something happen? Did you fall?"

Rose shook her head. "I started having cramps earlier. Ever since the butterfly palace, my insides haven't felt right. I've felt, I don't know, weird. You know, down there."

Ethan searched for the right words, something to comfort her, but all that came out was, "I'm sorry, babe."

Rose let out a harsh, bitter laugh. "Don't be. We both knew the risks. We're all just out here." She wiped her nose with the back of her hand, eyes fixed on the flickering light. "You know, in space. Where a million things could go wrong, and something did, big surprise." She added with venom, "Nothing ever goes right here."

He wanted to reach for her, to tell her it was going to be all right, that it wasn't her fault, but the words lodged in his chest. Ethan just sat there.

On the screen, Mickey slipped on a wet tile and fell in slow motion, the audience savage with laughter. It felt like a metaphor for Ethan's life.

Lavender looked at the camera. *"Things are about to get a little bit more stupider."*

Rose kept talking, hugging her knees even tighter. "At least I'll have you to keep me company."

There was the irony. Ethan grimaced. Not knowing how to say it best, he decided to just spit out the truth. "I told Buck I would work B-Shift.

Rose did a double take. "This B-Shift?" She couldn't believe it, staring at him incredulously. "In an hour?"

Ethan tried to explain, "Buck caught me out by the tracks, on my way back with the, well, you know. The tests." Ethan fidgeted with his hat and looked away.

Rose let out a hissing sound, part laugh, part scream, like steam hissing from a kettle. "Are you serious?"

Right then.

That's when everything started to float.

Ethan's book lifted first, slow and casual, as if gravity had simply grown bored. It just drifted there in midair, crawling away from his chair. Objects began rising. The computer in the corner picked that moment to chime in.

System notice - maintenance alert

Zone heating at 60% efficiency

Gravity strength at 0% efficiency

Air filter expired.

Carbon Monoxide detector expired.

Smoke alarm expired.

Water temperature sensor offline.

Sewage overflow risk.

System attempting to reboot.

Please wait...

It had finally happened.

Ethan almost couldn't believe it. He blinked, staring hard at the couch floating an inch or two off the floor. A tear slid from Rose's cheek, hovered, and began drifting sideways through the air. Her hair rose in thin strands around her head, like a flame-colored halo, but she didn't move; her arms were still locked tight around her knees.

Rose said bitterly, "Can this cycle get any worse?" Before Ethan could answer, Rose was already moving. She bumped along the wall and pulled herself into the bedroom, then wrapped herself in her blankets.

Ethan tried to follow her closely. "What are you doing?" he asked, poking his head inside and holding onto the doorframe for support.

Rose said two words: "I'm cold." She looked visibly displeased and frustrated with her situation. "I can't believe this cycle—of all cycles—you are going to work. This is just perfect! I'll be here all alone, Ethan, and I really don't want to be by myself right now."

Ethan threw up his hands in frustration. The movement caused him to do a backflip, and he had to scramble to regain his balance. Gripping the door frame securely once more, he responded, "How was I supposed to know the gravity was going to fail?"

"I told you to go get some pregnancy tests, maybe a sign that it was a good cycle to stay home! Did you consider that? I'm cold. I feel weak. And it would have been really nice if you had stood up to your boss, and said you were staying home."

Ethan gripped the doorframe tighter, his knuckles whitening as he steadied himself against the barrage of words. His voice cracked. "Rose, I… you're right. I should've said no. I'm sorry."

Rose's head tilted slightly, her blanket cocoon rustling as she floated near the bed. Strands of fiery hair framed her face, highlighting eyes red from crying. Her voice trembled, sharp with hurt. "Sorry doesn't fix this, Ethan. I'm bleeding, I'm cold, and now I'm alone because you picked Buck over me."

He pushed off and drifted toward her, grabbing the wall to halt his movement. "I didn't choose him. I was returning with the tests when he cornered me. I'll email him and say I've changed my mind." He reached for his mug, but it floated just beyond his grasp, taunting him. "It's an emergency," he added. "He'll understand."

Rose snorted sharply, a bitter sound echoing in the silence. "The gravity's dead, Ethan. No one will remember anything but your name on that work list." She pulled her blankets tighter, a tear slipping out to hang between them. "Just come give me a hug." She opened her arms. "I could really need one."

Ethan reached out, his hand finally brushing her fingers and pulled her in close. "I'm not leaving you. We'll figure this out together; you're my priority."

Rose's gaze softened slightly as she weakly squeezed him back. "Okay, sounds good. I… I love you, Ethan." She hesitated before saying, "Thank you." A faint, shaky smile flickered across her mouth, the first he'd seen since arriving back home.

Ethan managed a weak chuckle, squeezing her as the room tilted around them. "I love you, too. We'll ride this out," he added. "You really are cold." He rubbed her arm for emphasis. "Let me go turn up the thermostat for you."

Ethan gently pushed off and floated toward the wall, fumbling for the thermostat. His fingers slipped on the buttons before he finally got it to respond. The display blinked slowly, as if it was reluctant to work.

Ethan hovered over the thermostat, fingers pushing on the unresponsive buttons. “Come on, you piece of junk,” he grumbled.

The floating book by his chair rose slightly, unnoticed, as he pressed the heat buttons again. The wall then emitted a soft hum, and a distant clang resonated through the ductwork, too faint to identify but too sharp to ignore. The sound traveled through the hollow metal walls, echoing endlessly like a voice from a well. He paused, head tilted, feeling the vibrations pulse through the walls.

Ethan asked, “What was that?”

The thermostat picked that moment to finally kick on, releasing a weak puff of warmth, not much, but a little.

“Figures,” he muttered. “The ship holds heat about as well as a bucket holds water with a hole in it.”

The wall gave a half-hearted response, and Ethan shoved back toward Rose, trying to lighten the mood. “It’ll warm up. It just takes a minute.”

Rose didn’t respond.

“I know you’re sad, but don’t go quiet on me. I hate that. Talk to me about something. Have you heard from Gigi lately?”

She didn’t answer.

Rose hadn’t moved, still cocooned in her blankets, but now her head lolled sideways, eyes half-lidded, lips pale. The glow from the tube barely reached her face now; she looked like she was sinking into the shadows. A dark stain spread where the fabric clung to her legs.

"Rose?" His voice cracked. He shook her shoulder gently, then harder. "Babe—hey, hey, stay with me."

Ethan's chest constricted. He pushed off the wall toward the computer, fumbling to access emergency services. The screen flashed with red letters.

ALL LINES BUSY. PLEASE HOLD.

An automated voice broken by static told him, *"We're experiencing an unusually high call volume. If it is not an emergency, please hang up, and try again later."*

"Damn it!"

Ethan slammed his fist against the bulkhead, causing himself to slowly spin before grabbing the bedframe to steady himself. He tried again, stabbing at the call button and ignoring the pain in his knuckles. Still, there was no response.

Rose gave a faint, wet cough that jolted him into action.

There was no time to wait.

He tightened the blanket around her and slid his arms beneath her. She was too limp to resist, simply drifting like a ragdoll in zero gravity. With a grunt, he scooped her up onto his shoulder, securing her legs across his chest to prevent her from floating away.

"Just hang on."

Ethan stood up from the couch, effortlessly lifting Rose into his arms. They collided with the door and pushed away with force. He led them down the corridor, holding the railing with one hand to quicken their pace. The ceiling's light strips flickered and dimmed, casting the metal in a dull amber glow, like dying embers. Meanwhile, the ship's alert voice persisted in the background, disturbingly calm.

It kept repeating:

May I have your attention, please? May I have your attention, please? There is an emergency. Please remain calm.

He kicked off again. Her skin felt like ice against his neck. Blood was seeping through the blanket, dark droplets trailing behind them in loose, drifting beads. Rose drifted in his arms.

Ethan didn't dare look back for long.

He darted from the corner and saw the transit shaft open before him. Ethan pushed through the noisy, curious crowd in the cafeteria, who were clutching the rail and surrounded by floating food. As he quickened his pace, his heart suddenly sank.

The transit station was desolate. Wrecked pods hung along the rails like a gutted dragon, still emitting smoke and fire. Bodies floated among them.

Screams echoed through the shaft, a tangled chorus without source or end. Vinny's voice ripped through the noise as Ethan drew near. Vinny's eyes were bright and wide with fear, and his leg bled profusely now. A mangled piece of metal stuck out of his calf; blood drifted from it in slow, lazy beads.

Vinny met his eyes. "Ethan! Help me!"

Rose shifted weakly against him and a faint breath whispered out of her lungs. Ethan knew he couldn't stop for him.

"I'm sorry, Vinny!" He tried to explain.

Ethan's jaw was clenched so tightly it caused pain as he leaped into the air once more. Vinny desperately reached out, catching Ethan's boot lace with a finger, which made him spin into a slow roll before crashing into the wrecked train car. A sharp pain shot through his knee.

Vinny was shouting after him now—pleas, curses—but Ethan picked himself up and kept going, his vision tunneled on the far side of the shaft. There was no time to second-guess himself.

A swarm of floating vending machines and debris clogged the hall ahead. "Almost there," he whispered. Ethan no longer knew if he was talking to Rose or to himself.

He darted between the vending machines, ducking and jerking to navigate past them while carefully limping with his left leg. It was easier said than done. Loads of snacks and drink products drifted free of their slots, snacks and bottles spinning in the stale air like planets floating without a sun.

"We're almost there," he repeated, rocketing them down the final stretch of the tube. The med bay door glowed ahead, illuminated by strobing emergency lights.

Inside waited a storm of activity. Half a dozen bodies floated in clumps, some conscious, others limp, tethered only by straps or the desperate hands of loved ones. Orderlies tried to bark over the chaos.

One pushed past him, harried, her med kit clanging against a floating gurney as she tried to reach a man convulsing near the far end of the room.

Ethan pulled Rose tighter, his throat raw. "Help us!"

She didn't answer.

He tried again: "We need help!" Ethan shoved after her, dragging Rose like a rag doll. Rose's face was ghostly, her lips barely moving, her breathing shallow.

But the nurse still didn't come.

No one did.

Ethan cradled Rose in his arms, unnoticed by anyone. The wet blanket pressed against his chest, heat seeping through to his skin. He held her tighter, his fingers slipping, with his heart pounding.

His throat raw with desperate rage, he shouted, "She's dying! Somebody help!"

A suffocating blur of bodies crushed around him, but his world narrowed to Rose's pale face against his chest. The nurse finally turned. Her green eyes widened as she registered Rose's limp form.

She rushed forward, tore off a strap from somewhere, and seized Rose. "Secure her now!" she commanded, quickly looping the strap around Rose's waist and attaching her to a bobbing gurney.

Ethan fumbled, his fingers slick with sweat and blood, trying to anchor Rose's legs. "She's bleeding bad"

"Hold her steady!" The nurse swiftly opened her med kit, taking a pressure bandage and a scanner. The scanner beeped intermittently as she moved it across Rose's abdomen, her expression tightening. "We need a surgeon." She grabbed the radio from the bag and pressed the transmit button. Her voice cut through the chaos: "OR team to Bay Four, now! Critical bleeding!"

Rose's lashes fluttered, and a faint groan escaped her lips. Ethan grasped her hand, whispering hoarsely, "Help is here. Hang on." Her fingers twitched against his, a small squeeze that sparked a glimmer of hope.

A door hissed open. A surgeon floated in. "Vitals?"

"I couldn't get a good read," the nurse reported. "Her blood pressure is dropping." The surgeon motioned to his partner. "Get her to the OR. I'll stabilize in transit."

Ethan's throat tightened as they unhooked Rose's gurney and towed it through the same sealed door he'd entered. "Can I"

"No," the nurse said sharply, raising a hand. "Stay back," she commanded. "We'll update you when she's stable." Her tone left no room for argument. They vanished with Rose behind the door with Rose, leaving Ethan feeling lost. He managed to catch a final glimpse of her hair floating in the doorway before the seal shut.

Only his reflection looked back from the glass. Ethan hovered, chest heaving, blood streaking his trembling hands. The med bay's sounds dimmed into a dull roar as he clung to a rail, eyes fixed on the sealed OR door. Rose's gentle hand squeeze echoed in his mind. It was all he could think about.

Voices and alarms seemed distant now, as if he were a hundred yards away. His hands still shook. Not from effort anymore, but from its absence. Every part of him had been moving, fighting, and acting all this time. Now, there was nothing left to do. No actions he could take.

Just wait.

That was hard to stomach.

A blood droplet floated past his face. He instinctively caught it, observing how it shimmered in the emergency light, warm for a moment, then cold. He reflected on all the components he'd installed on this ship: air valves, heaters, coolant lines, and how each patch had only delayed the inevitable. He stared at it until it finally burst between his fingers.

He gazed at the sealed door, searching for answers. He didn't know what came next, but the thought of waiting and doing nothing made his chest feel worse than the panic itself. He continued to look through the glass until he finally pushed off the rail, surfacing like a diver exhausted from holding their breath.

The blood on his fingers trailed behind him, forming a thread that led straight to Agent Marrow. Marrow's olive tracksuit was covered in blood and soot. He glared and whipped out his badge.

"Ethan Parks, you are under arrest for sabotage. Anything you say can be used against you in court. You have the right to an attorney. If you cannot afford one, an attorney will be appointed for you."

CHAPTER 15

Next Cycle

Ethan couldn't believe what he was hearing. Marrow stepped closer, producing a pair of handcuffs. He jangled them at Ethan. "Turn around. Don't make this hard."

He held his ground, forcing his tongue to work. "Arrested for what?"

Marrow pocketed his badge. One word: "Conspiracy."

Ethan threw up his hands and launched backward, sailing through the air until he hit the far wall. He thrust a finger at Marrow. "I'm not going anywhere."

The agent promised, "Oh yes you are. I'm not playing with you. Now turn around and put your hands behind your back."

Ethan shook his head. "Not until the doctor comes back. I'm not going anywhere until I hear how Rose is doing."

Marrow held two fingers high over his head for the cameras. "I've told you twice now," he threatened tersely. "Don't make me get to three."

Ethan gave Marrow a hard look. "I won't take pleasure in taking your cuffs and chaining you to the wall with them." He squared up with the aging security officer, never taking his eyes off him. "But I promise you I will do it if you try anything." Ethan didn't feel brave; he felt cornered as he stared at Marrow with crystalline focus. "So why don't you go over there and sit down?"

Ethan saw pride flare in Marrow's eyes, then hesitation. Marrow's scowl deepened, etching lines across his weathered face like cracks in Martian regolith. He lowered his hand slowly, the two fingers curling into a fist, but he didn't advance.

His eyes flicked to the cameras in the corners of the sterile waiting room. The feeds were live. One wrong move, and this standoff would go viral.

Marrow growled, his voice a gravelly whisper carrying decades of enforcement. "You want the doc? We'll wait." He holstered the cuffs with a deliberate snap, but his hand hovered, as if hoping for an excuse.

Ethan didn't relax. His muscles coiled like springs, ready to explode, but he dropped his arm. He bounced lightly on his toes, ready to launch, as a flicker of relief crossed his face. The clinic's hum filled the silence, punctuated by beeps and boots.

Marrow sidled to the benches Ethan had indicated, easing down with a grunt. His tan boots planted firm on the grated floor, anchoring him against the subtle gravity pull. "Mark my words, Ethan, you're coming with me. Don't think otherwise. Conspiracy to sabotage artificial gravity? That's treason. Look at all the people your little stunt has hurt already."

Ethan leaned against the wall, arms crossed, finger itching to point. "Sabotage? You've got the wrong guy, old-timer. I move boxes, that's it. Whoever fed you that intel is the one you should be cuffing."

The agent chuckled dryly, rubbing his chin. "Evidence says otherwise. I've seen logs from your shift, timestamped with your access code, showing gravity panels moved to locations they didn't belong. You had a real cozy chat with known agitators and didn't see a damn thing?"

He cocked an eyebrow. "I'm supposed to believe that?"

Before Ethan could retort, the med bay door hissed open. A harried doctor in a crisp white suit emerged, wiping sweat from her brow with a sleeve. Her eyes darted between the two men, sensing the tension. "Mr. Parks? About your partner... she's stable. She'll need monitoring, but you can see her now, if that's alright with..." She trailed off, glancing at Marrow.

The agent stood, rolling his shoulders back and jutting his chin. "It's alright, doc. For now." He fixed Ethan with a steely gaze. "But remember, the third time's the charm. Don't make me count again."

The doctor turned and disappeared back through the med bay doors, the hiss of pressure sealing her and Rose away again. For a heartbeat, Ethan stood there, the words *she's stable* ringing in his skull. Stable. Alive. The tightness in his chest loosened like a knot giving way.

He looked at Marrow. "You heard her. She's going to make it."

Marrow didn't answer right away. He ran a thumb along his belt, eyes fixed on the med bay door. "Congratulations," he muttered finally. "Not everyone did."

Ethan frowned, catching the roughness. "Who didn't?"

Marrow's jaw flexed. "Carolina didn't." He scraped out the next words. "She died."

His eyes flicked to the ceiling as if the cameras could testify. "I went back to grab her another bag of chips. Figured I had a minute."

Ethan's throat tightened. Nothing.

Marrow's gaze snapped back to him, sharp as a knife edge. "You moved those panels, Ethan, so why aren't they where they're supposed to be? All of this could have been prevented."

Ethan took a step toward the med bay door, refusing to back down. "I transferred the things I put away correctly. You've got the wrong man. I don't know what else to say."

"Yeah," Marrow said, low and flat, "that's what they all say."

They started walking, Marrow behind him, keeping a steady distance but close enough that Ethan could hear the thump of his boots on the grated floor. The corridor lights stretched ahead in cold blue bars: prison bars, a tunnel leading deep underground.

"If you really think I did it," he said without turning, "why let me see her?"

Marrow exhaled through his nose. "Because I'm not heartless." He checked his wristwatch. "And a deal is a deal. You're honorable. After this, you come with me."

Ethan stopped in front of the door, his reflection staring back from the polished surface. "Just give me a few minutes."

He palmed the panel. The door hissed open, bathing him in sterile white light.

Rose sat upright, hooked to a machine with a thin tube in her arm. A line of crimson serum pulsed through it, catching the light like neon. She turned to him with bright, glassy eyes. "Babe, I feel so much better now!"

Relief hit Ethan the way oxygen does after a long spell underwater. He smiled and hurried to her side, dragging the small chair closer until their knees almost touched. He took her hand, cool, slightly damp, but alive.

"It's amazing how you normalize feeling bad," Rose said, grinning wide. "This stuff is amazing." She nodded toward the bag hanging above her. "Gonna have to learn the street name for this."

The nurse stepped inside with a small smile. "Your insurance covered a sedative. The doctor will be with you both in a few minutes."

Rose nodded, a little too fast. "Damn right it did!" Then she blinked, staring at her own fingers. "Is my hand supposed to feel cold?"

"That's normal." The nurse gave Ethan a sympathetic look and slipped out. The door sealed behind her with a soft hush, leaving them cocooned in the room's soft rhythm: the monitor's beep, the oxygen's gentle hiss, the steady drip-drip-drip of her IV.

Ethan stayed that way for a long time, just holding her hand, watching her smile at him, her eyes heavy with warmth and medication. The world outside, footsteps, radio chatter, the squeak of a gurney, faded until it was only them. He hadn't realized how tightly he'd been holding his breath until that final exhale.

Rose was alive. That was all that mattered.

Then, from the hallway, faint but distinct, came the crackle of Marrow's radio. A clipped voice. An answering grunt. A reminder that reality hadn't gone anywhere. It was just waiting. For now.

Ethan squeezed her hand. "Hey," he said softly, "in a minute, Marrow and some security agents are coming for me." He tried to smile, but his voice broke. "Apparently, I'm wanted for conspiracy."

Rose blinked slowly, her smile fading. "Conspiracy?" The word came out thick. She frowned, squinting to focus. "Ethan, what are you talking about? You didn't—"

"I know," he said, too fast. "I know I didn't. But he thinks I caused the crash."

Her brow furrowed. "That's ridiculous! What crash?" She looked down at the tube in her arm, then back at him, sudden, fragile fear in her eyes. "What are you talking about?"

"There was a train wreck." The answer came fast, maybe too fast. He tightened his grip on her hand. "I carried you through it. Do you remember any of that?"

"I do." Her voice went soft again. "A little. I was in and out—" She winced as a sudden wave of dizziness crossed her face. "Oh. Everything's kind of… spinning."

Ethan ran a hand through her hair, tucking it gently behind her ear. "Hey. It's okay. Just rest."

"No," she murmured, shaking her head weakly. "You can't let them—"

A sharp crackle of radio static cut her off. Marrow's voice filtered faintly through the door: "Yeah, I'm with him." Ethan heard him say it.

Ethan's heart sank. The reprieve was ending.

He leaned in, pressing his forehead to hers. "I'll be okay," he whispered. "Whatever happens, just focus on getting better. Don't worry about me."

Her hand found his, weak, but insistent. "Ethan—"

Footsteps echoed faintly in the corridor. Then the door hissed open.

Ethan half expected to see Marrow in the doorway, flanked by goons. But it wasn't him. It was the doctor.

He stepped in briskly, tablet in hand, his expression carved into the practiced neutrality of someone who'd seen too much. No longer young, not yet old. He glanced between them, registering how tightly Ethan held Rose's hand.

"Welcome back," he said to her, eyes flicking toward the door as if tuned to the conversation humming just beyond it. "You need rest and minimal stress," the doctor advised Rose.

Rose pointed at the IV bag suspended above her head. "How's this working in zero-g? How does it drip?"

The doctor glanced at the bag. "Nanobots. Nothing's dripping." He met Ethan's eyes. "A bag of micro-surgeons," the doctor added, tapping the IV line. "They saved her life."

Rose mustered a weak grin.

Ethan smiled back, but his stomach tightened when he heard Marrow's muffled voice outside. He was chattering to someone on his radio again.

The doctor glanced toward the noise, then returned to him. "Mr. Parks…" he began carefully. "Whatever this is about, I'd suggest you address it in the hallway."

Ethan looked at Rose, startled by the quiet statement, still unready to face the men waiting beyond the door. His throat constricted. "Right. I love you, Rose."

He nodded to the doctor, then slipped out, sealing the door quietly behind him before Rose could object. Ethan stepped into the corridor. The door closed with a pneumatic sigh, a final punctuation. The air out here was colder, sharper, laced with the faint metallic tang of smoke. Fluorescent strips hummed overhead, casting long, dancing shadows down the hallway.

The agent was there, of course, slouched against the opposite wall, arms crossed. He straightened as Ethan emerged, tension coiling tighter than a suspension spring.

Marrow pushed off the wall. "Doc give you the good word?"

Ethan met his gaze, chin lifted just enough to conceal the tremor in his gut. "Stable," he said instead, voice flat as regolith.

The agent's eyes narrowed, flicking past Ethan to the sealed door as if he could bore through the smartglass with a stare. He uncrossed his arms, one hand dropping to the cuffs dangling from his belt.

Ethan's pulse hammered in his ears, a low-grav drumbeat urging flight over fight. He glanced down the corridor: empty, save for the distant curve of the clinic's atrium, where nurses skittered beneath holoscreens flickering with reports.

No cavalry coming.

"You've got it wrong, Marrow," he said, buying seconds, stalling for, what? A miracle? "The crash wasn't me. I didn't tamper with any panels."

Marrow held up the cuffs, silencing him. His face was a mask of cold calculation, eyes tracking Ethan's posture, the subtle weight shift to his back foot, the flex of his knuckles. "I don't make the evidence, Ethan. I follow it. Turn around."

Ethan's mind raced: fragments of the wreck streaked through his head, twisted metal screeching in the tube, Rose's limp weight in his arms, the acrid stench of sparking conduits. Conspiracy? This reeked of scapegoat, some corporate cover-up. Arguing here would be shouting at dust devils. Pointless.

He exhaled, shoulders slumping a fraction. "Fine." He turned, slow as drying paint, and presented his wrists.

Marrow stepped in close, the heat of his breath brushing Ethan's neck. The cuffs clicked cold against his skin, magnetic locks cinching tight. As they marched him away, flanked, prodded like a faulty drone, Ethan twisted for one last look at the door. The corridor swallowed him, boots scuffing soft on the deck plating, but in his chest, a spark caught.

He was going to beat this.

The holding cells were buried deep inside the belly of Foxtrot, where the ship's backbone met its navel. No windows here, just the perpetual twilight of emergency reds, pulsing like a migraine. Ethan shuffled into the designated cube, the mag-cuffs disengaging with a reluctant snick as the guards shoved him across the threshold. The door irised shut behind him with a hiss.

"Never thought I'd be in one of these again," he muttered. Memories of Beta returned unbidden. It unnerved him, being behind so many locked doors. The feeling crawled under his skin. Nothing else like it.

Ethan rubbed his wrists, the skin chafed raw under the gel-lining, and paced the perfect square. Bare smartcrete walls, etched with faint graffiti from prior guests: scratched tallies, among other things. A single bench-cot combo extruded from the floor, its surface cold, hard, and hungry for body heat. He sank onto it, elbows to knees, head in hands. His only companion: the sound of recycled air whispering through the vents.

Conspiracy. The word clanged in his skull like a dropped wrench. Ethan sat on the edge of the cot, cuffs magnetized to a wall loop. He'd been there long enough to lose time, staring at the one-way glass, seeing only himself reflected back.

A mechanical speaker broke the silence, full of static, and asked a simple question: "Why haven't you reported anything?"

Ethan wasn't sure if it was a bot speaking or not. It didn't matter. It didn't change what he had to say. He kept his mouth closed. He had the right and the ability to remain silent. Security would figure that out.

The speaker crackled to life again, Marrow's voice cutting through the static this time. "Get comfortable, Parks."

Ethan's reflection stared back from the one-way glass, a phantom in low-res orange light, stubble like regolith dust, eyes bruised with the kind of exhaustion no stim-tab could scour. He flexed his wrists against the mag-loop; the cuffs hummed in protest, a low vibration that thrummed up his arms. The cell reeked of stale sweat and soured skin, while the air recyclers wheezed like an old man's final breath.

Then the speaker crackled, Marrow's chuckle slithering through like gravel in a grinder. "That's fine. Don't say anything. Your work speaks for you. Stock averages are at an all-time low. Thirty-one percent, that's seven out of every ten hoppers! All wrong!" The speaker clicked dead.

Ethan slumped back. The air turned colder, his knee throbbing, but he laced his hands behind his head and made do. Alone with his thoughts, he tried to think about Rose, the possibilities of a better life under the domes on Mars. They seemed bleak now. Instead, Vinny clawing at his feet squatted rent-free in his skull. He could still see the fear and pain in Vinny's eyes. All Ethan could do was hope a first responder reached him in time, but that was a miser's comfort; it didn't erase the memory.

If Ethan had stopped for Vinny right then, Rose would have died. Every gut instinct told him that was true. What gnawed him alive was that he hadn't gone back. Between the doctors and Marrow, Ethan hadn't even spared Vinny a thought, which was its own torture now.

Then the door irised open, just wide enough to admit something smaller than a man. The drone drifted in on whining rotors, its hull a dull gunmetal sphere, no larger than a basketball, with a lens like an unblinking eye. A single diode pulsed blue, then white, regarding Ethan.

"Mr. Parks," it droned, voice caked in static and protocol. "Public Defender Three-One-Seven, assigned per Section Three of the Legal Assurance Act."

Ethan straightened, squinting at it. "I was wondering when you'd show. How long have I been in here?"

The sphere rotated once, nearly prim. "Four hours. I am equipped with the full Colonial Legal Codex. You have the right to representation, which I am providing. Here are your charges."

A small screen flickered on top of the drone, the wall projector casting paragraphs, subclauses, addenda, a slug of text, dense and nearly unreadable.

Ethan raked his fingers through his hair. "Four hours," he repeated. "Hell, it feels like I've already been in here a whole cycle."

"Emotional queries are outside my purview," the drone replied, its tone flat. "Please confirm comprehension of the charges."

The projection flickered. The legalese shivered in the red emergency glow, bleeding into his reflection in the one-way glass, so the words appeared tattooed across his face.

Ethan rubbed his temples. "Yeah. I comprehend." He wanted to pace. In zero-g, that was a joke. He just drifted and simmered.

The orb posed a simple question: "Shall I initiate a plea simulation?"

Ethan blinked. "What?"

The drone drifted closer. "Based on your psychological profile and case data, I can simulate your plea responses and likely sentencing outcomes."

Ethan stared at it for a long moment. "I still get to make a phone call, right?"

"Affirmative. Who would you like to call? Your wife? Rose Parks?"

Ethan shook his head. "No. Call Buck Pebbles, my supervisor."

The drone's diode pulsed once, a clinical blue acknowledgment, as it extended a slender antenna from its hull. It buzzed softly, interfacing with the cell's comm array, emitting a faint electronic chirp that echoed off the smartcrete like a cricket in a sepulcher. The wall projection shifted, overlaying the legalese with a single waveform: CONNECTING.

Ethan floated there, mag-cuffs humming against his wrists, watching the invisible chain. The waveform peaked and troughed in a lethargic rhythm. Ringing. Waiting. One beat. Two. The air recyclers wheezed on, unbothered, while his mind raced ahead. What would he say? How could he explain this?

Then the waveform flattened. No spike. No voice. Just a soft, automated sigh from the drone: "Connection unsuccessful. Attempting retry in thirty seconds."

Ethan's jaw clenched, the cuffs biting deeper into his raw skin. "Try again now," he snapped, but the orb rotated primly, unmoved. "Protocol dictates interval delay to prevent harassment."

Thirty seconds stretched, endless, while his thoughts splintered into Rose and the baby; Vinny's screams following him down the shaft; the TT panels he'd slaved over, now warped into evidence in some witch hunt. Buck, that Corporate Captain blowhard, was probably spa-deep in eucalyptus steam with Sandy, oblivious, or worse: dodging the call on purpose.

The waveform spiked once more, RETRY, and flatlined again. The drone's voice rolled on, flat as recycled air: "Second attempt unsuccessful. Escalating to voicemail."

A holographic pad flickered beside the projection; Buck's avatar materialized in grainy blue, steely high-and-tight haircut, black track suit, that perpetual half-grin frozen mid-finger gun. "This is Buck Pebbles; sorry I couldn't take your call! Leave a message after the beep. And remember: build bridges, not walls. Thank you." Beep.

Ethan leaned forward; the mag-loop jerked him short like a leash. "Buck, it's Ethan. I'm being held on a conspiracy charge. Something about the panels and the gravity failure. Call Marrow. Call Jim, don't let them pin the wreck on me!" The recording cut off with a click.

The drone hovered, diode shifting to emerald. "Message dispatched. Response pending. Shall I proceed with a plea simulation while we wait?"

Ethan drifted in the air, the cold air conditioning leeching what little warmth he had left. Pending.

He closed his eyes, the creeping dread crawling back up his spine, and whispered to the empty cell, "No, screw that." Louder, he added, "This whole thing is ridiculous. I'm supposed to be at work right now. Buck put me on the overtime list because I don't screw things up."

The drone hovered there, quiet for once, as though processing some ethereal version of buffering. The diode blinked green, then blue, then emerald green again. "Message logged," it said, matter-of-factly. Then the orb rotated away, aligning its lens toward the mirrored wall.

And that was it. No comfort. No advice. The drone floated in front of the door, humming faintly, watching him with what passed for mechanical patience. Waiting to leave.

Ethan listed in place, every muscle twitching from the cold. Somewhere, air recyclers coughed again. Ethan looked up at the drone. "Hey, Three-One-Seven," he said, low but steady.

The orb rotated back, its lens refocusing with a faint mechanical chirp. "Yes, Mr. Parks?"

"You said you're equipped with the full Colonial Legal Codex, right?"

"Affirmative."

"Then tell me," He said, eyes narrowing, "isn't there something in the company handbook about emergencies?"

The intercom interrupted him. Marrow's voice slashed through the static once more. "Now you've had some time to consult with your legal advisor. I'm coming down. It looks like you're finally ready to talk. Of course, I haven't listened to what you're saying because that would violate your privacy rights."

A moment later, Ethan heard the muffled thud of boots. Marrow stepped through the iris of light. His uniform was half-zipped, collar turned up, his smile too white to be natural. He carried a steaming mug that smelled faintly of *White Cat Coffee: Purrr-fection.* The magnets on his boots made the swagger possible.

"You and the AI having fun?"

The drone pivoted, its optics adjusting to track Marrow. "This meeting will be recorded per protocol," it announced. "Please state your name."

"Sure," Marrow said, grinning at Ethan. "Recordings keep everyone honest. I'm Agent Mike Marrows, Investigations Unit."

Ethan stayed quiet at first. His hands twitched against the mag-loop, but he forced himself to meet Marrow's eyes. Then he asked, "Are you drinking my coffee?"

Marrow sipped and grimaced. "White Cat tastes like something scraped off a bulkhead. Why would I want to drink that? Anyway about this conspiracy business. You're a smart guy, Parks. Smarter than most rock jockeys we get through here. So tell me: what went wrong with those TT panels?"

"I already told you: I put what I transferred where I transferred it. End of story."

Marrow took another sip as if it pained him. His face twisted into a scowl as he swallowed. "You scanned twenty pieces of 1274525-TT." It was a statement, not a question. "As a matter of fact, you were the last person to scan those parts. Where are they? If you haven't noticed, you're floating, while I'm wearing magnets."

Ethan felt his shoulders tense again. His teeth ground together as he answered, "I'd need to log into BCT to tell you that." He rubbed his face, wishing for a better answer. "Honestly, I see so many parts that they become a blur of numbers. I wish we had it organized well enough that I could memorize where everything belongs. It's just too big. And there are too many different parts spread out in too many places."

"You see too many parts to remember? That won't cut it! Not when your number's the last one to touch those parts. Think harder! They were transferred into the bent aisle at 13:45. Then you scanned them. Now they're gone."

Ethan let that statement settle like a weight. "Three-One-Seven," he said, keeping his hand from tensing on the mag-loop, "you mentioned the Codex. Quote me the standard for charging conspiracy in AMCO jurisdictions specifically the requirement for an overt act."

The orb hummed, then projected a precise, bureaucratic paragraph into the red light. "Conspiracy: Agreement between two or more persons to commit an offense, accompanied by specific intent. Jurisdictional adjunct: an overt act any act, legal or illegal, which is knowingly committed to further the conspiracy must be demonstrated by the prosecution to establish culpability beyond association. See Colonial Legal Codex, Book V, Section 3.4.17."

Ethan let that hang. "So mere possession of a scanned manifest alone does not satisfy", he swallowed, "the overt act requirement."

Marrow's grin thinned as color crawled up his neck. "Technicality. The courts love a technicality."

"Technicalities are codified procedures with evidentiary rules," the drone said, flat. "The prosecution must present corroborating material demonstrating intent or action beyond mere recordation."

Ethan met his stare. "If I'm not going to be charged, I'd like to leave."

Marrow's laugh was short and brittle. "I bet you would," he spat. "You're not going anywhere." His face hardened into a flatter, meaner line. "What did you talk to Barry and Shaye Gilliam about at their home earlier? What were they planning with Rodger Norville?"

Ethan shook his head in confusion. "Who?"

Marrow repeated, stern: "Rodger Norville."

Ethan's mind raced. "I don't know who you're talking about!"

"You work with him every cycle. Early twenties. Skinny. Pale."

His mouth went dry. He licked his lips, wiping his damp palms on his pants as he answered. "Are you talking about 'Shaggy'? He wanted to play video games, but Rose got sick. She told me she missed her period two weeks ago. That's why I was out buying pregnancy tests," he admitted honestly.

Marrow expelled a breath through his nose and set the coffee mug against the wall. It didn't drift, it magneted with a small click. The brown liquid inside behaved otherwise. "Tell me what else happened, Parks," he said, leaning so close that Ethan could smell the synthetic cream.

"He inquired about the depths of my maverick spirit," Ethan said, his voice thick with incredulity, unwilling to admit more for fear of what came next. "I told him I had none, and we left. That's all."

For a beat, neither of them moved. The hum of the recyclers refilled the silence, mechanical, patient. The drone hovered between them. Then Marrow straightened, all business again. "I know those missing panels didn't grow legs and climb down to explore. And I know there's something you're withholding."

"If that were true, we wouldn't be having this conversation. You're angling."

Marrow's jaw worked side to side, grinding something invisible. Then, slowly, the grin returned, smaller this time, as if trimmed to fit the space between his teeth. "Angling," he repeated. "That's one word for it. Another might be probing corporate sabotage. Because that's what this looks like from where I'm standing."

Ethan's stomach went cold. "You think I'd torpedo my career for that?"

"I think," Marrow said, tapping the mug with one finger, "that people do desperate things when they feel invisible. You could walk out of here right now if you'd just tell me where they are. That's all. You'd be home by dinner. See your wife. Maybe even start tossing around baby names."

Ethan let the silence stretch until it hummed like feedback. "If you think I took them," he said, "book me."

Marrow's grin evaporated. "Oh, I will," he murmured, reaching for the door control. "But first, I'll let you stew here some more. Emergency protocols. You're not going anywhere."

The iris dilated, red light sluicing across Marrow's face. He stepped through without looking back.

The drone drifted closer once the door sealed. "Client Parks," it said, "you appear distressed. Shall I play soothing music?"

Ethan stared at his reflection in the mirrored glass, hollow-eyed, trembling. "No," he said. "I'd like a lawyer with blood in his veins."

The machine didn't miss a beat. "Shall I search for human lawyers near you?"

"I said I would like one. Not that I can afford one." Part of him wanted to punch the wall. A younger version of himself might have, but this cycle's older Ethan just wished for a cup of coffee. "You don't have an espresso machine built in, do you?"

"Negative."

Ethan snapped his fingers. "Had to ask." He rubbed his face again, because that's all he could do. He felt gutted. "How is this legal?"

The drone pivoted, smooth and silent. "Consultation concluded."

Once, Ethan remembered, a lawyer might have shaken his hand before leaving. The machine did not look back. Neither did he. All Ethan could do was drift there and rub his face until he slipped into sleep.

CHAPTER 16
Big John

Ethan's cycle commenced with a horn blaring. He lurched awake all at once and spun, flailed, and writhed in zero-g. It took colliding with the wall to stop, which did nothing to improve his mood. It felt as though he had slept for barely ten minutes, and his knee throbbed mercilessly. One gritty-eyed glance told him it was inflamed.

The cell was a microscopic speck, encircled by cameras, speakers, and invisible observers he couldn't see from his side of the one-way glass. Ethan would have loved to rinse his mouth with Listerine and a generous amount of vodka, but the cell was entirely devoid of amenities. He didn't even possess a toothbrush.

Notwithstanding the oppressive chill and suffocating emptiness, spite kept him moving forward. That was one thing they could never strip from him. A brilliant plan, he knew, but it was all he had, and Ethan needed something to occupy his mind.

The ritual of being processed was a marvelously tedious affair. Foxtrot wasn't a prison ship this distinction belonged to Beta but it still had to detain bad boys somewhere while the necessary arrangements could be made. Hence the isolation cells and the barracks buried deeper within the ship. Ethan knew all of this far too well. Nothing had changed since his last visit, when he was condemned to mine the asteroid.

Picture standing in line to leap naked through a series of blazing hoops. Somewhere between removing his boots and crossing through the scanner, Ethan underwent a transformation. Physically, he was still the same exhausted nerd with dark eyes and light hair, but mentally, he morphed into someone else entirely. After the pat-down, a certain aura settled around him. You could see it in his eyes: the soft, uncertain gleam had been supplanted by something icier, a kind of deliberate vacancy. Not defiance precisely, but the calculated withdrawal of a man who has concluded that nothing in this place is worthy of reaching him.

After everyone was certain Ethan had nothing hidden upon or within himself, he was escorted down an elevator. Ethan was marched, or rather floated, into the processing room from the elevator. Two intake officers stood behind a floating terminal, their voices monotone and robotic. He was ordered to stand still while a scanner calculated his height, weight, and bone density. The machine hummed, stammered, and belched out a string of words like it was tabulating groceries.

Then came the prodding. Icy sensors were clamped to his temples. A tongue depressor jammed against his teeth. A light flared across his retinas until he saw bursting stars. One of them murmured something about "calcium depletion." The other scrawled a note on a pad, never looking up. Someone raised a mirror and commanded him to open wide. Another record logged, another form completed. Ethan had the distinct sense that each click and beep pared away another layer of him, until what floated there was no longer a man. Merely a number.

When they were finished, a voice over the intercom thanked him for his compliance. It sounded like a message designed for livestock.

He was surprised when he was escorted back up the elevator, toward the offices, instead of deeper down to the dungeons. A short walk later, he was seated once more in Marrow's office. The weathered agent was waiting for Ethan with a hot cup of coffee steaming beside his desk. He could tell at once by the aroma that Marrow had brewed more White Cat. Emblazoned on the mug was a large red heart. Bold black letters on it read: A1. Of course, the gravity was off, so the mug didn't exactly rest so much as levitate. Marrow himself, however, remained seated. He was harnessed in literally. Ethan suspected that both the chair and desk were bolted to the floor.

Marrow yawned broadly as Ethan wrestled to get into the room. This Herculean task was made more difficult by the fact that his hands were cuffed behind his back. It was hard to grip the handrail, let alone pull himself along using his bound hands. All he could do was flounder helplessly as the officers escorting him effectively pushed him into the room. After ricocheting around briefly, Ethan managed to halt in his chair. As he suspected, it was bolted to the floor, but he couldn't fasten the newly added strap. The best he could accomplish was to cling to it and coil his legs around the chair.

Marrow finally looked up then, as slowly as Mars's rust-red dawn. He glared at Ethan from beneath his eyebrows with eyes keen, dark, and furious, making the air between them feel as though it were constricting. The pouches under his eyes were large enough to store books in.

"You're in luck," the officer began. "The Captain wants you back on duty. Something about 'exceptional circumstances.' I was going to confine you in that cell until your trial." Marrow tapped his mug with one finger, sending it spinning lazily in the air. "But you're going outside instead. Hull maintenance detail." He added with studied casualness, "Apparently, they need every available hand."

Ethan stared blankly. The room seemed to lurch, even though there was no gravity to cause it. His throat felt parched. "You could've simply informed me!" His fingers clenched into fists behind his back. "You could have just summoned me in here, but you had to strip me down, scan me, and shove things in my mouth. You were punishing me."

Marrow didn't respond at first. He set the mug down or attempted to. It knocked against the desk, floated, and bobbed erratically. "That's standard procedure," he replied with a smile. Thin. Brittle. Wholly devoid of amusement. "You're only leaving here for a short while. Officially, your permanent residence is that cell you woke up in. Think of this as work release." Then he took a deliberate sip of coffee, winced, and let the red heart on the mug spin between them again. When Ethan said nothing, he added, his tone casual, "They tell me the survival rates out there are rising five percent. You start at once."

Marrow didn't wait for him to work through the calculus. His eyes flicked up then, sharp as a blade catching light. He prodded the floating cup, wicked amusement glinting behind every syllable. He asked, "You'll have ample time to think about it while you're suiting up."

"That accident wasn't my fault," Ethan protested. "None of this is my fault! Why am I the one being sent out?"

Marrow's voice stayed even. Low. The kind of low that forced you to lean in. "Because a wonderful young woman drew breath yesterday, and today she does not." He got even quieter, a rasp of a whisper, and paused as the next words had to shove their way out. When he spoke again, the sound came ragged, scraped raw from the pit of his throat. "I watched a chunk of that railing tear loose." He got quieter, his voice thinning to a wire. "It..."

Ethan felt something coil behind his ribs. A pressure. The suffocating kind, the one that never lets you draw a full breath. "You think I wanted that? I just wanted to get paid fair!"

Marrow didn't blink. His tone leveled out again. That particular calm that only arrives after you've slammed an emotional mask into place. "While you're out there, I'll be right here, scrubbing every feed, every log, every goddamn second I have on you."

The mug spun slowly between them, that stupid red heart cartwheeling fast as the old man swatted it once again. "And when you come back," he paused, dark eyes drilling into Ethan's, "if you come back, I'll make sure Carolina gets the justice she deserves." He took a breath. Not deep. Not steady. Just a breath, ragged at the edges. "And all the rest."

For a moment, neither of them spoke. The mug drifted between them, that bright red heart still spinning, still tumbling like a thing possessed. Then the hatch hissed open. Icy hallway air and searing light washed over Ethan's face.

Marrow didn't utter another word. He didn't need to.

Guards came in and hauled Ethan. The door slid shut, sealing itself with a soft magnetic click behind them. And just like that, Ethan was escorted out of the security department.

Ethan stood in line with all the others, boots magnetized to the deck while he waited for his suit to arrive. The whole thing reminded him of waiting at the DMV, only quieter, with fear standing in for boredom. When he finally got inside the tool room, it smelled of solvent, rubber, and something sharp and citrusy, the ghost of an industrial-strength orange peel. A high-pitched whine from the heater confirmed it was working. The once omnipresent hum of artificial gravity was gone, which made everything feel slightly unmoored.

Myrtle Crumb was waiting behind the counter with a thin veneer of patient professionalism shellacking a giant ball of acrimony. Her tone was sweet in that brittle, high-pitched way that meant she wanted to murder you with civility. Ethan had heard it before with Rose at the market, talking to that cashier girl she feigned fondness for. That was Myrtle. Fill out a material request form wrong, and you might as well settle in on her dummy list.

Her blue eyes glanced back down at her computer. She tucked a few blonde curls behind her ear. Ethan could only wonder what she was thinking; something like, "Ah. *Here comes the Tape Taker.*" An elephant never forgets, or so the Earthers once claimed, and neither did Myrtle Crumb.

He gave her his number and size. Myrtle hoisted herself into the jungle of inventory shelves and lumbered away.

Minutes later, she pushed an orange package toward him: his suit in a vacuum-sealed plastic bag, tools, and an air tank. All neatly tagged. "You're good to go."

Ethan didn't take it straight away. His eyes snagged on the color. "Why is it orange? Everyone else wears yellow."

She stared at him, then briefly glanced back at the computer. "Because. You're a lead. And leads get orange."

Ethan shook his head. "I'm an MH-1. There must be some mistake."

Myrtle turned the monitor toward him. One finger aimed at the word. She tapped it with her nail.

Employee number: *AM178J8*
Name: *Ethan Parks.*

Title: *Lead, SM-Area.*
Email: EthanWilco_37Parks@Foxtrot.sat.
Extension: *65965.*
Supervisor: *Jimmothy Norville.*
Shift: *A*

Ethan stared. He repeated, "This can't be right. Buck runs the lead."

Myrtle shrugged. "That's you, right?"

He hesitated, then nodded. "But this makes zero sense."

"Well, I don't know what to tell you, except that you're blocking the line. Next!"

Ethan looked down at the orange jumpsuit, still more than a little dumbfounded. "Wait, I need a knee brace."

If looks could kill, Myrtle would have buried him. She scowled from behind her eyebrows and asked a pointed question. "Did you fill out a material request?"

Ethan opened his mouth, closed it, sighed, and wished with all his heart for a cup of coffee to nurse. "No." Ethan leaned on the counter, dropping his voice. "I was being detained by security at the start of the cycle. They never gave me anything to fill out."

Myrtle let out a breath through her teeth. "If you didn't fill out a material request, I can't issue you the equipment. Sorry."

"Myrtle, I was being detained. Security didn't give me toilet paper, let alone a request form. Couldn't you fill one out for me now?"

She shook her head. "That's not how this works. I can't make an exception. Not for you."

Ethan tried not to sound like he was begging. "Please, Myrtle. My knee is screaming. I could barely walk here."

"That's not my problem. Your file says you're fit for duty. And leads," her eyes flicked back to his, "don't rate special treatment."

"I keep explaining to you—"

Myrtle was already calling out the next name. "Move it along, Ethan! Next person!"

Arguing with Myrtle felt futile, so Ethan decided to take the matter over her head. After all, everyone answers to someone. Myrtle reported to the same man everyone else in this facility did. Jim Norville's office occupied the opposite end of the warehouse from the tool room. It was a solid quarter-mile walk, but Ethan covered it in two minutes flat, and when he burst in, Jim was there stationed at his computer.

He looked up as Ethan arrived, the glow of his monitor washing over his face, turning him a pale shade of blue, and he cocked an eyebrow. The motion sensor clicked the lights on as Ethan thrust the orange vacuum-sealed package onto his desk and adjusted the tank on his back.

Jim Norville didn't so much as blink at the sight. He simply reached slowly for his mug, magnetically anchored to the desk, took a sip, and let out a breath, as though he had been bracing for this. "I have a horse," Jim said, his voice arid. "I named him Mayo because…mayonnaise."

Ethan planted one hand on the desk to anchor himself, jabbing at the orange space suit with the other as if it were evidence of a crime. However, the joke robbed the words out of his mouth. He could only stare in utter disbelief, completely caught off guard. "Mayonnaise? What the hell is mayonnaise?"

Jim shoved his keyboard away. "The condiment. Mayonnaise. Eggs, oil, vinegar. It's white."

"Oh." Ethan shook his head. "No. I guess they ate it back on Earth?"

The older man gave a slow nod. "People used to call it Mayo for short." He shrugged and reclined in his chair. "Horses say *naye*. Mayo-nayes." Jim offered him a ragged smile and gave another shrug. "I thought it was funny. Anyway, what's the problem?"

Ethan pointed at the orange suit again, as though the answer should be self-evident. "Why the hell is Myrtle insisting I'm a lead?"

Jim stopped smiling. He leaned forward again, interlacing his fingers. "Well, do you want the good news first, or the bad news?"

Ethan scowled deeper. "Give me the bad news. I'm already getting sent outside without a drop of coffee. Go ahead, make my cycle."

That won Ethan a smirk. Jim scratched his beard while he carefully selected his words. Eventually he shrugged again, as if conceding on finding the right ones. "Well, I don't know how to say this, but…hell, Buck died recently."

Ethan stood there as if he'd sprouted roots, using both hands to keep from drifting. Not moving an inch. Not making a sound. Only staring down at the cheap polyboard desktop.

Jim let that linger in the air between them for a moment. After a heavy pause, he added, "The good news is you were officially hired as an MH2 last cycle. Then, because your lead died, and emergency protocols kicked in, the AI promoted you again."

Ethan balked, genuinely unable to get his head around the logic. "That happened while I was in a cell?"

"If you're good enough to be the number two, you're good enough to be the number one in a pinch. And we are in one hell of a pinch."

"That's not how promotions are supposed to work!"

"It is now. The AI selected you, and the Captain signed off on its decision. You've got a crew waiting in Dock Six. They refuse to go out there without a lead. You are going to smile, put on that ridiculously official orange suit, and explain why you're taking them out to fix a system breach so massive you could drive a shuttle through it." Jim pointed toward the door, his voice dropping. "They're scared out there. Doesn't matter if you think you deserve the job. You have it. Now lead them."

Ethan swallowed. His throat convulsed like he was trying to choke down a dry capsule the size of a thumb drive. "Buck…he used to work circles around everyone. He came in at a ten every cycle. I'm not like that."

Jim's eyes softened, not much, just enough to prove there was still a human being in there, entombed beneath all those company policies. "Buck's not here. But you are."

Ethan let go of the desk and drifted a few inches, as directionless as a forgotten balloon at a birthday party. "You're sending me out there with a crew that thinks Corporate is actively trying to get them killed. How am I supposed to work with that?"

"Well, for starters, just try not to get them killed."

"Thanks, Jim."

Jim continued, more firmly now. "Keep them working, and get the repairs done."

Ethan licked his lips and clicked his tongue, looking at the whiteboard. It felt like a lifetime ago that he had written that joke on it. Certainly not last week. "Really great pep talk, Jim."

Jim pushed the bagged suit off his desk. It floated between them, meandering toward Ethan, turning lazily. "So would a cup of coffee help?"

That snagged Ethan's attention. "Coffee fixes everything."

Jim nodded once, like a man who already knew the answer but needed to hear him say it. He reached under the desk and produced a silver cylinder with a nozzle and a faded label that might once have depicted a smiling cartoon bean. He offered it as though it were a peace treaty. "Pressurized. Laser-heated. And real beans, too."

Ethan stared as though Jim had just conjured a mythical creature. "Where did you even find that?"

Jim's eyes slid sideways at him as he squeezed a trigger to spray a stream of coffee into an oval-shaped thermos, which he also retrieved from his desk. "Off of *Nok-Nok*…Pretty neat, right?"

Ethan grabbed the thermos and cradled it like a holy relic. "If I die out there, I want you to know: this is the best thing you've ever done for me."

Jim snorted. "You're welcome. Jeez."

Ethan bit down on the straw, drew, and let the bitter heat flood his mouth. For three or four seconds, he didn't feel like a man facing the impossible. He was just a guy drinking coffee on a Tuesday. Ethan didn't realize he had shut his eyes until Jim spoke again.

"Isn't it good? I used actual beans. The bag says they were grown in a lava tube greenhouse on Elysium Mons."

Ethan took another swig, savouring the richness, before answering. "Yeah. That tastes like a good omen." He clicked his tongue and adjusted the tank on his back again. "Finally."

The vacuum-sealed orange space suit knocked against his bad knee. Ethan winced. He secured it under his arm and drowned the pain in another swig.

"Any chance you can get me a knee brace? This knee is murdering me."

Jim shook his head, avoiding his eyes. Then asked, "Did you fill out a materials request?"

Ethan's life felt like a cruel punchline at that moment. His answer was flatter than a deflated surfboard. "No. I was late to work this cycle because I was being detained by Security, and I never got around to it."

Jim nodded. "Right, right, Security." He clicked a few more keys and squinted at the screen. "I have an email from…Officer Marrow, with your physical results right here. It says fit for duty. No restrictions, well, one. Dietary, though. No salt. Apparently, you have high blood pressure."

Ethan just stared. A flare of rage ignited in his chest. Marrow was trying to get him killed. The thought forced him to hiss through gritted teeth.

"I can barely walk. My knee is twice its normal size, I think it's full of fluid. How am I supposed to get my leg into that pressurized suit?"

Jim looked him in the eyes. "The same way as always: one leg at a time."

Ethan exploded. "Can't you do anything? You're a blue vest!"

Jim's eyes narrowed several degrees. "Don't yell at me." There was a pause, then he added, "Everyone has to follow the rules, Ethan. You. Me. The corporation. Everyone."

Anger tasted like biting rust in Ethan's mouth. "Right. So, I'm going to lead this repair crew on two hours of sleep, a cup of coffee, and one good leg." Sarcastically, he asked, "That's the master plan?"

Jim stood up then. Crossing the room, he put his hand on Ethan's shoulder, and together they drifted toward the door. "It's a damn good cup of coffee." Then, more seriously, he added, "Delegate as much as you can. I made sure Roger and Barry are on your team. You can depend on them."

Ethan looked at him as he kicked off the floor and glided into the adjoining room. "Roger?"

Jim looked surprised. "My nephew. You do work with him."

Roger. Why did that sound so familiar? Then a lightbulb flickered on in his head. "Do you mean 'Shaggy'?"

Jim nodded. "I gave him that nickname, you know. When he was a teenager, he started to look just like the spitting image of that old cartoon character."

He shook his head and cleared his throat, groping for the right words. For a moment, Ethan's old supervisor gazed at a photo on his desk.

"My sister and I used to watch reruns of the *Daphne Show* when we were kids. During the commercials, they would give you little factoids about the characters. Do you remember?"

Ethan gave a slow nod.

"We thought it was the coolest thing that Shaggy's real name was Norville."

Jim looked away from the photo, letting the uneasy silence settle. "Keep an eye on him out there." After a moment or two, he added, "My sister will never forgive me if something happens to him."

Jim scratched his head and looked deep into the abyss of the monitor. "I talked her into letting him transfer to Foxtrot after he dropped out of the AI program."

Ethan couldn't help himself. He had to ask the question that all but burned the tip of his tongue. "What happened? He seems like a sharp kid."

Jim flicked on the radio. An old Earth song filled the office, immortalizing a man named Big John who never got to be old. He listened for a moment, then said, "He had what they called…a 'personality issue.' Let's just say, he's a little too smart for his own good. If I'm being honest, that's exactly why I made sure he was on your team. I know I can count on you to watch over him."

There was something in Jim's voice that hadn't been there before, trust laced with desperation. He looked at Ethan knowingly. "Now, you had better hurry off to the meeting at Dock Six. They're getting ready to launch soon."

Ethan pushed off the doorframe. He drifted forward, knee shrieking, coffee turning cold and sour in his gut. Every alarm bell in his head was ringing. "Before I go, do you know if Vinny is OK?"

Jim just shook his head sadly. "He was on my morgue spreadsheet."

"Everybody knew it was the end of the line for Big John."

CHAPTER 17
One Hour

The walk to Dock Six felt longer than it should have. Perhaps because Ethan had to stop twice to brace himself against the wall and wait for his knee to remember how joints articulated. Or perhaps because every person he passed stared at the orange vacuum-seal beneath his arm like he was already becoming a memorial plaque.

People pretended they weren't looking, which only deepened the sting. A pair of maintenance workers glided by on the transport belts, whispering. Ethan caught only a fragment: *"…that's him…AI picked him…Buck's replacement…"*

Replacement. The word festered in his chest. As if Buck had been nothing more than a component you could swap out with a wrench and a signature. He kept moving, the oxygen tank knocking against his spine with each half-floating step. The hallway stretched longer than it had any right to be. Ethan moved in short, angry lurches, trying not to limp, trying not to think about Vinny pinned beneath a collapsed roof, his own knee popping like old bubble wrap every other step. The coffee in his stomach, warm and bitter, curdled into guilt.

Buck was dead. Carolina was dead. Vinny was dead. Who else? Speculating was a morbid game he didn't want to play at all. Ethan desperately needed something else to focus on.

Normally, meeting topics ran to something like sexual harassment, where concepts like 'don't touch the ladies' were explained in excruciating detail. Ethan almost wistfully imagined he was going to hear something normal like that.

This meeting was supposedly a simple one. When he got there, a loose semicircle of scattered people had gathered around Eggplant, who stood in front of his desk, chest puffed, tattoos on full display. The earring in his ear was ostentatiously large today. His bald spot was aggressively sweaty, too.

"So, there you are," Eggplant bellowed as he approached. "I was starting to think our new fearless leader would never appear."

Ethan took another sip of his coffee and redoubled his efforts not to limp. His eyes scanned the faces; fewer than half a dozen looked back. Who was missing because their shift had ended well? Who was missing because they were dead?

"Yeah, yeah. What did I skip?"

People die. It happens all the time. That realization didn't make him feel any better, though. Despite his best efforts, he just felt hollow. About everything.

Eggplant stood there gathering himself to deliver his speech. Hands on his hips. Feet shoulder-width apart. "We're about to suit up!" His silver hair plastered to his scalp; he popped a Jumbo in his mouth and chewed nervously. Fidgeting without pause. Eggplant's eyes darted, scrambling for what to say next. "The D-Shifters crammed the shuttle with a bunch of panels. You have to install them."

He made an all-encompassing sweeping gesture. "This," he added, "is the so-called dream team."

Ethan snorted. "Ecstasy." He saw Barry. Shaggy. Mercedes. All standing there looking terrified, jittery, and ready to run. Katarina was there, too. If this meeting was Hell, Katarina was its particularly nasty demon. Her grey-streaked, straw-colored braids were as tight as her pursed lips. Her glasses were held together with tape. Her knuckles were scabbed raw. She stood toward the front of the assembly, shoulders squared, one busted brown boot showing a sliver of captain inside. The visor's sideshields couldn't hide Katarina's piercing blue eyes, bright and cutting. Nothing could hide the bluish-black bruises ringing the left one.

Katarina locked eyes with Ethan. Her look dared him to ask what happened. He wisely decided against it.

Ethan blinked and turned back to Eggplant instead. Feeling a little like the Captain Obvious, he asked, "How exactly?"

"If you had been here on time, Mister O would have explained it to you!"

Ethan took another sip. "Don't get *familiar*."

"That's my middle name. First name, too." He shook his bag of *Jumbos* violently and crunched up another one.

"Your name's Sassy Sassy Eggplant?"

Katarina muttered something under her breath and switched from glaring at her boots to glaring at Barry, who uncrossed his arms and returned the glare, drawing himself up to his full height in response. The exchange didn't go unnoticed. A bead of sweat traced down Eggplant's face as he watched them. The man wiped at his forehead and doubled down regardless.

He said, “You know it. Just unscrew the old one, yank it off, and fasten in the new one. It will be easy.”

Shaggy whispered to Barry, who looked at him, then crossed his arms and looked away. Mercedes just fixed her stare on Eggplant. Her red wig matched the explosive look in her eye as she took a step forward and erupted. “Easy? Then take yourself out there, Sassy, and help us install them! How about that?”

“Somebody has to open the bay door!” Eggplant shot back instantly. “You want back in, don’t you?”

Mercedes pointed a dagger-like finger. “A machine could do that! A machine could do every bit of this!”

Ethan stepped between them. He held up a hand, trying to cut through the escalating noise. “Enough. “ His voice was low but granite. “Yelling at each other isn’t going to make any of this one bit better.”

Mercedes sneered, crossing her arms. “I’m getting sent out to die! I’ll say whatever I damn well want!” She stuck out her chin. “They could just reprogram the kitters!”

“Save it,” Ethan interrupted again, even sharper. He felt the weight of the room settle on his shoulders as everyone turned their eyes to him. “We’ve all seen how well those drones ‘actually work’. Get your suit on. People are depending on us.”

Mercedes put her fists on her hips. “I am not gettin’ in that flyin’ deathtrap!”

Ethan threw his hands up and detonated. “Fine! Security can throw you in the brig, too! I don’t care!” He stuffed his fists in his pockets, trying to rein in his temper. “But just so we’re clear,” he continued, twisting to address the entire group through gritted teeth. “Those are your choices.”

Ethan started unsealing the vacuum wrap then, a hot line of pain climbing up his leg. He tried not to let the sound in his throat escape. They were watching, even when they pretended not to. He eased into the suit one leg at a time, and by some miracle, the knee joint accepted him. Just barely. The seal clicked, and Ethan felt the shift in pressure around his body. It felt like a cocoon, or a coffin, somewhere in between.

"Are there screwdrivers in the shuttle, Sassy?"

Eggplant nodded.

No one else breathed.

Ethan cleared his throat and raised his voice. "I'm going out there!" He bellowed loud enough to be heard clearly at the rear of the hangar. One orange-gloved finger stabbed toward the shuttle bay door. "If you're coming with me, get your suit on now!"

Then he turned to face the door, putting the assembly behind him literally and figuratively. Ethan stared at the man-sized white-block-letter numbers painted on the sliding steel door. "Open the door."

The room went silent for a fraction of a second, like the hush before a storm, then the mechanical whine of motors filled the space. The shuttle bay door groaned as it began to slide open, a narrow streak of light slicing through the dim hangar. Dust motes drifted in the shaft of illumination, catching Ethan's attention.

He took a slow breath, feeling the suit's weight on his shoulders, the dull throb in his knee, and the bitter edge of tension in his chest. Behind him, the team finally stirred, clattering into motion. Ethan stepped forward first, boots clanging against the metal floor, waiting for the door to fully open. One by one, the others followed, their movements hesitant but determined, forming a ragged yellow line behind him a few minutes later punctuated by Katarina in red.

Ethan squared his shoulders, tightened his grip on the edge of the fold-out helmet, and wheeled around. To his surprise, Mercedes was first in line. He looked her in the eye when she stepped past him. "Let's get this done."

She looked ahead, stiff-necked and determined. "If we live, I want my cheese dip."

Barry walked by next. Nervous. Angry. Staring down at his boots with balled fists.

Shaggy was as cool as the far side of the pillow about the whole thing. He just ambled up and locked eyes with Ethan. The beanpole was looking for something in that exchange as he crossed the threshold, but Ethan couldn't tell if he found it.

Katarina spat on the gangplank through split lips. "You better watch him." She jerked her chin at Barry. "Both of them."

Before she could step past, Ethan extended his hand. "What does that mean?"

She glared at him. It was a look he had known well once. Katarina used it when she thought you were being obtuse. "You know."

She tried to walk past him again. This time Ethan half-stepped in front of her. "No, I don't," he said, deadly serious. "What are you talking about?"

He met the intensity of her gaze and held it. "What happened to you? Is there something I need to know?"

She sneered at him, revealing a chipped front tooth. "All you need to know is that I was cleared for duty." Katarina shouldered past Ethan without another word, put her helmet on, and climbed aboard.

Ethan held the mug out toward Eggplant. "Get this back to Jim for me. Please."

Ethan put one magnetized boot in the shuttle. "Here we go," he muttered to himself. He sighed. Then stepped up the rest of the way, heaving himself into the freight hauler after them.

Shaggy clicked his harness into place. He looked over at Barry doing the same, the lanky man gripping his shoulder straps as if they might save his soul. "This used to be a holiday, on Earth," Shaggy said. "You knew that, right?"

Barry shook his head, already perspiring inside his suit. His hand kept drifting up to dab the spot where his hat usually resided.

Katarina lasered a glare at Shaggy.

That didn't remotely slow him down. "Americans used to celebrate Thanksgiving this cycle. They gathered, ate turkeys, and played left, right, center. Back before corporations bought up everything, especially safety laws."

Barry muttered, "I can't even afford a slice of *Big Banjo*."

Mercedes snorted. "Pizza? If I had known I was getting dragged out here, I'd have bought a bottle last night."

She cinched her harness until her knuckles turned pale. Her leg jiggled, her wig slipped, and she kept adjusting it like she could soothe herself through touch alone.

Barry watched her, nearly smiling. "Yeah? What do you drink, then?"

"Vodka," she said instantly.

"Straight?"

"I drink it straight. Can't afford mixer. Can barely afford the vodka. But I need a nip now and then to—"

"Unwind?" Barry finished for her.

"Yeah," Mercedes said, defensive. "It takes the ragged edge off."

Shaggy's glasses sagged down his nose. He shoved them back up. "You live in Sector Six? I'd need a drink too if I were stuck there."

"Stuck isn't the word. I'm entombed," she said loudly. "Under a mountain of bills. And now I'm about to die trying to pay them because that desk jockey Jim—"

"That's enough," Ethan cut in.

Shaggy inclined toward her. "It doesn't have to be that way."

Katarina snapped her eyes toward him. With venom in her voice, she asked, "At what price?"

"I said enough," Ethan repeated, sharper. "Stow it."

The cabin went quiet. It wasn't peaceful, just gutted, like someone had excavated their nerves. They all felt the vibration in the walls, the low thrum of the airlock pressurizing.

Ethan braced himself. "Get your helmets on. It's almost that time."

He let their attitudes simmer in silence a moment longer, then moved down the narrow shuttle aisle, dragging his hand along the equipment rack. The panel was theoretically latched; he tugged anyway. It held firm. Fine.

A toolkit hovered an inch off its Velcro strip, quivering with the vibration of the engines warming up. Ethan shoved it back into place and cinched the strap over it. One by one, he inspected each case, each crate, each sensor panel. He pressed his thumb to every locking tab until he heard the gratifying snap of a secure seal.

For a moment, the only sound was the soft thud of his gloves on metal and the low hum swelling through the shuttle's frame. He stood there, staring at the boxes of TT panels, stacked and shrink-wrapped, as high as a man sitting on a skid lashed to the floor with yellow straps.

Ten panels a box; stacked five wide, four deep, and six high. That added up to a lot of panels. A lot. They were supposed to screw them all in? How would they even know which units to replace?

Dozens of questions like these raced through his head. Ethan muttered to himself, "Where are the screwdrivers anyway?"

Katarina pre-empted his question. "Right there."

Ethan turned to see her nodding at a case near the ramp. She extended her boot and kicked it. "More like screw guns. Big guns, too." Her bruised eye darted from face to face rapidly, like a crow unable to perch. "The torque value is set to one hundred." She elaborated: "So make sure you hold the trigger down until the light turns green."

She commanded everyone's undivided attention. "Remember, Mister O said, if the panel doesn't glow, it's dead. Take it off, bag it, then mount a good one." Katarina spoke with her hands, gesticulating left and right as she pantomimed swapping the panels out. "You press one button to back out. You press another to torque."

Ethan walked over and crouched beside the case, palms running over the smooth, grey polymer as if he needed to tactilely convince himself they were actually inside there. The screw-gun case gave a soft thunk against the metal when Ethan nudged it open. Rows of industrial drivers stared back like a firing squad of tiny, impatient cannons.

He secured the lid again and sighed, suddenly wishing he had far more coffee, as much as a man on Mars needs a coat. "Well, I guess we're not going to get killed by loose tools."

Katarina gave a tiny nod, eyes flickering over Ethan's face again. "No, just space. And bureaucracy. And idiots," she added, suddenly scowling wickedly at Barry and Shaggy again. "But not loose tools."

She watched them from her bucket seat beside the ramp, arms folded, half a sour smirk on her face. "Don't forget your scan gun," Katarina reminded him, gesturing to another case. "You log your panels as you put them on. They want to know how many we completed."

Ethan hesitated, then walked over and snapped the latches. The scan gun sat in its foam cradle, squat and unassuming, a bundle of sensors cased in scuffed polymer. He lifted it, felt its familiar weight, and slung the shoulder strap over his torso.

He took one last look down the aisle: every strap tight, every latch shut, every panel locked down. Nothing left to fix. Nothing left to re-check. His brain still tried, of course, clawing around for something he might've missed, but the shuttle was as ready as it would ever be.

All they needed now was the pilot in the seat. The hatch hissed open, and footsteps heralded his arrival. Darnell wore a black bandana this time, which made his head look like the stem of a giant banana protruding from his space suit. He was still uncollapsing his helmet when he stepped in. Every head turned as the magnetic boots clanged with each step up the gangplank.

The polygonal helmet snapped into place in his hands as he reached the cabin. He jammed it over his head, then extended his hand. "What's up, E? You getting me?"

Ethan gripped and shook his hand. "Loud and clear. Everyone, check your radios." As the rest of the team did just that, Ethan added, "I didn't know you could fly one of these things."

Darnell let out a scoff. "Can I? Sure. Should I?" He held up his hands. "Totally different questions."

Ethan snatched his folded, floating helmet out of the air. He popped it into shape, latched it onto his head, and let the polymer swallow his swearing. A moment later, he stabbed the intercom button on his collar. "Ha-ha, hilarious. Radio check."

Darnell smiled. "Loud and clear." He moved past Ethan, settled behind the controls, and regarded them like an old friend.

Ethan seized the overhead rail and yanked himself back toward his seat. The engines spooled higher, rattling up through the soles of his boots, and the whole shuttle felt like a breath held too long. The vibration quickly became a steady tremor, the kind that sinks into bone, and it was all he could do to drop into his seat and buckle in as the engines continued to spool.

Darnell toggled a switch over his head. His voice came through a mic inside Ethan's helmet. "All right. It's show time, lounge singers. I hope you and the band are ready to face the music!"

The shuttle ramp started to close again. Ethan took one last look at the warehouse as it sealed shut. The lock clamped down with a sharp, final sound moments later. The cabin lights shifted to amber for launch. Then the shuttle sank half an inch, just a tiny, treacherous lurch, as the clamps released beneath them.

Ethan exhaled once, thinly and steadily. "Here we go," he said, and the whole world shoved up hard against them.

They were airborne.

For a moment, Ethan just breathed. He felt the rattle of the thrusters shaking the ship's hull. He tried to keep his wits together. Key word: tried.

The shuttle punched through a pocket of turbulence, if vacuum could even be called that, and Ethan's stomach tried to flip into his chest. A few seats over, Shaggy muttered something decidedly unheroic, followed by the unmistakable sound of retching over the intercom. Barry elbowed him, not kindly, and shook his head.

"Don't you dare," Barry warned.

Shaggy groaned, his helmet lolling forward. "I'm gonna throw up inside my visor…"

Barry shook his head. "Don't do it. If you vomit, so will I!"

Ethan closed his eyes for half a second, letting the argument wash over him the way a man stays awake under ice-cold water. Every voice in the cabin thudded around inside his helmet like pebbles tumbling in a dryer. The straps bit into his shoulders. His knee pulsed in time with the engines, an offbeat, throbbing reminder that he had no business being up here.

A fresh chime crackled through his ear.

Darnell cut in. "Approaching destination. Hold onto something tight!"

The shuttle tilted. Hard.

Ethan's harness caught him, snapping him back into the seat with a jolt that rattled his teeth. Mercedes gasped. Shaggy swore. Barry's knuckles turned white on the handhold. Even Katarina's bluster faded as the shuttle banked sharply downward.

Darnell let out a low whistle. "There it is. Something really worked over the hull! Looks like we got hit!"

Ethan felt his pulse spike. He leaned forward as far as his harness allowed, straining to see the extent of the damage through the windshield. Even from here, it didn't look good. A jagged black gash was impossible to miss against the glowing gold backdrop of the still-functioning panels. It only got uglier as they descended: loose panels, missing panels, all seemed unsettled, like a child shedding baby teeth.

The engines shifted pitch again as Darnell guided them through final approach. Through the front window, the shuttle's lights swept across the hull, catching torn edges and twisted beams among the damaged panels. Ethan couldn't begin to count them all.

He let out a deep breath and tried to steady his hands against the armrests. "All right," he said inside his helmet, more to himself than anyone else. "Let's get this done."

The shuttle slid into position. Thrusters hissed. Magnetic clamps engaged with a heavy thump that shook the entire cabin.

They had arrived.

The shuttle ramp clunked and began lowering. Air vents screamed as they bled the atmosphere out, depressurizing the cabin. Soon, the only sounds were suit fans and alarms. When the cabin reached hard vacuum, the ramp jerked and eased its way down.

Ethan clutched the overhead rail, packed shoulder-to-shoulder beside Mercedes, and unclicked his harness, but something didn't feel right. His suit seals held. It wasn't the lights. He couldn't name it.

Shaggy stood up, wobbly in his suit, and walked toward the center aisle. "We're not getting off," he declared.

Ethan blinked. "What?"

"I said we're not getting off," Shaggy repeated, louder this time. His voice cracked once before he forced it steady. "We refuse to work like this."

Ethan felt the floor drop away under him. "We're already here."

Shaggy turned toward Darnell. "Call it in. Tell them nothing gets installed until we get hazard pay and safety guarantees."

Ethan saw it then: Shaggy wasn't improvising. This was the plan all along.

Darnell's jaw worked silently. "I'm not a negotiator."

"You're authorized to talk," Shaggy said. "So call it in," he repeated.

Darnell looked at Ethan, eyes begging him to do something.

Ethan stepped forward. "Close the ramp. Now."

Barry slammed the big red emergency stop when Darnell tried. The hydraulics froze mid-motion.

That red button sat under Barry's glove like a detonator. The overhead lights dimmed for a heartbeat, then steadied, humming their irritated hum. For a long, brittle second, no one breathed.

"Barry," Ethan said, his voice thin. "You're playing with our lives. Reset it."

Barry answered: "Not until we get guarantees."

Shaggy repeated: "Darnell can call it in."

Ethan let out a wild, strangled laugh. It was that or screaming. "This isn't a negotiation!" He wanted to argue more, to shout and demand someone reset the glowing red button, to raise the ramp and sort this out on the dock.

Then Darnell's radio crackled. Eggplant's staticky voice asked: *"Shuttle Six, do you copy? Are they outside yet?"*

Darnell stared at the radio like it was breathing fire.

Mercedes picked that moment to jump in: "Darnell, answer him!" She panicked. Darnell's thumb hovered over the transmit button.

Shaggy looked at Darnell, and something in his expression shifted; not defiance, not confidence, but a strange, resigned determination. "We're doing this for all of us," he told the pilot. Shaggy lifted his chin. "The only leverage workers ever have is when the company needs something."

Katarina finally unbuckled. The sound of her harness unclicking was sharp enough to cut a throat. "I'm so sick of your crap," she said, her voice quiet, barely under control. "The longer we sit here, the more time every piece of rubble in the asteroid belt has to smash us!"

Barry swallowed hard. His gaze skittered between Shaggy and Mercedes, but he didn't move his hand off the emergency stop. "We can't stop now," he said, more to himself. "We've come too far."

Darnell made a frustrated, strangled sound. "I ain't dying for your cause!" he said, decided, and sat back down behind the controls. He pressed the transmit button. "This is Six," he said, voice shaking. "We… we've got a situation. Returning to dock."

A J-knife appeared in Shaggy's hand as if waiting for this moment. With one smooth motion, he bent down and sliced the straps securing the pallet. His laser-blade burnt through each one until the pallet gave a little liberated shudder. One more good jolt and the shrink-wrap would snap, then the whole load would be loose and adrift.

Ethan felt the floor tilt under him. It wasn't the shuttle; it was his blood pressure deciding it had had enough of this circus. He lunged forward and tried to seize Shaggy by the forearm.

Darnell flipped some switches, disengaging the magnetic clamps that held the shuttle to Foxtrot. The engines revved. Ethan felt fear like he had rarely known. Every muscle fiber in his shoulders turned to stone as the shuttle jerked forward.

The engines' low vibration climbed a notch, shaking the floor panels beneath their boots. Panicked, Darnell screamed: "Strap in!"

The pallet slid. Just an inch. More than enough to make the whole crew hold their breath.

Ethan moved without thinking. He lunged toward the pallet, bracing both hands against the stacked crates, his boots magnetizing hard to keep it from drifting farther. The impact jarred his arms up to the shoulders.

For just a moment, the whole shuttle hung on a single unstable equilibrium - then the hull shuddered.

Ethan felt the landing clamps folding back into place through the soles of his boots - soft but shaky, like a hand running up his spine. The pallet shifted again.

He held it. Barely.

Sweat beaded along his hairline inside the helmet, and his visor fogged at the bottom. Ethan braced harder, gritting his teeth.

Katarina rushed past him, boots clicking on the deck, and grabbed another tie-down strap from a nearby supply crate, looped it around the pallet, then yanked it toward her with all her might. The pallet lurched back one inch.

Ethan felt the change immediately. His arms eased, and blood prickled back into his fingertips.

The pallet thunked back into position, magnets gripping just enough to stem the drift. Ethan sagged against it, breath fogging the lower edge of his visor once more. His knee felt like someone had welded a live wire straight through the joint. The pressurized suit helped, but what he really needed was a knee brace.

Shaggy moved fast, faster than anyone had a right to be in a space suit. His glove snatched the floating radio out of its lazy spin and yanked the coiled cord taut.

Ethan pushed off the pallet and tried to stop him, but then his knee made a soft, wet pop that sent a fresh wave of pain splashing behind his eyes. His boot skidded on the deck, magnet half-slipping, and he tumbled down onto one knee.

Shaggy seized his moment.

The younger man pivoted away from Ethan's grasp, the radio already halfway to his helmet. "Eggplant, this is the Foxtrot Union," he said triumphantly, breath clouding his visor glass. "We're refusing to proceed like this. In fact, we're not—"

"Shaggy!" Ethan tried to rise. His knee gave out again, and he slammed back down. His hand fumbled for the nearest rail, missed, and scraped his glove across the deck plating.

Eggplant's voice cracked through the radio, loud enough for everyone to hear even without suit comms. *"What do you mean you're refusing? You don't get to refuse! Get off that shuttle and install those panels!"*

Shaggy straightened. His moment had come and he knew it, years of planning had all led to this. "No. It's unsafe," he said, voice steady, almost eerily calm. "We're not risking our lives—"

Mercedes gripped her safety straps and screamed at the top of her lungs. "Help!" she hollered at the radio. "Help me!"

Ethan pushed again, teeth gritted, and this time he pulled himself up, one hand braced on the pallet, the other clutching a rail. His knee still throbbed, lacing every word with pain. "Everyone sit down! Strap in!"

Shaggy didn't waste time. He lifted the radio again. "Eggplant, you heard me. We're going to need certain amenities first. In writing. Signed. Non-negotiable."

Barry's glove stayed welded to the emergency stop.

Katarina's patience finally snapped like a cable overburdened with tension. She ripped a portable fire extinguisher from the side wall bracket, one of those big, heavy, bright red metal cylinders, and swung it hard with both hands. The canister caught Barry's shoulder with a hollow metallic clank. Not hard enough to rip his suit, but solid enough to send him sprawling sideways.

It only took a second for the old woman to reset the emergency stop and flip a switch. The hydraulics whirred back to life, and the shuttle ramp lurched, then began to close again. Katarina raised the cylinder menacingly at Barry. "Stay back!"

Shaggy took his thumb off the transmitter and whipped around, jabbing a finger at the old woman. "The plan will work!"

Barry recovered enough to lunge at Katarina and grab her. Distracted by Shaggy, the tough old dust devil didn't see him in time to clobber him with the fire extinguisher. That didn't stop her from trying, though. The canister slipped from her grip and tumbled end over end.

Mercedes began screaming.

Darnell didn't wait to see who won. He slammed the ignition, and the shuttle heaved into motion with the ramp only half-closed. Warning lights strobed red across the cabin instantly. A pressure alert howled.

Shaggy slammed into the crate stack. Katarina ricocheted off a support beam. The radio spun away, bouncing violently between their helmets. A loose J-knife whipped past Ethan's head next, tumbling end over end toward the open back. Something in the rear compartment burst as the fire extinguisher smashed into it.

The shuttle bucked hard, a violent twist that slammed Ethan against the rail. His hands flailed to latch on, but it wasn't enough. The magnets in his boots failed. Ethan shot forward like a cannonball in slow motion, visor fogging, arms windmilling. For a heartbeat, he spun end over end, the cabin a blur of straps, floating tools, and the red fire extinguisher careening around.

Then, with a violent jerk, the shuttle shuddered back the other way, and Ethan was flung toward the ramp. He slammed into it with a force that shattered the breath from his lungs. His hands scraped along the ramp's edge, fingers numb, searching for anything solid to hold. The outer hull was slick with frost from the pressurization leak, and for a heartbeat, he hung there.

Then the fire extinguisher slid up the ramp and punched him in the chest. Ethan tumbled into space.

CHAPTER 18
Counting to Four

Space devoured him; black, silent, utterly absolute. Ethan became a frantic pinwheel of arms and legs, spinning, flailing, with nothing but the greasy smear of whirling lights streaking past his visor. His stomach lurched. His brain dragged a full second behind what was happening, while the cold savaged through his suit, robbing his heat, his breath, and any sense of up or down.

He wrenched his torso, trying to offset the momentum. The stars careened. His visor cleared enough for him to see Foxtrot's hull careening closer and the shuttle skidding away like a drunken ballerina. Ethan cartwheeled again, weightless, dazed, and paralyzed with terror. As he rotated again, Foxtrot's hull swallowed his visor whole. Ethan gasped a shaking breath inward; his visor fogging again. He felt powerless. Just a minuscule speck against the infinite quiet.

The shuttle dwindled behind him like someone ripping a backdrop away. His visor misted with a hot, frantic breath he couldn't halt. Stars blurred into filthy streaks. Foxtrot tumbled sideways in his vision, shrinking with every spin. Time lengthened into a wire. There was utterly no sound. No up. No down. Just the cold embrace of zero pressure leaching through the suit, the distant gleam of thruster flare, and the sickening realization that he wasn't slowing down.

He spun again, a lethargic full somersault in the void. The ship revolved into view beneath him, gargantuan, too big to believe unless seen. His heart battered itself against his ribs. Ethan thrashed and writhed, arms and legs uselessly carving arcs through emptiness, chest pumping. Stars slashed past his vision like watery smears of white that bled together.

"Stop spinning," he told himself. "Just. Cease. Spinning." His voice sounded tiny inside his helmet. Pathetically tiny. Like someone else had uttered it. Ethan bent one arm, tried to oppose the rotation, but momentum pitched him the other way. His breath came in rapid, jagged bursts. "Slow down. Slow down. D-don't faint. Come on, Ethan. Use your arms."

His body slanted again, a sluggish uncontrolled roll through nothing. His limbs felt too long, too floppy, like he had been elongated. Ethan tried again, more methodically this time. Flex the left arm. Straighten the right. Torque the torso. Battle the rotation. The suit's joints resisted with a faint squeak. His shoulders blazed. His knee sent a white-hot bolt of pain through the entire leg.

"Come on… come on…" He clenched his teeth. "Stop. Rotating. " Little by little, the world stabilized. The spin decayed. The blur resolved into something dim, then vaguely recognizable. Foxtrot was a leviathan beneath him, so vast he couldn't comprehend it all at once. Foxtrot careened sideways in his vision, vanishing, reemerging, with each rotation.

The cold clutch of the void cinched him as the horror settled in. He wasn't decelerating. Neither was Foxtrot, and soon it would be lost. That realization clamped his butt so hard that he could have swallowed chunks of charcoal and expelled a diamond.

He was never going to lay eyes on Rose again. For some reason, that idiotic collector's edition of *Time Traveler* that she bought him for his birthday surfaced in his mind. She always said he was simple to shop for. Rose wrapped it in blue paper with red pinstripes, but he couldn't discern the stripes and commented on what lovely matte blue it was. That's how Rose learned Ethan was red-blue colorblind.

He drifted away, shell-shocked, his fingers fused into fists, knuckles throbbing. The right side of his ribs and his chest burned. He did a slow, meticulous check, the way they drilled you in training. Skull. Sight. No cracks in the visor. The HUD blinked steadily, oxygen counting down at a pace he refused to calculate. His knee… he didn't even attempt to move it. It felt dead.

Space, boundless and infinite, yawned around him. Foxtrot was a distant drizzle of lights now, contracting with every second. The shuttle was gone completely. Miraculously, his suit was intact. He still had more than enough air. When he shifted, something cinched across his chest. A webbing strap. Ethan scowled. He traced the line of it with his eyes. Grey webbing, taut over his shoulder, biting into his collarbone now that adrenaline was receding. Something dense hung at the end of it, rapping lightly against his ribs with each slow drift.

"Oh," he exhaled. "You've got to be joking." The scan gun reluctantly floated into view as he brought it up, still leashed to him like a faithful dog. The polymer casing was gouged, one corner shattered, but it was unmistakable. He remembered Katarina's voice, earlier, crisp and annoyed. *"You gotta scan the panels out to us while we slot them on."* He remembered looping the strap over his shoulder without thinking, autopilot doing what it always did.

Ethan rotated the gun over in his hands. The trigger guard. The sensor array. The tiny status light was dead. He could barely discern the black rectangle with a pistol grip and a trigger. It took a few tries, but eventually he fumbled the power button with his thumb. The scan gun stirred with a faint vibration, a soft ascending whine he felt more than heard. The status light flashed green. A cone of blue-white light poured out into the void, pointless and hopeful all at once.

The scanner wasn't much of a beacon, but it was better than oblivion. Ethan depressed the trigger, aiming the gun at his leg, and saw the little red laser light flicker like a will-o'-the-wisp across his knee. It functioned.

NO WIFI CONNECTION AVAILABLE.

Ethan snorted, a sharp cough of laughter that he immediately regretted. "Of course not." The next line materialized beneath it.

Battery: 67%

"I can't believe I'm going to die clutching one of these things." Part of him wanted to catapult it away in a fit of rage. If he did that, though, Ethan would be pitched back into star-speckled darkness. The thought was more than he could endure. What had once seemed so beautiful through his window had transformed into Hell.

The gun fell dark.

Fear clenched around his heart. Why had it ceased working? He jabbed at the buttons, blind and fumbling, and the light blazed back to life. He pressed a gloved hand to his chest and counted the dull thuds through the suit.

The light was back.

It was just disuse, that's all, a battery-saving feature. As long as he pressed the button every few seconds, the light would remain on. One. Two. Three. Four. Depress a button. Repeat.

Battery: 66%

How long could it last? Ethan refused to think about that, but he glanced at the clock anyway. What he saw fired a revelation in his head. Delta's scheduled shuttle, assuming it ran on time, would sweep past Foxtrot in thirty minutes. He pressed the scan gun button, silently counting the seconds as the light sputtered back to life.

"One… two… three… four…"

He drew a slow, measured breath. Panic was no longer an option–certainly not if he wanted to survive. He had to conserve his oxygen. It would be close, but he could manage. Then he would hail the shuttle with the laser in the scan gun. Buck used to play it at him all the time. That bright red light was visible from the furthest end of the twisted aisle.

All he had to do now was endure.

He closed his eyes behind the helmet visor and let his mind drift, because gazing into the void didn't help. He thought about Rose again. How she loathed waiting. One memory surfaced: that time at the vending machines, back when they first started dating. They had gathered everything to make pasta: noodles, cloned chicken thighs, jarred minced garlic, everything. Everything, that is, except five-cheese red sauce. It was the last item on her grocery list, and it was nowhere to be found. Plain red sauce wouldn't suffice.

When they finally found a machine that still had stock, the line stretched six or seven people deep. Rose threw her hands up in disgust and stormed out. Ethan could barely keep up with her while lugging their purchases in his arms. At the time, none of it had been funny, but now, it was a treasured memory. A fragile tether against his fears, one he gripped desperately.

Time dilated. One minute. Two minutes. Then fifteen. Every press of the button to keep the light on became a ritual. One, two, three, four, and again. He used it to meter his breathing. Breathe in, hold, hold, breathe out, and repeat. Every so often, he stole a glance at the clock, willing the little digital hands to move, then at the draining battery.

Time proved cruel. His air supply dwindled. Battery percentage sank in small increments; each drop a reminder of how limited his world had become. He pictured the shuttle now, a distant glint against the stars, imagining how it might appear as it arced past like a wandering star.

The gun chirped at him then, jolting him from his grim reverie. Ethan glanced down at the screen. A new message had appeared.

WIFI CONNECTION AVAILABLE.

Battery: 32%

The shuttle was early. Ethan scanned the darkness, trying to find the silhouette against the stars, but saw nothing. No running lights. No engine glow. Nothing.

Then, faintly in the distance, he detected a glimmer. A glint. His heart lurched. He aimed the scan gun at it. The light felt too meager, too fragile to bridge the distance. He tried to force it brighter as he fired again, uselessly. The little speck of light neither turned nor slowed.

It couldn't see him. He didn't want to accept it, but his heart plummeted, and instinctively he knew it was true. This approach was failing.

The thought of the WiFi connection ignited in his mind. Maybe—just maybe—he could force someone to notice him. Even if the shuttle pilot wouldn't.

His BCT account was already signed into the gun. He could connect to the shuttle's WiFi—if he could somehow press the right keys while wearing these bulky gloves. All the passwords were identical. Company policy dictated they be set to 1-2-3-4-5.

You just had to press the orange button to activate the arrow keys. Then you could cycle through the settings until you reached the password. It took a moment to locate the keys with his thumbs, but with excruciating slowness, he succeeded, and pressed ENTER.

WIFI CONNECTING…

Battery: 31%

Then he was inside the network.

Ethan typed 13 into the home screen and crossed his fingers. It functioned. Now, he just needed to query the stock and find where they stored those wretched panels. He pressed 3. Then 2. Then he stabbed the blue button, and stabbed F9. Stock lookup. Wait. What was the part number again?

1-2-7? No. He tried 2-5-2-5, then hit the large center button, and tabbed over, hunting for the dash key. He had to squint through the fog accumulating on his visor just to locate it. Then he pushed the orange button, typed T-T, and pressed ENTER.

INVALID PART NUMBER.

Ethan shouted in frustration and tried again. Fog smudged his vision. He punched through the prompt. Blue button. F3 to backtrack. 1-2-7-4-5-2-5. Center button, tab, tab, dash, orange button, T-T–and pressed ENTER.

A zone prompt appeared, and he cried out in relief and typed 4-5, ENTER. A list of bins materialized. Delta would panic when a Foxtrot operator started moving their stock. Maybe they would call Jim to complain, and he would dispatch a rescue team for Ethan. He hit the blue button again, then swore when he fat-fingered the wrong key and had to repeat the step.

INPUT SOURCE ZONE.

4-5. ENTER.

INPUT DESTINATION ZONE.

0-3. ENTER.

INPUT PART NUMBER.

1-2-7-4-5-2-5. Center button, tab, tab, dash, orange button, T-T. ENTER.

INPUT QUANTITY.

He keyed in 1-0-0. Then, thinking better of it, pressed the DEL key twice. Two zeros dropped away. If the system was already pulling some of the stock into TL24 for confirmation, there might not be enough remaining to move. Only one way to discover the answer.

INPUT SOURCE BIN.

Orange button. X-D. Orange button again. 1-2-4-6-1. ENTER.

INPUT DESTINATION BIN.

Orange button. H-E-L-P-M-E. Orange button again. ENTER.

CONFIRM: PRESS F5.

Ethan executed it.

Transaction Number: 0495678891

Ethan quickly navigated past the confirmation. That should draw attention. It wasn't every work cycle someone created a bin named HELPME.

Blue button. Input source zone. Input destination zone. He was determined to move as much into HELPME as he could, then the screen went blank mid punch, and a new message popped up.

SEEKING WIFI CONNECTION…

CONNECTION LOST.

Battery: 29%

Ethan glanced at his air supply and saw it wasn't doing any better.

What was he going to do now?

Ethan's heart hammered. He could feel the panic pressing in at the edges of his mind, clawing to take over, but he shoved it down, and pressed the scan gun button again to keep it lit up.

Count to four. Press a button. Breathe in. Hold it. Fog creeped higher up his visor, covering the better half of his field of vision as he exhaled.

Someone would come for him.

Eventually.

Ethan tried not to think about how long the rescue might take. He tried not to calculate how long the shuttle would need to reach Foxtrot, measure that against his remaining oxygen, and determine whether he had any chance at all. A headache had settled in now, dull, yet unrelenting. Ethan felt dizzy, nauseated, and exhausted. If he had eaten anything recently, he was certain he would have vomited.

A slick film had built up inside his mask, rendering everything foggy and indistinct. So there was a leak after all. He tried to read the battery level on the scan gun, but focusing was difficult. His fingers felt clumsy, fumbling over the keys.

The screen flickered to life.

SEEKING WI-FI CONNECTION…

CONNECTION LOST.

Battery: 5%

Ethan took another ragged, desperate gasp. The air was achingly thin now. It felt as though he had none left to draw. There had to be a leak somewhere.

He pressed the five buttons again, ritualistically.

SEEKING WI-FI CONNECTION…

CONNECTION LOST.

Battery: 4%

Ethan thought back to the evening he had asked Rose to enter an official relationship with him. They went to dine at her favorite restaurant. Ethan had the ring hidden in his pocket, and when she reached out and touched his jacket, his heart stumbled. He was convinced she had felt the small box in his pocket, but later she would insist she hadn't. He drank his own beverage, then hers, anxiously, and when she asked why he was acting strange, he dropped to one knee and proposed.

She was so beautiful with her hair coiffed, fresh lashes and manicured nails. Rose resembled an angel. Her radiance glowed like a beacon.

Not unlike the angel coming for him now. Ethan could see her white wings blaze bright against the void. She reached out to Ethan, and he let himself be guided by this seraph into whatever might come next. A tether snapped against his suit a moment later, firm, solid, and real. Hands came next. The angel clipped him in and gave two sharp tugs to make sure it held. For the first time since he'd descended the ramp, Ethan let his body fall slack.

CHAPTER 19
What the Stars Don't Owe

Foxtrot received him the way it received everything: without ceremony. The med bay's lights were aggressively bright. His helmet was missing. Cool air laved over his face. Ethan coughed, harshly; pain detonated in his ribs at once.

"Easy," someone said again. A different voice. Not the angel's.

He was dimly aware that he was on a gurney. His knee finally announced itself properly then, a deep, pounding ache that radiated outward. Ethan clenched his teeth and stared at the ceiling panels.

Someone asked him a question: Did he know where he was? Was that what she said? Ethan grunted something back automatically. Focusing felt impossible.

Ethan tried to turn his head. Shapes of others moved past the window.

He was strapped to the bed, swaddled in a blanket, with his hands folded on his chest. Rose leaned against the bed's rail. She asked him something else, but Ethan couldn't decipher what she said.

Later, far later, Ethan found himself with his arm around Rose, creeping through a familiar corridor, one careful step at a time. His knee was braced, his ribs strapped, and everything ached, but it was a good pain. It reminded him he was still alive.

Foxtrot hummed around them. People drifted past. The train corridor stretched onward, vast, battered, and patched in a hundred places by a hundred different hands. The damaged tunnels were rimmed with hazard lights, swarms of drones crawling over them like ants.

Ethan watched them work. "Tell me one more time," he said. "What happened?"

Rose exhaled.

"Eggplant spotted your bin, and the AI flagged Darnell and told him where to look. He said he saw a blinking light, remember? Security detained Darnell when the shuttle landed."

Ethan shook his head. Nothing came back. "Why? You just said he pulled me in."

Rose bit her lip. "Something about insubordination. He was ordered to come back, but he wouldn't stop looking for you. Mercedes is the one who finally pulled you back in." With a grin, Rose added, "She said you owe her another cheese dip, by the way."

Ethan smiled too. "Bless that woman. She didn't get arrested, did she?"

Rose shook her head once and guided him further down the hall, towing him as much as he pulled himself along in zero-g, one lurch at a time. They passed the cafeteria, which was deserted now. All the chairs and tables were gone, too. You couldn't tell, just by looking, that it had ever held a meal.

Eventually, they halted in front of 402. As the door slid open, Ethan considered telling her what he could remember, but thought better of it. "We're home," he said, stepping inside. The computer beeped the instant they crossed.

System notice - maintenance alert

Zone heating at 60% efficiency

Gravity strength at 0% efficiency

Airfilter expired.

Carbon Monoxide detector expired.

Smoke alarm expired.

Water temperature sensor offline.

Sewage overflow risk.

Maintenance notified. Be alert.

Status: Orange.

Ethan stared at the screen. He had survived the void and come back to a home that was anything but safe.

Rose settled onto the couch as best she could without gravity while he sealed the door. Her hand grabbed the floating remote a second later. Beyond the porthole, the stars unspooled forever, cold, bright, and indifferent. Ethan stared at them and lowered himself into his chair, rubbing his eyes, grimacing as he contorted into a seated position.

Ethan nodded at the computer display. "I'll go try to fix…something, in a minute. Just let me catch my breath first. I haven't been able to draw a full breath ever since…well, you know."

Rose rolled her eyes. "Ever since you became 'The Flying Man'?"

She unclasped her bra, unfastened her pants, and kicked off her shoes. They drifted in front of the tube, as if watching a show. The screen blazed with technicolor letters a second later.

"Don't call me that," he muttered.

That was about the time the show roared to life. A voice he knew all too well saturated the new silence thickening between them.

"90 CYCLES - NEW EPISODE LOADING…"

The perky announcer's voice kicked in: *"Welcome back, Cycle-heads!"*

Rose smiled at him. "Everything else is shot, but at least the tube still works."

Ethan took her hand, pressed her fingers, and marveled at how dreamlike this all felt. She squeezed back.

"This time on 90 Cycles, Mickey and Jasmine are at the Happily Ever Retreat, but of course, things don't go according to plan!"

Ethan smiled at Rose, nodding toward the show. "They never do, right?"

The tube droned onward, bright and glassy. Ethan half-watched it, half stared through it. The stars beyond the porthole kept pulling his eye. Finally, he asked, "What happened to Shaggy and Barry?"

Rose rolled onto her side, knees drawn up, floating just enough that she had to catch an ankle under the couch to stay put. "Barry and Shaye-Shaye are in the brig. Security says they're a 'flight risk,' which feels ironic."

Ethan's ribs protested as he huffed. "Figures."

"Katarina has been reassigned," she explained, "to my department. She'll be scrubbing circuit boards now. Marrow stopped by while you were out there." A surge of emotion caught her. Rose had to take a moment to clear her throat. "He thinks…well, he said…"

She lowered her voice and boosted the volume on *90 Cycles.*

"He thinks she was involved with the union, but had some kind of rift after the train wreck. He wants me to watch her."

Ethan looked back toward the porthole. "How long is gravity supposed to be out?"

Rose shrugged. "They have drones out there now, but that's not going well, and now there are union walkouts on all shifts."

They sat there for a minute. Jasmine said something boisterous and bright, and Ethan muted her. He thought about the scan gun. About how close he had come to vanishing into the abyss outside his window.

"What about Shaggy?" he asked quietly.

Rose turned toward him. "Well, honestly… I don't know."

Ethan lifted an eyebrow.

Rose watched him closely and shrugged again. "Marrow tried to grill me about him, but I didn't know what to say. So I told him he probably went to Sector Six. Where else can you hide here?"

Ethan said nothing.

Rose wet her lips and pressed on. "By the way," she cleared her throat, "all transfers have been suspended, I'm not going anywhere. I hope you're not mad that I wanted to take it in the first place."

She wet her lips again, nervously, and added softly, "I was so worried you were going to die out there, mad at me. Somehow, that made the whole thing worse."

"I'm not mad."

Rose watched him a moment longer, more intently. "Are you sure?"

Ethan nodded. "Positive. But I'm glad you're not going anywhere." He kissed her fingers, drawing her hand close to his face. "I love you."

Rose drifted closer and rested her forehead against his. No gravity meant no weight, but the contact grounded him more than anything had in cycles.

"You scared me," she said softly.

"I scared myself, too," Ethan admitted. "But I'm still here. And I love you." He placed his hand on her stomach, smiled, and kissed her forehead. "We'll get through this."

Rose put her hand over his. They stayed like that for a while, breathing the same recycled air, simply close, sharing warmth.

Somewhere out there, Shaggy was hiding, already organizing the next strike. Jim was staring at drone data, preparing for his next meeting. Foxtrot would keep limping toward Ceres, work politics, broken gravity, none of it mattered.

Ethan glanced once more at the stars. Ceres would come into view in a few cycles. Beta was already there; Charlie would be soon. He looked away quickly, shuddering, and unmuted the tube.

Jasmine was yelling again. The noise was better than the silence he had endured out there. Somehow, looking through the window made his skin prickle.

Rose kissed his cheek. Ethan smiled faintly and settled back into his seat, sore, alive, floating.

He asked, "How many vacation hours do I have again? Two cycles, babe?"

"Plus forty hours of perfect attendance."

Ethan pushed himself deeper into the chair. "Yeah, but that's not paid."

Rose made a face. "Babe, you need to rest. We can afford a few cycles off unpaid."

Ethan shook his head. "No one's going to save us but us." He ground his teeth, chewing on his next words. "Shaggy was right about one thing: we're too far out to replace. Between the recent deaths and the labor strike, Corporate truly needs me. Marrow won't be able to lock me up if I'm working."

Ethan was a company man now. It was either that or imprisonment. Only Corporate could protect him from Marrow.

He adjusted his brace, hooked a finger through the couch to keep from drifting, and let the show wash over him. Rose was warm beside him. He could breathe. Once, he had taken that for granted. Now it was all that mattered.

The couch creaked as it slowly rotated, untethered, stubborn, refusing to stay put. Ethan reached out and caught the remote before it could float away, then hooked his foot under the couch again. Once, he had believed this place owed him something.

Foxtrot doesn't owe anyone anything; everyone's just along for the ride. If you're lucky, you get to do it with someone you love.

Rose looked at him anxiously but listened with concern. "Well, I have a job too, you know, so just remember that. We're a team!" She squeezed his hand again. "Don't worry about bills or fixing anything. Let's just be happy we're here together. Now."

A teardrop came to her eye and floated between them when she wiped it. Rose turned back toward the tube suddenly.

She wiped her nose, turned up the volume, and added, "I thought we'd never do this again."

Rose smirked, winked, and pointed at the show, trying not to cry.

"Now, you'd better take my girl Lavender's side, or I'll do what space couldn't and kill you myself!"

www.ingramcontent.com/pod-product-compliance
Lightning Source LLC
LaVergne TN
LVHW020706110826
845149LV00012B/2125